THE CAROUSEL

a novel

STEFANI DEOUL

Ann Arbor
2016

Bywater Books

Bywater Books First Edition: November 2016

The Carousel was originally published by A&M Books, Rehoboth Beach, DE in 2010.

Printed in the United States of America
on acid-free paper.

Cover design by
TreeHouse Studio
Winston-Salem, NC

Bywater Books
PO Box 3671
Ann Arbor, MI 48106-3671

www.bywaterbooks.com

ISBN: 978-1-61294-089-2 Print
ISBN: 978-1-61294-090-8 Ebook

DEDICATION

For my family

She drove. And she drove. And then she drove some more. She drove with a purpose born of desperation. If she could drive fast enough, far enough, perhaps she could disappear. Perhaps Columbus was wrong. Perhaps the world was flat and there would be a time and place in which she could just fall off the edge. Vanished. Gone. So she drove. Seeking a release she did not know how to find. The monotony of the asphalt became her cradle. The broken white lines the safety bars of her crib.

Night or day made no difference. As long as her head was erect she drove on. When driving was no longer possible she pulled the car over and slept, wrapped in her steel cocoon.

I was once like you

Had a nine to five and a mortgage due

That rat race got to me

First it ate me up, then it set me free

One day it buried me alive

I snapped and almost lost my mind

I crawled out just in time, to go

Walking . . .

Walking on sacred ground

Janis Ian & Jess Leary

 Through the yellowed haze of her headlights, Millie Hickson saw the strange car parked outside as she pulled in to open for her morning shift at the Old Town Diner and Gas. Even at this hour, before dawn's early light made its appearance, the vehicle appeared unremarkable but for the layers of dust and mud consuming every inch of it. It wasn't even possible to guess its color, but it attracted attention just by being there. Millie Hickson had been opening the morning shift for years and the early crowd was pretty much a set group.

Cautiously Millie turned into the lot and parked, all the while eyeing the car for any sign of movement. For a brief moment she thought she glimpsed a body slumped against the seat, but the fogged windows prevented any real view. She debated whether or not to call Tom as she carefully exited her car.

Her white waitressing shoes softly crunched the gravel as she made her way toward the diner. The wet chill air of a Northeast morning made her shiver. Millie paused again and inched her way back, circling the strange car. Another gust of wind blew, this one knifing right through her. So much for detecting. She clutched her already closed coat closer and headed inside—warmth taking precedence.

The moment Millie flicked on the fluorescent lights she hit autopilot, the mystery of the car left behind with the slamming of the door. She set the walls echoing as she grabbed the heavy-duty metal coffee pot and put up the first brew. That accomplished, she began to check the stations, refilling the sugar, setting out the creamers and cursing the night crew— in what had become her morning ritual—for a job half-assed done as always.

The ringing of the door opening made Millie jump. Her eyes registered a woman—though she looked more like a teenage boy, her jeans and thread-bare sweater hanging off her thin frame, her shortish black hair falling lank over her eyes. There was something about her that seemed virtually translucent, a lost child, frightened and fragile.

"Morning," Millie called out.

The woman looked up and registered her with a blink.

"You can sit anywhere, but you're early. Charley's the short order cook and he doesn't come on 'til six. So you got about ten minutes to wait."

For a moment Millie didn't know if the woman heard her. Then slowly her eyes rose, blinked, and again looked down. She cleared her throat and then, almost as if it was something she had forgotten how to do, she spoke, "Can I get a cup of coffee?"

"Now that's the one thing I do have. Got some truckers who pull through early so I always start it first. Brand new pot, fresh brewed." Millie continued this boisterous litany as she made her way around the Formica counter. She wasn't sure why, but somehow it seemed like this would be the only way to keep the woman from fleeing. Not like whether she stayed or left was such a big deal, but there was something about her, about the way her eyes opened like huge pools inviting you to jump in only then quickly closing. It was like standing at an empty pool and fantasizing it filled with water only in reverse. Whatever. It seemed to be working.

As Millie grabbed a cup and saucer, pulling the spigot down, the woman gingerly approached the chrome edge of a red vinyl barstool. Her fingers made a motion as though to spin the stool, only they never really touched.

"Here you go, hon. There's cream and sugar if you need it and my name's Millie," she continued rambling on, tapping at her plastic nametag. "You need anything else, you just ask."

The woman wrapped both of her hands around the cup, trying to absorb its heat. The unrelenting shimmer of the diner with its sparkling chrome and fluorescent lights assaulted her senses. The rows of cakes staring blankly out from behind their refrigerated shelves set her stomach churning. The constant cheerful chatter of the waitress, whose red hair clashed vividly with the hideous pink uniform, continued this attack on her senses. Everything seemed to be reeling.

§ § §

The quiet of the bathroom was like a tall drink of water. She leaned against the wall, the light green tile, like a chilled glass, dripping its icy sweat onto her forehead. Gradually the white noise pounding her brain began to recede. Slowly she pulled herself off the tile and turned toward the mirror. Her hand reached out toward the face reflecting back—it was the face of a stranger.

She sat on the toilet, nestled securely in the tight confines of the stall. Time passed. It was so safe, so quiet. She didn't want to leave.

§ § §

Millie juggled some plates and continued with the coffee refills. She breathed a sigh of relief when she saw the restroom door swing open.

§ § §

How long had she been gone? It had gotten so busy. More people, another waitress, the kitchen "pick-up" bell chiming. The dizziness threatened once again to engulf her. It was too loud, too bright. She struggled for air. It was too hard. She looked up.

Millie's eyes tracked the woman's entrance and honed in on her. Millie stopped pouring, stopped moving. Through the din Millie could hear her own heart pounding. She realized she was holding her breath, willing this woman to find her way back out.

Millie's plea registered as though it had been spoken out loud. The woman looked up and met the waitress's eyes and clung to them, an unseen rope for her to grasp. She knew she could grab this line, that somehow it would be okay, that this waitress could help her through. Slowly she inched her way, using her fingertips to clutch and hug the walls—a not-blind woman's Braille, pulling herself along. Finally she reached it, her corner of the counter, her oasis, her hand once again gripped her cup.

The ringing counter bell sliced through this unseen thread. "Hey Millie, pick up already, would ya?"

"Hold your horses, Charley." Millie turned, grabbing the assorted plates of eggs, toast and pancakes, stacking them at angles along her left arm and hand. Her right hand grabbed the syrup. Plates in hand, Millie passed back through the counter divide, sliding by the dollar bill tucked neatly under the edge of the saucer.

§ § §

She wearily fled from the discord of the diner and went to pump gas. Struggling to keep a hold of the pump, to manage the thick black hose, which seemed to wriggle and writhe in spite of her attempts to tame it. The glare from the morning light of a winter's sun added another throbbing beat to her already aching head. She looked away. Her eyes took in the lot next door to the diner—a junkyard. She squinted at the sign, THE TOWN DUMP. The pump clicked, she replaced it and sank back into her car.

As she pulled out, something her eye must have unconsciously, unseeingly caught, and yet somehow registered, forced her to brake. Backing up she stopped alongside the junkyard. She could see nothing. She wanted to turn around, put the car in gear and go, but she knew it was too late. Dread forced her from the car. Leaden legs carried her onward. Her head screamed "no" even as her hands reached out and grasped the chain link fence. She pressed forward as though this would help her focus. It was there. "Turn away now," she commanded, closing her eyes, rocking back from the fence. "Too late," her brain intoned. "But maybe you're imagining things," came the doubtful reply. She re-opened her eyes. It was still there.

§ § §

Lyle Johnson walked the eight blocks as he had done every day for nearly fifty years now. To an outsider this was the kind of place where they claimed nothing ever changed. But he knew they were wrong. Things did change; you just had to know where to look. Once he had been young, strapping Lyle Johnson, jauntily making his way down the street, stopping to make sure "Old Misses Wallis" was okay, flirting with Elsie Smythe of the bluest eyes to be found for miles. Now Mrs. Wallis was long gone, her house sold four times over. Elsie Smythe had married a naval officer and took off to see the world. And as for him, he was no longer strapping or jaunty, just "Old Man Johnson," leaning more on his walking stick, growing weary in mind, body and spirit.

Lyle looked at the houses—houses he passed every day. Like him, they seemed weary, no longer young and enterprising. The wood frames had once sparkled with promise, their colors bright, trims neat. Now, they were chipped and faded, the paint and the promise ravaged by time. Once the lawns were well-tended patches of green, now they were space savers for rusted out cars and bikes, for weeds and dirt. Even the sidewalks were no longer smooth and even. Tree roots and water had wreaked their havoc, transforming a daily stroll into a mass of uneven cracks and fissures leaving treachery in their wake. Yep. Everything changes. Just not everybody sees.

Lyle glanced at the boy as he turned the corner. He sat off to the side, his arms wrapped around his legs, his chin on his knees. The old man passed him, continuing his steady gate, past the junkyard up to the diner.

§ § §

They say weariness can consume you. What they don't tell you is—not fast enough. She was so tired. She knew she should just get up and move on, but she couldn't. Everything hurt. She hadn't known that hair could hurt, that teeth could ache, and that even fingernails could share the pain. She hadn't known that turning numb would be such a painful ordeal.

§ § §

As he entered Millie looked up and smiled, "Morning Lyle, the usual?" Millie no longer waited for a response. The question was just a kind of polite ritual. Six days a week since the day she started, Lyle Johnson came in and ate the same breakfast, rain or shine, summer or winter, year in and year out. About the only thing that ever changed was which jam he put on his toast and Millie knew that was only because she changed which jam packet she put on his plate. He came in precisely at eight-thirty. Left at nine o'clock. Didn't matter how busy or full up the place was, the first stool to the left of the counter divide was for Lyle Johnson and everyone knew it. And if by chance you weren't a local, not to worry, a local would be sure to educate you real fast. As far as Millie was concerned, the President of the United States would be told that stool belonged to Lyle Johnson and he'd just have to sit somewhere else.

Millie grabbed a clean cup from the upside down stack, flipped it over and reached for the spigot, "Hey Charley, poach one, slice of whole wheat toast."

Lyle Johnson polished off the last sip of his refill, glanced down at his watch and reached for his walking stick, "See you later, Millie."

Down the stairs, over by the fence, Lyle saw the boy was still sitting exactly as before. Mindful of the stranger Lyle pulled out his keys and began to untangle the chains holding the gate closed. As he finished, the boy slowly unraveled his arms and stood up.

§ § §

She moved cautiously into the junkyard, aware he was watching her. Her hands were clenched deep inside the pockets of her jeans, balled little fists, nails digging into her flesh. Her shoulders hunched about her. Her eyes never stopped scanning, her heart racing a mile a minute.

"Hey boy, can I help you with something?"

She pulled her eyes away and turned toward the voice. "I thought I saw a carousel." The hoarse whisper was more statement than question.

"Yep. Or what's left of one anyways. It's in the back. Been there oh, at least, um, forty years now." Lyle began to pick his way through, the young boy following right behind him. "Yep. Must have been the summer of sixty-five. Bought it off some Carnies." The memory made him chuckle. "Said this was it, they'd had it. They were going to San Francisco and become hippies. Get some of that free love that was goin' around. Yep. Hunk of junk it was too. Didn't run, had pieces missing. Funny, thought people would want it but didn't work out that way. Seems to just hang on year after year."

Lyle's voice trailed off as he realized he had lost his audience. The young boy stared, mesmerized at the sight before him. "Well boy, that's it. What do you think?"

Lyle watched as the boy circled carefully around the ruins. Slowly he made his way back around, stopping at a horse lying on the ground. He knelt. Lyle watched the hand come out of the pocket and almost reverently stroke the horse's nose. It was as if the boy was listening to hear what that old piece of wood had to say.

Lyle watched the hand run over the carved mane and, in its caress, Lyle suddenly realized he wasn't watching a young boy, but a girl. A skinny little thing. He continued to watch, waiting to see what she would say.

She sat stroking, feeling, listening for something only she could hear. Her eyes kept scanning the broken pieces. They were most likely the desolate ruins of an Old Parker County Fair. Probably had been a thirty- eight foot carousel, its thirty-two horses and two chariots spinning brightly around, music piping, carrying a brass ring of good fortune for one happy-go-lucky rider. Now there were maybe eighteen, maybe nineteen horses left, and some of them, she could tell even from where she crouched, were damaged beyond repair. No longer a carousel, they were barely even a herd. More than forty years of neglect and exposure to the elements echoed their pain to her. Slowly she made contact with each one. Lyle watched and waited, waited and watched.

Her head tilted down toward the horse where she began. Finally she seemed to have an answer. Never getting up, she spoke to the old man. "I want to restore them."

Lyle snorted, "This ain't no museum. This is a junkyard. I sell junk. You want them, you buy them."

"Can't buy them. But I can make them whole," she said, struggling to construct an argument that might sway the junkman. "Probably be worth a lot more to you whole. There's probably a whole lot of people who would pay big money for a restored horse."

Lyle sat himself back on a pile of assorted junk. His right hand rocked his walking stick back and forth as though it was a metronome keeping beats for the thoughts in his head. He looked at the girl squatting down, her hands still touching the horse. "How do I know you can fix it?"

"Can't make it worse."

Lyle looked at her hands, white knuckled now, clutching the horse's mane. He searched her face. Didn't quite know what he was looking for. She held his gaze. Something 'bout her eyes reminded him of Elsie Smythe, although he certainly couldn't say what, and darned if he wasn't just thinking of Elsie that very morning. The walking stick continued its steady beat. Lyle sighed, silencing the stick's rhythm, "Well, like I said, been here about forty years. I suppose if you were to restore it, I'd at least get me some room back here." Lyle used his stick to get upright. "Yep. I suppose that could be worth it."

She watched as he walked slowly away. She released her breath, unaware that she had even been holding it. Gingerly she leaned her head down against the horse, "It's going to be all right."

She sat there waiting for him, just like yesterday. Well, almost just like yesterday. As Lyle drew
closer he could make out piles of tools and such.
He knew he told her she could work on the
horses, but he wasn't ready to see her at this
hour. His annoyance mounted. Well he didn't
rightly care how gung ho she was feeling. He
had a sign right on his fence—Business Hours
Monday through Friday, 9:00 AM - 12:00 PM,
1:00 PM - 5:00 PM, Saturday 9:00 AM - 3:00 PM,
Closed Sunday. Lyle peered over, yep, it was
hanging right there. She was just going to have to wait alright. He
was going to go and have his breakfast and then come and open up just
like his sign said. Yep. It wasn't as if he didn't have it spelled out in plain
English!

Lyle continued to walk stiffly by, deliberately ignoring her presence in
his driveway. Of course, he reasoned, maybe she can't read. He climbed
the steps to the diner and turned back around. She hadn't moved.

"Okay Missy, here's what I'm gonna do." Lyle paused as she stood up.
If she heard him change from "boy" to "Missy," she gave no outward
reaction. "I'm gonna open up the fence so as you can get your stuff inside
and get started on account of your being here waiting and all. But then
I'm gonna put the lock back on and go have my breakfast 'cause like this
here sign says, I don't open until nine o'clock!"

Lyle punctuated his annoyance at having his morning ritual interrupted
by pointing to the posted sign. The girl stood there, realized he was
waiting for something. Slowly she blinked and then looked down. With a
large sigh, Lyle leaned over and grabbed the chain.

She heard the chains settle and the lock click back into place. Grabbing
some of the bags, she twisted her way around the maze of junk toward
the back. One by one she laid out her tools, placing them gently around
the first horse.

They were all store-bought new, glistening the way your brand-
spanking new back-to-school shoes shined that very first day. These
tools had no scuffmarks, no tales to tell. As she laid them out her eyes
canvassed the rest of the junkyard. She didn't even know what half of
these things were supposed to be. How many hours had someone slaved

to save enough money to buy that thing, that precious thing, which now lived here? So many things, so much history, once so dear to someone, now piled haphazardly, discarded and long forgotten. She looked back to the horse, "But not you, you were never discarded. Just tucked away. Tucked away, waiting for me."

"Hey Lady!"

Somewhere in the recess of her mind she heard the cry.

"Hey Lady! You deaf or something!"

Again, the voice, shrill and insistent, shrieked through the air. She turned and her eyes took in a young boy, maybe eight, maybe nine, stopped in the parking lot, his feet planted defiantly on either side of his black bike. Even at this distance she could make out a face full of freckles, each freckle fiercely distinct as if they were individually rising up to help him issue his challenge.

"Hey Lady, whaddaya think you're doing, huh?" The boy never paused in his shouting. "That's Old Man Johnson's place and he don't open until nine o'clock and it ain't nine o'clock yet!"

The boy stared determinedly at her. If she only had language left to give, she might try and answer him, tell him it was okay. But she didn't, and it wasn't, so she couldn't. Instead, she thought absurdly of *High Noon* and in her mind began counting paces. Suddenly, the boy dropped his bike and went flying up the stairs.

"Mr. Johnson!" the boy's screech began outside and continued as he pushed through the glass door so hard it nearly shattered. He continued tearing through the diner like a house on fire, knocking into Millie who in turn nearly dropped Mrs. Jeffer's tea into her lap. The dozen or so customers scattered throughout felt their hearts drop to their stomachs. All the normal sounds of breakfast just stopped. "Mr. Johnson, there's some lady in your junk yard, probably stealing all you got!"

Almost before Lyle could put down the toast he had just been about to bite into, over half the diner was out of their seats and making for the door. Lyle struggled to get to his feet and gain some attention, "Hang on Billy Ray, everybody, it's all right."

"But Mr. Johnson, I ain't lying, I saw her," the young boy whined. He could feel his spotlight slipping away.

"I know you did Billy Ray," Lyle patted the young boy's shoulder, "and I'm really thankful you're as smart as you are, coming in here to get me so fast, but this time it's all right, I let her in." Lyle could feel the whole diner staring. What he had started as a kind of apology quickly became a defensive challenge. "She's gonna fix up that old carousel."

The disappointment to this somewhat dubious announcement was palpable. What had rapidly become a major thief who they could all race out and nab turned out to be a merry-go-round repair lady (as she was instantly dubbed), sapping all the wind from their sails.

Lyle Johnson leaned over and reached for his cane, making his way stiltedly past the still suspicious Billy Ray Ryan, through the still-staring crowd and out the door. He didn't even wait for his free refill.

§ § §

Each hammer blow resounded, firm in its ability, lonesome in its unaccustomed surroundings. At last the makeshift shelter was complete. It wasn't much to look at, some two-by-fours and tarping, but it would provide more than a working spot in the midst of the chaos of the yard; it would provide shade and some protection. The openness was too much, the exposure too great. This would be much better.

Lyle Johnson walked home for lunch, having once again locked the girl in. She didn't seem to mind, leastwise she didn't say anything, but he felt real strange about it anyway. He had never locked a person in before, but then again, this way she wouldn't be bothered by customers. She sure didn't talk enough to sell anybody anything. But still, locking her in, he wasn't sure if he was doing the right thing. She didn't seem quite right. On the other hand, he'd lived long enough to understand that different people got different ways about them and she didn't seem quite not-right either. He just wasn't sure. Yep. Just wasn't sure.

Lyle paused and looked down the block. There was a time he knew them all, called them friends. Trusted them to watch his back and they trusted him to watch theirs. Those days were long gone. He locked her in 'cause he had to look after himself. Yep. There was a time if a man stole from you it was 'cause he was hungry. Yep. Once even thieves had honor. These days you had to look after yourself, lock your doors and windows. His eyes searched the block again. How many times did he turn on the news and see some story about someone who died and no one knew for weeks on account of they didn't have any neighbors to check up on them.

Nope. These days you check up on your neighbor and you're being too nosey. Yep. It's a fact. People just don't take pride in being neighborly anymore. You just got to look after yourself.

§ § §

She looked at the horse lying on the ground. Miriam. She knew it was Miriam as soon as she saw her. The armor surrounding the pony's head was chipped and weathered, but life was still there in her eyes, still playful, teasing, prancing despite all she'd been through; she knew she could bring her back. That the diseases ravaging her could be stopped and Miriam could stand as proud—maybe even prouder—as she ever had.

She felt her hands shaking and wrapped them quickly around her body, never breaking eye contact with Miriam. She felt another tremor and decided she should take a break, maybe eat something. Maybe just get back in the car and keep on driving. Yeah right. If she could have done that she wouldn't be here now.

She walked to the gate. It was locked. She had forgotten. Or maybe she never really knew. She couldn't remember. It really didn't matter.

§ § §

Lyle cleaned up the crumbs his sandwich had left and rinsed his utensils, setting them in the drain board. He could never understand why people who lived alone couldn't rinse their own lunch dishes and instead, stacked them up for a whole week in the dishwasher, waiting until they had enough to wash. Seemed to him it used up a lot more energy that way than by just washing his own plate then and there.

As he locked his door, he thought again of the girl locked in his yard. Maybe she was hungry, she sure was skinny. He could feel his earlier anger mounting. She wasn't there even one day and she kept interfering with his routine. It was absurd. Yep. Downright absurd!

He made it to the end of his walkway before giving in. The problem with having a thought is you've had it and now there's no way to get rid of it because it's already there. Yep. No point in pretending otherwise.

§ § §

She turned around and walked slowly back. There was no running. Hell, she couldn't even walk out! This was stupid. What made her think she could breathe life back into this carousel? She should have kept driving. She should have at least thought about what this would entail. Her lungs fought her, begging for air. She had been driven by emotion, by desire. Maybe just sheer exhaustion. She had not stopped to think. Wanting and believing is not the same thing as being able. Closing her eyes, she slid down along the fence.

The white noise began to engulf her. Captive, captive, captive, the chant began in her head. A fleeting vision of climbing the fence danced tantalizingly across her eyes. Breathe, she ordered herself, trying to stop the panic. Prisoner! Her clenched fist knuckled against her forehead. No, he will be back. If she could only force her fear back in maybe it would help. Prisoner! Her mind continued to taunt. Her fists knuckled in, meeting each barb with equal force. Without warning, she felt her hand pushed gently. It was as though it was being nuzzled.

She flashed open her eyes, stared down at her hand. There was nothing there but still her fist unclenched. The white noise began to fade and she heard a familiar mocking. "God you think too much. Try just going with the feeling, jumping on in, following your heart." She tried to shake it off. "Your heart silly, not your head," the amusement in the voice was not hidden in the admonishment.

She opened her eyes. "Well there you have it!" With a deep breath she unfisted her fingers, pushed herself upright and stepped away from the fence. She stared at the broken-down menagerie strewn before her. I follow my heart and now I have a whopping headache!

She got up and paced—first left to right, then right to left, always stopping at Miriam. Miriam was probably not the place to start, but Miriam was everything. If she could bring Miriam back to her, she could do anything. Without Miriam, it wouldn't matter.

Gently she sat down on the ground and took Miriam's head, positioning it in her lap. She looked into the eyes, unmoving, unblinking, but still somehow filled with trust. Gently she leaned down and rubbed her forehead between those eyes. It was a pledge of love, a promise to try.

She rose and found the bags she had brought, opened one and removed a pair of rubber pants and a jumbo rubber apron. Another bag held the dichloromethane and the brushes. She looked around and breathed a sigh of relief as she spotted a spigot inside her cage. Grabbing the bucket she made her way toward the outer wall of the small shack that was Lyle Johnson's office.

It was time to begin. With infinite care she started the arduous task of stripping away all the abuse and neglect, shedding layers to find the beauty hidden under the paint, cracks and chips—the beauty designed by a craftsman so many years ago.

Miriam would have laughed at her. Probably said something like, "Knock it off. Strip off all my war paint and what you find may be many things—but definitely not beauty!"

But she knew Miriam was wrong. All that war paint was a façade. An exterior created to keep the world from seeing all the beauty hidden beneath. Just layers of defense.

It is astonishing how you can live your life, dragging through, day by day, slogging through the muck, and be content—if not happy—and then, suddenly, someone comes along to make that existence seem barren. To make you see you were living but you didn't have a life. If it were a TV commercial, Windex-Man would knock on your door, spray your eyes, and with the quick wipe of a tissue a layer of grease would disappear, making the world actually sparkle. That was Miriam's gift. She was born to be Windex-Man. She challenged life at every turn, making everything vibrant. She was fire and light. Miriam always insisted vehemently that ignorance was not bliss.

Her hands gently traced the horse's brow. She was no longer sure Miriam was right.

§ § §

She drove the three and a half miles to the campground she had found the other night. Come summer it would probably be jam-packed, but it was too early in the year for anybody but the foolhardiest fools to come out. Only a crazy person would be out here now. How poetically accurate.

"If you can be sardonic and witty in your head I don't think you are fully mad and certainly not mad as a hatter!"

She pushed her hands to her ears, "Shut up." She didn't want to talk now. She just wanted to find quiet, a small piece of silence for just a minute.

It was not to be. She sat on a stump listening to the night noises. It's a strange thing how loud random sounds become once it gets really quiet. There really isn't any such thing as silence because the air fills with all this other noise. Leaves rustling, animals talking, even the creaks and groans of the earth. It's air filled with sounds the daytime won't let through.

Before she left she had finally sifted her way through the horses. She hated it. It was like carousel triage. Which could be saved, which were too far gone. Now there were only fifteen to contend with, and three of them were iffy at best.

From his vantage point high up on the ridge Sheriff Tom MacElwain watched her. If she had looked up, even from this distance, she would have been able to guess law enforcement. Partly it was his posture, a stance so erect it felt chiseled. Partly it emanated from his eyes, hawk-like. They didn't simply survey the terrain; they sought any prey that hadn't taken cover. His eyes could cover miles, taking everything in, reflecting nothing back. And Tom MacElwain didn't like strangers. Strangers meant trouble and he didn't want trouble on his turf. He wished he owned a pair of those fancy night binoculars. Damn! Why did it have to be such a black night? There was no big old moon to help him see, not even a sliver of stupid Cheshire Cat grinning in the sky. He turned, slinking silently backwards into the dark.

Below, she opened a brown paper bag, took out a banana and began to eat her dinner. The peel went back into the bag and she pulled out a can of tuna and a can of Coke. Dining had become mechanical. Chew and swallow. Sip and swallow. Her stomach lurched, but she persevered. She was unaware of the eyes watching her.

Sheriff Tom MacElwain had returned. He now watched her through the night scope attached to his hunting rifle. In the cross hairs, she was his prey. His earlier annoyance turned to adrenaline as he followed her every move, the rifle tracking, his mind creating a vivid tableau of himself as the great hunter.

She stood up. The great hunter tensed. She put her empty cans into the bag, opened the car door and set the bag on the passenger floor. She reached in to grab something from under the seat. Her hand felt around; he leaned forward taking aim. She pulled herself out of the car, her hand clutching ... he squinted into the scope ... toilet paper?

She tore off several sheets, reclaimed her brown bag from the front seat floor and walked into the woods. As she removed her pants and squatted, it crossed her mind that there was a slight absurdity to moving into another part of the forest for privacy, as though it made any difference where she peed. What made this section of the woods more appropriate as an outhouse than the one she had been dining in? Not that you'd want to eat and use the same place for a bathroom, just that with no one around, she still went searching for privacy. Space designated place. She had read stories, everyone had, of crazy people leaving their feces wherever they were. She guessed she wasn't crazy enough yet. All those miles and she still had some marbles left. Space. Place. Floor-planning the great outdoors. Old habits die hard, harder than we know. Even the wilderness must be divided to provide appropriate housing.

Rolling his eyes he set down the rifle. "Damn," Tom muttered, trying to stamp his feet and not make any noise, "it is a cold fucking night."

She emerged from the bushes, opened her car trunk and leaned down.

"Fuck!" He hadn't been paying enough attention when he settled in. "Stupid fucking mistake," he cursed. He couldn't see into the trunk from his angle. "A god-damned eight-year old could do better." This was not going to be his night. Before he could even shift himself to a new sight line, she straightened out. He lunged for his scope.

She stood there looking at the mess in her trunk. Her eyes focused on a big white plastic bag with a tie. Her hands trembling, she loosened the tie and still holding the bag closed, moved her nose to the opening. Her vise-like grip softened just enough to allow for a small opening. She pushed her nose into the plastic and breathed, her eyes squeezed shut, sucking in as much air as her lungs would allow. Lifting her head, she released the air. She paused and leaned back into the bag. This time she seemed to draw in what she needed. Her left hand closed around the bag as she carefully replaced the tie.

One hand shut the trunk as she emerged, her other clutched a blanket. She climbed into the back seat and locked her door. Reaching into the crack between the front seat and the reclining portion, her hand slinked down in the small space. Her fingertips scrounged until they found a leather cord and she felt the ring it held. Lying down, eyes closed tight, she rubbed the circular metal like a talisman as she prayed for sleep to come quickly. Don't think, just sleep, she begged herself, don't think, just sleep, willing, pleading, a pounding litany.

She didn't hear the man lower his rifle, slip backward into the night, walk the mile to where he'd parked and drive off.

§ § §

Jess Kastellon lowered herself from the window as she had done so many times before. She knew they wouldn't know she was gone. They had changed her bedroom when they discovered she was sneaking out, moved her across the hall, away from the exterior porch overhang. They never realized she could reach the old maple tree. Before that day was over, Jess Kastellon had climbed that very tree and tied a rope 'round one of the branches. Now, her fingertips gripped the sill and her legs dangled free. She stretched and twisted, using her toes to reach for that rope. Finally, her toes caught the very edge and she worked it up between her legs, rubbing it along, first one side then the other until her knees finally grasped it. She let go of the ledge and dangled precariously upside down as the rope swung like a pendulum, back and forth.

In the midst of the swing Jess pulled herself upright and climbed onto her branch. There was no fear, no question of falling. The movements were choreographed, in complete control. Jess paused for just a moment, just long enough to remove the sneakers she had tied around her neck and lace them up.

She shimmied her way down the tree, wishing she could wear her boots but they were too hard to hold onto. Besides, they made too much noise when she jumped down. Still, boots were better, tougher. There wasn't anything Jess Kastellon couldn't do when she wore her boots.

At this hour the world was her kingdom. Set free by the stars, Jess became a Knight in King Arthur's Court prepared to do battle, a Musketeer out to avenge an insult, a cowboy riding to lead a posse or maybe a General in the cavalry, rushing in to save the day! She was Annie Oakley, Jemima Boone and Calamity Jane all rolled into one. Her fine steeds could best anybody. She swung down the last branch, dangled and dropped.

Tonight as she made her way to town, she was only Jess, wanting to see—needing to see—if Billy Ray was telling the truth. Billy Ray Ryan liked to tell stories. It's a fact. He was always bragging about this or that, and some of them were whoppers. Jess knew that and she didn't think Billy

Ray was smart enough to be making this one up, but she didn't know for sure. So she needed to check it out for herself. She snuck up to the fence, looked in.

There they were—her horses. Here's where they stayed, safely corralled, waiting for new adventures. Jess had ridden each and every one of them in her nightly quests.

§ § §

She bolted upright. Something had jarred her wide-awake. What was it? Her eyes darted nervously. Her hands reached out frantically, checking the door locks. Everything seemed still. But. "What is it?" She pressed her fingertips to her head, squeezed her eyes shut. "Think."

It was Miriam. She could hear her. She was talking to somebody, to a little girl, but it wasn't her. It couldn't be her. Miriam couldn't have known her when she was little. It wasn't possible. She curled into a ball, pushing her body as deeply into the seat as she could.

§ § §

"It's okay, Jess," Miriam said softly, her voice laced with loving patience. "It's a good thing."

Jess' small hands clutched one last time at the fence. It was time to go. She walked home, very small against the night. She wished she had worn her boots.

§ § §

The old lady lay awake in the dark. It was hard to know her age. She only knew she was older than she could count anymore. She had been feeling that something was happening. She could feel the change in the air that night. She knew something was up.

She didn't bother to get out of bed. Didn't bother to turn on a light. Wouldn't make any difference. Her eyes had stopped working years ago. At the time, she thought she'd be lost without them. But now she knew different. She knew that eyes only give a person one kind of sight. Now she could smell change, hear the difference carried on the wind and feel truth in her bones. She didn't tell anyone what she knew. They didn't want to hear. They didn't believe her when she spoke. They believed only what they could see, not what she could tell them. She no longer told them anything. She left her voice behind with her sight. She kept what she knew to herself. Just like tonight. Tonight she knew. She didn't know what it meant, but she knew for sure change was in the air.

The sight of the car in the parking lot brought a grim smile to Millie's lips as she pulled up. She wasn't really sure why, but the feeling was a peculiar kind-of self defense reflex. There was just...something—a resentment of some sort. Into her mind popped the opening from *Mission Impossible.* "Your mission, Millie, should you decide to accept it, will be to force the merry-go-round repair lady to speak." Millie gave her mascara a final check in the rear view mirror and chuckled—a bit maliciously.

Millie opened her car door, and with her hand still holding the door handle, turned in her seat and contemplated for a last brief second. Suddenly Millie popped-out, swung the car door behind her and made a beeline toward the dirt-encrusted mound across the way. What was it Daddy always said, something about "the best offense being a good defense?" Or was it the other way around? Who cares? It's time to engage.

She gave her keys a slight toss, grasped them and turned. Without waiting to see how she'd be received, Millie crossed directly in front of the mud-clad car, stopping at the grill to holler, perky as all get out, "Coffee will be ready in five minutes!" That pronounced, Millie whipped herself around and headed to open up.

§ § §

She sat frozen, not quite sure what had happened. Instinctively her hand reached for her car keys, turned the ignition on.

§ § §

Millie heard the car engine turn over but forced herself not to turn around. Let her run. No skin off her nose. Finish unlocking the door and get to work. Millie turned off the alarm, turned on the lights and got on with the side work. Just as she finished placing out the fresh creamers, the jingle of the door opening announced a customer. Millie smiled to herself. "Gotcha!"

She had put the car in gear fully intending to peel out of there, to continue her trip into oblivion. Instead, she had let it idle and looked over toward the junkyard. The sigh she heaved was full of anguish and resignation. She wasn't going anywhere. She reached for the keys, turning the car off, pounding her fists against the steering wheel. Defeated, she accepted the challenge and made her way toward the door. She entered, and sidled silently over to the counter.

Millie got up from the table she'd been working, gave the countertop a quick wipe, poured a cup of coffee and set it down. Without pausing she returned to her side work. Only the sound of the glass sugar container being unscrewed and re-screwed broke the silence.

She played with the spoon, cleared her throat, played with the spoon some more. "Thank you." It would barely qualify as a whisper.

Still, Millie considered, it was a start. She had engaged the enemy and come out on top. All right, so it wasn't exactly mission accomplished, more like . . . The bell rang again, signaling the arrival of another person. As Millie rose, she caught the woman quickly drop the spoon and wrap her hands around the mug, effectively shutting down.

"Hey, Millie honey," a voice boomed from an enormous bear of a man. "How you doin'?"

"Hiya, Joe." Millie tried to keep her annoyance at bay and grabbed for a cup, "Just pull in?"

"Drove all night." Joe Norstak leaned across the counter. "Just so I could get to you. You sure are one pretty sight for these road-weary eyes."

Millie rolled her eyes. She'd heard it all before, some more silver-tongued than others, but all of it had been said before. One of these days, she vowed, someone was actually going to surprise her. She spared a chagrined glance at the strange, quiet woman and realized that this morning she had no patience for Joe and his games. "Charley's running a bit behind," Millie called out, managing to hold her voice steady as she placed the now-filled cup down in front of the big man.

"Aw, c'mon Millie." Neither the presence of the stranger at the counter nor Millie's non-response registered. Nothing ever deterred Joe Norstak's morning flirtations in the least. "Let me take you away from all this. Hop in my truck and we'll drive, just you and me, to the ends of the earth."

"Let's see, just you, me and your brother, Rudy. Now doesn't that sound cozy?" The front door chimed again as Charley blew in. "Ah! Saved by the bell! Morning Charley. You got here just in time. Joe needs his eggs scrambled—with saltpeter." Millie shot Joe her mock glare, honed to perfection over the years. It occurred to her, and not for the first time, that if someone actually did have an original thought, she might just take them up on it.

Millie stopped behind the counters to put the ketchups away. She quickly refilled the woman's coffee, not waiting for, nor expecting comment, knowing the moment had passed.

§ § §

The morning had started out cold and damp, the mist providing steady moisture. As the day wore on, the sun rose steadily. She stopped what she was doing long enough to remove the raggedy blue sweater, revealing what had once been a white, and what was now simply a dingy, t-shirt.

At first her mind raced with thoughts she could not complete. She tried to make sense of the night before, tried to think what had happened that morning. The thoughts seemed incapable of settling. She knew she had once been capable of cohesive thought, but she couldn't seem to remember when. Now thoughts were like butterflies, pausing, teasing and somehow just tantalizingly out of reach. Just when you thought you might catch it, the wings flapped and lifted off with ease, leaving you stumbling about wildly, tangled in a drunken dance of arms, legs and gravity. Thinking was now a very busy, very manic, very unprofitable pastime. It was easier not to think. Calmer.

Whoosh. It was a gentle sound accompanying the soft nylon brush as it moved over and over, rubbing, massaging, currying the limbs of the horse, removing the grit and the grime and the garish layers of hastily reapplied paint. Her muscles rippled gently with each motion. There was great comfort in stripping paint. As long as she kept moving the nausea stayed at bay. Her stomach could have a moment of quiet. The swells of emptiness rocked gently by her rhythms; the feel of the brush as she rubbed away the years, uncovering fresh smooth surface. She wondered where the paste was that could dissolve her layers, let her brush away the ugly coating of life.

She felt her presence. Didn't even need to look up to know that the eyes watching her every move belonged to the little girl of the midnight visit. She had wondered when she would come.

Jess stood there watching the lady. She didn't say anything, didn't move any closer, she simply watched.

Lyle Johnson looked up from the day's paper. His window allowed him to oversee his entire yard. He watched Jess watching the lady. Lyle smiled. Jess Kastellon, now there was a young hellion for you. Faster and smarter than a whip. Yep. Always running, always in a hurry—places to go, things to do. Yep. She was a right little hellion that Jess.

Lyle thought that perhaps he should make introductions. Of course, that was hard to do when he didn't know the name of the lady sitting in the middle of his junkyard stripping his horse. Yep. His eyes traveled back and forth between the two. What was he supposed to say? See Jess, this here's some lady. Lyle watched as Jess moved a step closer. He thought back to that day, when little Jess couldn't have been more than three. He'd been in the office when Sharlyn Kastellon had come running, screaming for that child. Sharlyn had taken Jess and her twin sisters for lunch at the diner, but Jess had slipped away. Sharlyn thought she had been kidnapped. Lord, things got crazy. People running pell-mell from the diner, Sheriff Tom driving up, his lights flashing and siren blaring. Lyle, himself, rushing over to help. Before they could get organized, Jess had appeared screaming, "Mama! Mama! Look what I found!"

Lyle laughed to himself remembering how Sharlyn kept trying to hug the little girl, who just kept pushing and squirming and screaming. Finally Sharlyn put the child down and Jess started tugging and pulling, heading straight for the junkyard. Well, naturally everybody had to follow. This tiny little bitty thing had just about the whole town marching along right behind her. Darned if she didn't just sashay her little self right up to those old carousel ponies and say, "Look Mama, HORSES!" in a voice more awe inspiring than, than, old Reverend White on a Sunday sermon roll.

"Lyle Johnson, care to share the joke?"

Lyle jumped. He'd been so busy remembering he never heard Sheriff Tom come in. Lyle's eyes still shone wet from laughing. "Been thinking back on that day Little Jess got herself lost."

Tom laughed, "Had the whole town turned upside down as I recall. Sharlyn screaming, people running all this way and that." He paused thinking about it and then, laughing once again, "Probably the most excitement we'd all seen since Frank Hayworth's dog ate Greta Lyon's petunias and she chased him down that street wearing nothing but her birthday suit!"

The two men howled with laughter reliving the spectacle. "Yep," Lyle wiped his eyes, "That sure was quite a sight."

As their giddiness abated, Tom turned his attention out the office window. "Jess doesn't look too happy with our new visitor."

"Yep." Lyle grinned.

The two men continued to watch, unobserved. The lady kept on working. She hadn't asked Jess to come. Didn't want her; didn't need her. Jess kept on staring.

Tom watched the scene for another moment, then let his eyes wander around the office, his tension escalating as he glimpsed the old tackle box that passed for Lyle's cash register sitting right out on the counter. "Well I think I'm going to go get myself a cup of coffee." He gave Lyle's shoulder a squeeze before continuing. "Lyle Johnson, you be careful now, you hear me?"

Lyle smiled. "Yep. I hear you Sheriff. I hear you."

Tom strode resolutely across the tarred driveway. Reaching the landing leading up to the diner door, he turned back one more time. His face was expressionless, but his eyes, hidden by sunglasses, were cold. Sheriff MacElwain did not like strangers.

She finally looked up. Pushed her hair out of her eyes and allowed herself to make eye contact with the little girl, "Are you just going to stand there all day, or are you at least going to help?" The question came out stilted, harsh, even to her own ears.

Jess rocked back on her boots for just a second. Then, never taking her eyes off her target, she began to move slowly around the fence.

The lady reached into the bag that held a small rubber apron and gloves. They'd been waiting. She showed Jess how to apply the paste and gently use the brush to loosen and remove the paint. She sat back down and cradled the head. Jess sat down by the tail and set to work. Their lives suddenly joined by the horse between them. Neither one said anything. Lyle watched for a few minutes, then picked up his paper and went back to reading.

§ § §

She awoke slowly beginning the arduous procedure of unraveling her cramped body from her makeshift back-seat bed, amazed to see the morning. It seemed a lifetime ago since she had slept through the night.

Millie turned in her sleep, her blankets tossed about, her arms hugging a pillow. Tom MacElwain smiled at the sight before him, leaned over and kissed her cheek, whispering, "Duty calls." The sheriff settled his hat and as he exited the small A-frame house. Millie burrowed deeper into the covers, neither willing nor ready to face the day. A smile played on her lips, as she drifted back toward her dreams, God, she loved Sundays!

She paced around her car in In the nearly empty parking lot. She hadn't even thought about Sunday. Even if she had, she would not have known today was Sunday. She looked at the locked gate, at the sign that read, "Closed on Sundays." Her hand anxiously shoved her hair from her forehead. She hadn't thought about Sunday.

She sat down near the fence. Stood up and paced. Sat back down. Maybe he would think of her and come and open up.

Lyle Johnson's voice rang out with an "Amen." It had been a fir service, a good, solid service. The young pastor, Reverend William D .ton, was shaping up just fine. Lyle remembered when this young man with his long hair had first arrived almost three years ago. Lyle didn't think much of him then, but, yep, Lyle had to admit he was coming along just fine.

Jess Kastellon hated Sundays. She sat fuming and fidgeting in her pew. Sharlyn leaned over, "Enough Jess. Just sit still!" Sharlyn laid her hand across her daughter's lap in an attempt to stop the squirming machine that was Jess. She looked forward, praying for God to grant her strength.

Jess eyed her sisters, singing up within the choir, with contempt. She hated church, hated having to wear a dress and absolutely hated having to sit still. She couldn't figure out why God cared whether or not she wore a dress. She certainly did not care whether or not God did.

Jess continued to fidget as Reverend Dalton droned on, reciting the week's upcoming activities. "Boring!" she proclaimed to herself. She turned in her pew just as Billy Ray did. As their eyes met he stuck out his tongue at her. Before she could react, she heard her mother's, "Jess," in that well-known tone. Jess slunk down in her seat, her foot kicking the bench in front of her.

As the choir sang its final hymn of the morning, the Reverend made his way down the aisle, throwing open the doors to reveal the sunshine of a near-perfect Sunday. Lyle stood up, moving stiffly into the quay of handshakes and well wishers.

"I'll tell you Mrs. Kastellon, Jennie and Joanie sound more like angels with each week." The two girls giggled as the Reverend spoke. "You must be very proud." Sharlyn hugged the girls to her, smiling her thanks as she stepped from the church. Lyle listened from his place in the line, noting Reverend William Dalton tactfully said nothing about little Jess' antics. Yep. He was coming along just fine.

The line continued forward and Lyle looked up into the Reverend's outstretched hand. "A fine service Reverend," he said, moving to allow Billy Ray to tear through the doors with Jess right on his heels, shrieking something about "killing him." The Reverend and Lyle exchanged knowing grins. Stepping back, Lyle donned his going-to-church hat.

"Why thank you Mr. Johnson. I hear you've had some excitement down at your shop this week?"

"Yep." Lyle politely touched his fingers to the brim of his cap and turned before the Reverend could ask any more questions. He most assuredly had not figured on how much attention this lady was going to create. As he headed toward the street he eyed several of the biddies with suspicion. Wasn't a body allowed to do some fixing up without it being a cause for discussion! Nope. He never would have thought painting some merry-go-round ponies would be such a major event.

She knew he wouldn't be coming, but still she couldn't leave. She stared at Miriam through the fencing, staring until the links began to blur. She could remember the cold metal of the hospital. She could remember being able to see Miriam but not being able to touch. The bars of the bed, they were icy, frozen barriers. All those machines, steely, reflective, ominous in their sparkle.

Her eyes began to burn. She didn't blink, didn't look away. She let the pain take over. It felt like pin pricks sparking from within. The burn grew. She would not blink; she would not turn.

"Hey, hey, hey, it's a busy day."

She would not answer.

"Didn't your Mama ever warn you your face could freeze like that?" Miriam's laugh rang loudly, "Ha ha! I know mine did! Ooh ... nice face ... could be freezing ... Now that would be a sight!" Miriam teased and joked, lurking all about.

She begged the burn to glow red hot. Make the pain something she could feel.

"Now, you have got to learn to lighten up." Miriam continued on, chastising, "You know what you always say, wallowing does not become you."

Miriam's voice swirled all around her, teasing her, taunting her. She blinked. The movement freed the tears she had locked behind the pain. "It's so fucking easy for you to say." She didn't know, didn't care, if her rage was from anger or sorrow. She screamed at Miriam, screamed at the world. "So god damned fucking easy!" Her hands shook the fence.

§ § §

Jess tore through the streets. She was late. It wasn't fair. Her thoughts collided angrily, her backpack bounced in rhythm with her pounding feet. It wasn't fair. She did everything good all day just so Ms. Winters wouldn't make her stay late and then Billy Ray went and threw that spitball at Miss Donna-Goody-Two-Shoes and she got blamed.

Jess' indignation spurred her racing feet on. It wasn't fair that she had to stay late and clean the blackboard. Ms. Winters should have known she didn't do it.

Fueled by her thoughts, Jess made it from the school to the diner in record time, but she was too busy being angry and doubled over trying to catch her breath to notice what would otherwise have been a major achievement. Taking in huge gulps of air, Jess finished her complaint with her most furious logic, If *she* had thrown it, she wouldn't have missed!

Jess straightened up and raced through the junkyard opening. "Hi Mr. Johnson," she shouted as she passed by, grinding to an abrupt halt in front of the lady.

She looked up, her eyes taking in Jess. The hair blown every which way, the untied shoelace, the red cheeks and the runny nose. For just a moment they took each other's measure. Then she nodded.

Jess twisted out of the backpack, dropping it where she stood. She quickly pulled on the rubber clothing, grabbed a brush and sat down by the horse's tail. Jess' face quickly became a study in concentration, her mouth hanging open as she began to curry the horse clean, pausing for just a moment, wiping her nose on her sleeve, then returning to the task at hand.

Lost in their concentration neither heard nor noticed the car pull up and park, facing the fence. A middle-aged woman was driving. She jumped out, as far as her considerable bulk would allow someone to jump and lumbered up the diner steps leaving the elderly, no, ancient woman sitting in the passenger seat.

"Hey, Millie?"

Millie glanced up from the back corner booth where she was grabbing a bite and counting her tip money, "Hey Nan, what can I do for you?"

"The plant just called." Nan Walsh puffed as she spoke, the hurrying about having nearly done her in. "I can get some overtime if I can come on in. Could you do me a favor and bring Gran a piece of chicken and a piece of lemon pie tonight?"

"No problem."

Nan went to reach for her purse; Millie waved her off. "You're a doll. I appreciate it."

Millie grinned, "Just remember that next time you're baking cookies."

"You got it."

Nan retreated down the diner steps, climbed back into the car. "It's okay Gran." She started up the motor. "I'm gonna take you on home and Millie'll bring your dinner on over tonight."

Gran continued to stare out the window with unseeing eyes, giving no indication she had heard a word. Nan simply patted her Grandmother's hand and put the car into gear. Gran continued to stare straight ahead as the car backed out.

Neither Jess nor the merry-go-round repair lady ever looked up.

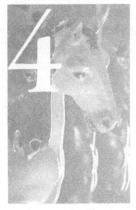

It was raining as they left the movies. Millie waited under the old Embarcadero Theatre canopy while Tom went to get the car. Once an architectural triumph, proudly proclaiming "downtown" as the place to be, it now played second-run double features, its glory days long gone. Two necking teenagers used the rain and its darkness for cover. Saturday night at the movies. Millie smiled a smile both wistful and indulgent as memories of sweet sixteen swirled through her mind.

Millie peered through the rain looking for her ride. She tried not to notice the boarded up stores across the way, tried to keep the depressed reality away. Yet unbidden from the recesses of her mind came that riff on an old folk song, "Gone to Walmart everyone . . . " Cars splashed by, lightening split the sky. Millie raced to climb into the patrol car as it pulled up, the passenger door flung open wide from the inside.

She watched Tom as he drove, tall in his seat, his hand loosely framing the wheel, the king of all he surveyed—at ease no matter what the road conditions. She always liked watching him drive, taking comfort from his ease. The car was strangely silent, the police band turned down, allowing the sound of the windshield wipers to set the tone.

Millie felt strangely oppressed. She thought she should probably say something, anything, but she couldn't find a place to begin. It didn't used to be that way. Millie felt herself growing more morose. Maybe it was the necking teenagers. The rain on the roof tinned fiercely, relentlessly. Maybe it was just the storm. Neither one spoke as they headed on home.

Tom leaned forward; turned the defroster up, its noise somehow breaking into the self-imposed silence. "Want to stop for a coffee?"

"Sure."

He signaled for a right turn and the neon sign of the diner slowly became visible through the downpour.

As Tom swung the car into the lot, his headlights picked up a small shadow in the rain. Tom and Millie looked at each other in amazement, and then both reached for their door handles.

Without knowing why, but knowing she had to go out there alone, Millie turned around, her left hand gently touching Tom's shoulder, her head softly shaking, "Tom?"

He looked at Millie's face. He sat back in his seat, his jaw grinding.

Millie opened the door, the foul weather sucker-punching back the yell in her throat, landing it somewhere in her stomach.

Tom wiped the windshield with his sleeve, leaning forward over the steering wheel, attempting to see into the storm. He wiped and squinted, wiped again and squinted some more, then sighed and leaned back to wait.

In the half dozen or so steps it took to reach her, Millie was already soaked through. For just a moment the two stared at each other. Millie reached out a hand and pushed her rain soaked hair from her eyes.

"The tarp pulled loose." It was a hoarse plea, a plea for understanding, a plea for help. She had driven over in the rain, thinking it would be better to get the car away from the dirt of the campground, which was rapidly turning into mud. She thought she'd stay in the back of the parking lot. That she would be okay there.

As she drove the storm grew rapidly worse and she began to feel sick. She knew the mess would be there before she saw it.

Millie simply nodded, walked back to Tom's car. The window slid down. "The tarp blew off." Millie kept her voice as matter of fact as the storm would allow, "See if you can get a key from Lyle and tack it down. We'll meet you at my place." She turned back.

"Hey Millie!" Tom's yell was barely audible. He watched as she paused, turned back and stared, the rain sluicing its way down around her. She made no effort to move back toward the car. After a brief hesitation she turned back around, the night quickly enveloping her.

Millie reached out her hand, took the woman's keys and steered her back toward her car. With some fumbling, she managed to get the woman into the passenger seat, herself into the driver's seat and the car turned on. As she located the headlight switch, her passenger curled into a ball, her teeth chattering. Millie shifted into reverse.

Tom watched the car take off. "Fuck." It was a statement.

By the time Tom arrived back at Millie's, it was well past midnight. There was no letup in the storm. Millie held the door open as he came up the walk. He took off his coat, hat and boots, exchanging them in the mudroom for a cup of steaming hot coffee.

"It's done. I got lucky. Joe and Rudy pulled in right as I got back with the key from Lyle. We managed to get it nailed down good." He paused, sipped the coffee, got up, opened the fridge and added a drop more cream. As he stirred, he turned back around and leaned against the counter. "Where is she Millie?" The question was a demand despite its deceptively casual tone.

Millie sat down, picked up her own coffee. "She's sleeping, Tom."

He took his time, put his spoon in the sink. "She can't stay here."

"Of course she can." Millie answered him calmly, picked at a non-existent spot of lint on her shirt, her mind still churning with thoughts of their arrival. Millie had hustled her in, set the teakettle on. The woman had stood there dripping all over her kitchen floor. Her teeth wouldn't stop chattering.

"I'm sorry." She tried to talk.

"Hush."

They didn't say anything else. Millie led her to the bathroom, turned the shower on hot. She turned to look and realized that the woman was barely upright. So she reached back in, turned the shower off and filled the tub instead. Millie turned back around, held out her hand for her shirt. When there was no response, Millie moved over and gently began to undress her, the eyes of the woman no longer seemed focused.

"Jesus!" Millie swore under her breath as she lifted off the tee shirt. The woman's body was emaciated, each rib easily countable. There was a still puffy scar circling the inside of her left breast. Millie guided her into the tub, rolled up her shirtsleeves, and then carefully, matter-of-factly washed her clean. She wrapped her in a towel, sat her down on the toilet.

The tea kettle screamed downstairs for all it was worth as Millie raced across to the bedroom. She grabbed a clean nightshirt from the dresser and raced back out, the drawer left wide open. Slamming the stove to off, Millie galloped back up the stairs and rushed back into the bathroom. Her charge was still sitting upright, her eyes closed, still shivering.

Millie touched her shoulder, watched as her eyes popped open, struggling still unsuccessfully to focus. Millie stripped away the towel, dressed her. As she went to help her up, Millie paused, felt her forehead and reached for the medicine cabinet. She grabbed the aspirin, and while cursing child safety caps, managed to extract two.

"Look Millie." Tom's voice called her back to the present.

Millie didn't bother to wait for the lecture she knew was coming. Tom was using his world-weary-as-though-you-were-three-years-old, voice. "No, you look Tom." Millie had had enough. "She was soaked through. She doesn't appear to have anywhere to go. I'm not about to send her back out into that rain. She stays here tonight."

Millie got out of her chair and crossed to the counter. Carefully she took the mug from Tom's hand, kissed his cheek. "I'll call you first thing in the morning so you'll know I'm still alive." She paused, looked at the set of his jaw, attempted a joke, "At least, you better hope I call, else you'll be hard pressed to prove you didn't do away with me."

Tom didn't move an inch.

"Tom?" Millie wrinkled her nose.

Nothing changed. Not his stance, not his stare. When he finally turned, the intensity of barely suppressed rage followed him into the mudroom. "I'll call first thing."

Millie shut the door, returned to the kitchen. She rinsed his mug, left it in the drain board to dry. She wiped her hands on the towel hanging on the refrigerator door handle and left the kitchen, turning off the lights.

In the hallway, she turned into the guest bedroom where the stranger was tucked in. Millie watched her sleep, concern darkening her eyes. The woman thrashed about, tossing and turning, sweat pouring out.

Guided by the light from the hallway, Millie picked up the washcloth she had left earlier by the bedside, sat down and stroked the fevered forehead. "Shhh, it's okay." Millie softly crooned words of comfort.

She seemed to settle, then thrashed violently. "No, no, no, Miriam, oh God, no!" It was a desolate cry. It reminded Millie of the sound a lone coyote makes looking for his pack. Her eyes filled with tears of compassion for this woman. In the dark of the night she knew without being told that these cries came from a place deep within her soul, a place where pain is stored.

"No!"

The fitfully sleeping woman felt a hand brushing gently through her hair. Miriam was here, soothing. It was okay. Miriam was here. She could rest.

§ § §

Tom sat in his den, grimly and methodically breaking down his gun, cleaning each section thoroughly. The room was dark, but he didn't require light. His hands knew the way, working a pattern of motions owned by the very fiber of his being. The grinding of his jaw kept beat. When he finished cleaning, he reassembled the weapon and stared at the now glistening gun.

Slowly the grinding began again. His hands reached back down. The clock ticked off the minutes as he began the process over again.

§ § §

Off in the distance a phone kept ringing. "Why won't it shut up?" Slowly, groggily, Millie came awake. Painfully, she realized she was on the floor. The ringing stopped. "Praise the Lord." Millie's head hit the floor. She listened to the raspy breathing broken only by a cough.

Millie attempted to sit up. Wasn't working. Her back did not care to cooperate. Once again the phone started to ring. Shit! It had to be Tom. Slowly she rolled herself onto her stomach. With a groan she pushed onto her elbows, then onto her knees. Her hand fumbled open the top button of her black jeans, her chest heaved with effort, sucking in air. The phone stopped. Shit!

As she used the edge of the bed to pull upright, Millie looked out through the window and saw the rain still coming down. She gazed down to the stranger tucked in the bed. Finally, the woman seemed to be sleeping quietly if not serenely. Millie smiled, placed her hands behind her back and attempted to stretch.

Back in her own bedroom, seated on the edge of the bed, she dialed. "Good morning," Millie croaked into the phone.

"Where the hell have you been?"

"Yes, I slept well, how about you?" Millie reached for her cigarettes, lighting one, inhaling deeply, and letting the smoke burn in the back of her parched throat. As she exhaled, she reached for an ashtray on her end table and caught sight of the clock. "Are you just fucking nuts!" Millie's voice shrieked into the phone. "It's eight o'clock on a fucking Sunday morning. What the hell are you doing?" Millie sucked in another drag, exhaled loudly and hung up the phone. Cigarette in hand she stumbled into the bathroom and took in her own reflection. Jesus she looked awful. Shifting the cigarette to her left hand she leaned on the sink. Her right hand touched and pushed at the bags under her eyes, made darker by the rings of dead mascara streaks, remnants from the night before.

§ § §

She was chasing the merry-go-round ponies. All she wanted to do was climb on, but they wouldn't stop, wouldn't let her catch up, grab hold. Why won't they wait for her? The faces of the ponies loomed large, their teeth jutting out, gleaming huge and white. Miriam spun by, gaily waving to her from her perch on the huge white steed. "Wait, wait for me," she begged and pleaded. But still they spun by, laughing, gleaming, taunting. Their colors formed fantastic swirls all around her, imprisoning her in their streams. She fought to get loose, she ran frantically. They laughed louder, their mouths beginning to foam.

She bolted upright in the bed, reached out blindly. She pulled at the nightshirt. She was soaking wet, all clammy. She ran her hand around the back of her neck; it came away drenched. Slowly she looked around at her surroundings-she was sitting in a four-poster oak bed, wrapped in a plaid flannel down comforter. She let her hand touch it. Absurdly she thought of *The Little Princess*. She was Sara Crewe waking up after the Indian servant had worked his magic. There was a dresser with photos but it was too far away for her to see. Her eyes began to water from the effort. She sank back down. It all hurt.

Suddenly the waitress was hovering over her, feeling her forehead. Then she was gone, leaving her alone again, her world spinning.

Coming back, Millie looked down at her, at the tears running down her cheeks. Gently she helped her up, giving her more aspirin and a glass of juice.

She managed to get the aspirin down and a sip of the juice.

"All of it."

Slowly, painfully, she complied. She tried to sink back down, but a hand moved toward her and she flinched.

"Shh, it's okay." Millie spoke slowly as she placed herself in the woman's line of vision. Then Millie settled on the edge of the bed, allowing the woman to track her movements. It was as though she were a wild animal who needed gentling. Millie raised her hand, palm down, and moved it up toward her forehead, not turning it over until she reached her destination. As Millie kept her eyes in contact with the merry-go-round repair lady she remembered the first time their eyes met and knew that somehow, even then, this woman had become her charge. "Well," Millie quietly spoke, "Now you need to shower and I need to strip this bed and change the sheets." Millie paused, "Do you think you can manage a shower?"

She nodded, began to inch forward. At the edge of the bed she ordered her body to move upright. One foot in front of the other; one foot in front of the other. The order developed into a chant running through her brain. It wouldn't stop making her dizzy.

"Ah shit!" Millie lunged from her position stripping the pillowcase and grabbed hold in just enough time to help break the fall.

Her glassy eyes burned with tears. She could see Millie's lips moving, but it was Miriam she heard. She reached her hand out to touch the lips.

She jolted awake to her hand being stroked. As she tried to jump and pull away, the hand held firm, keeping contact, never breaking its rhythm. As the hand kept pace she fell back into her pillow, feeling the motion, a steady metronome of warmth penetrating and carrying her back into a quiet sleep.

§ § §

Millie slammed four juice glasses down on the countertop. She grabbed the pitcher and began to pour. Juice sloshed everywhere. Damn. Looking at the mess, she glanced at the clock. Eight. It was only two hours into her shift and it felt like ten. Her hands wrapped around the glasses she hustled through the counter divide. Feet like lead, head too heavy, nerves way frayed.

Millie smiled as she served the orange juice, but even that felt strained. The edges of her lips were too taut, the fringes of her mouth muscles began to spasm from the attempt. Her head continued to pound so intensely it might have been competing with the storm still raging from the night before.

Lacey walked into the diner and looked around in shock. The place was packed. The "pick-up" bell was clanging trying to get someone to pay heed. Lacey spotted Millie in the center, moving like a whirling dervish, trying desperately to get the orders out. "Hey Millie," she called out in greeting while tying her apron, "What the dickens is going on?"

Millie flew by, "Order in, Charley." She stuck the paper in the metal contraption and gave it a spin, "Haven't got a clue. Apparently everybody and their brother decided to have breakfast out this morning. Could you pick up on two?"

The kitchen bell chimed. "Pick up."

Millie grabbed the order, made her way down the counter. "Here you go, Rudy. Three over with ham, country biscuits." She grabbed both the ketchup and the Tabasco sauce. "Enjoy your breakfast."

Millie glanced past Rudy to see Tom arrive and grab the end seat at the counter.

"Hey Millie."

Before she could answer, Charley rang from the kitchen, "Pick up." Millie looked down at Tom and half smiled in apology. A curious thought crossed Tom's mind. "Saved by the bell, huh Millie?" For just a moment Millie's smile dropped altogether, but then she shrugged and hurried away.

Tom continued to perch on his stool watching as Millie loaded up the plates on her arm. Lacey came by, grabbed a pot of coffee, flipped the cup over in front of him and poured. Absent-mindedly he nodded his thanks and began adding cream and sugar.

Millie made her way back through the restaurant and down the counter, pausing to refill coffee as she went. "Hey Joe," she welcomed the bow-legged trucker as he grabbed his stool next to Rudy, "You're late."

"Aw Millie, you do care." Joe smiled, batting his eyes. "See Rudy, I told you she cares." Millie rolled her eyes, pulled the pen from her apron pocket and simply waited. Joe was one of the few regulars who actually didn't order the same breakfast every day. "Accident on the interstate, four cars." Joe closed his menu, "I'll have a number three, whole wheat, scrambled."

Millie jotted as he spoke, ripped off the order sheet with a flourish. "Order in Charley."

"Pick up."

Tom continued to sit and watch. Millie looked down the counter and shrugged again. Their eyes met. With an air of resignation Tom drained his coffee and stood to leave. At the door he paused, but never turned around. Millie watched him walk away.

§ § §

Miriam reached for her. Her hand burned warm in Miriam's. She could feel her. If only she could just lower the bars and climb in, hang on and just go to sleep. So warm, so safe. It was all good. Safe, warm, love. Safe, warm, love. Don't want to go. Safe, warm, love. Want to stay here. Safe, warm, love.

"Not your time." She heard it but it didn't make any sense. She heard it spoken from the hand that was holding hers. But that was stupid. Everyone knows hands can't talk.

This time she allowed the rhythm of the stroking hand to move her from sleep to consciousness. Gently, lovingly, she was moved through the transition. She didn't know why she trusted in this hand, but she did.

Now as she opened her eyes she took in a pair of deep brown eyes, recessed into a face withered with age. If wisdom were a portrait, she would paint this old woman. All that a lifetime of love and honesty could teach seemed etched into each crease.

She knew there had been a question asked but she couldn't quite remember. The hand paused for the briefest moment and then began again. This time an ancient voice accompanied the caress.

"Let me tell you something about grief, child." The voice came low and steady, unhurried. "Now this ain't to say you can take one person's pain and measure it against another person's, 'cause pain don't work out that way. This is just a story 'bout how you can make it through. I was twelve years old when I married Walter." For another moment the hand paused, caught in a memory. "Had fourteen children—thirteen of 'em lived, too. Little Daisy, now she was stillborn. Buddy, he was just three when he fell down an old mine shaft. So that left twelve. They all grew up, went out, made their way in the world. Luther, now he was killed in the war. Rachel died in 1949. Tuberculosis. Isaac died in 1964. Heart attack. Robert died just one month later." As she ticked off each child in her mind, a face came and went. It was like going down the staircase in a big old house with each picture named and framed, frozen for eternity. "Lawrence, my, he died in a car accident in 1969, coming to visit his Momma. In 1974 we buried Martin and then, for the next five years I buried one more child each year. That left me just Walter Jr. I buried him in 1999."

Slowly the hand stopped stroking and gently grasped the one beneath it. It held on until she raised her eyes to meet those of the old woman. Almost as if the old woman could see the tear-filled eyes that finally looked up, her voice shifted and grew deliberate. "Grief will eat you alive child," the grip of her hand tightened, its strength so much firmer than its frail, withered casing, "You've got to let it go."

She lay still, frozen, on the pillow. She wanted to take her hand back, but she couldn't. She didn't ask the old woman who she was or how she knew. It didn't matter. Tears scalded her face as they overflowed. "I can't." The words rasped their way out brokenly. "It's too big. Too big for me."

§ § §

It was only late afternoon but already dark outside as Millie came into the still house. At least the storm stopped raging and the rain finally slowed to background patter. She set her purse on the kitchen counter, looked around. Something felt different.

She climbed quietly up the stairs and peered into the first room. The woman was still there, sleeping calmly. Millie continued on down the hall to her bedroom.

Her nightly routine had gone unchanged for years. Come home, take a shower, and wash away the grease and the sweat. Do the standard household chores and make unkept promises about the bigger ones. Eat a light dinner if Tom was working nights; maybe go out if he was on days.

Tom. Millie's body, already tired, sagged under the weight. Millie supposed she should call him. She just didn't know what she would say. She didn't know what it was about the merry-go-round lady that mattered. She just didn't have the energy.

"Energy," Millie sighed, "Where does it all go?" Once she had drive and desire and energy to burn. Now it seemed getting through the day took all the energy she had.

Millie took off her shoes and sat on the edge of her bed. She supposed she should take her shower, but somehow that suddenly seemed to require more effort than not. There were so many things to be done— bills to be paid, living room to dust, uniforms for the laundry, her promise she would organize her closets. The mudroom floor was still coated in mud from the night before. "God, I am too tired."

Millie tried to think when she had become so tired. She couldn't remember. Her heart clenched. She couldn't remember.

There was a soft knock on the open door. Millie turned to face her, both ashamed and defiant to be caught. For a brief moment there was no sound. There was only the recognition of their shared but separate pain.

Millie now understood what she couldn't tell Tom. She couldn't tell him how much it all hurt. How lost she was in her own world. How frightened she was. How hard just getting by had become. He wouldn't understand. She wasn't sure she did.

The woman looked at the waitress, remembered her name was Millie. "I'm sorry." She managed to get the words out.

"Me too."

§ § §

Millie broke the silence. "Can I ask you a question?" They sat in the kitchen, mugs of black tea in hand. Millie looked at her, watched as she managed to finish the last bite of a single piece of dry toast. Millie's pajamas were absurdly big on her tiny frame. Millie first thought maybe she would ask the lady her name, but then again, it kind of felt like the time for introductions had passed. Besides, she had accepted not knowing and now it felt oddly too personal. "How'd you get the scar?"

She stared at Millie over her hands wrapped around the mug. It wasn't the question she thought was coming. She never blinked. For a long moment it seemed she would not answer. Instead she wondered idly just how old this sort of brownish-purple Mikasa china pattern was. It wasn't even eggplant; maybe puce? It somehow didn't seem to fit the waitress. She wasn't sure why she thought that. She took a sip from the mug, watched as the pajama sleeves slid back when the mug lifted and then back down as she lowered her arms. When she did speak her voice was so matter of fact, they could have been chatting about the weather. "I tried to cut my heart out." Lovely day, isn't it? Do you think we'll get more snow this season?

"Oh." Lame, but genuine. Millie didn't know what to say, but then again, she found she was not surprised either. It all seemed to make perfect sense.

"I was trying to stop the pain." She paused for just a moment. "It didn't work." This time she managed a slightly wry grin although it looked more like a grimace. "When I got out of the hospital I just got in my car and drove. I thought maybe if I could get far enough, fast enough, I could leave it all behind in the rear view mirror." This time the grin twitched, "That didn't work either." The tears welled but she managed to hang on.

§ § §

Millie undressed for bed, snippets of the night's conversation still running through her head. *It's the moments*, Millie could see the woman as she whispered, raising her hand, fingertips together, searching for the words that could convey the importance of what she was telling *I didn't know how to live in the moments*. Her fingertips suddenly dropped apart leaving an outstretched hand and an empty palm, *and then there were no more moments to live in*.

Millie glanced about her bedroom. It had been her parents' room growing up and after they died she had migrated into it. She slept there, but was sad to realize how little she had done to make it her own.

Millie looked at the pictures strewn about the room. Pictures her mother had chosen and framed once upon a time. She saw the little girl she once was, beaming at the camera, hand over her heart, so proud of having learned all the words to the Pledge of Allegiance. There was another picture of herself, packed up to head for college, the promise of tomorrow written all over her face. She gently stared into eyes that were once giddy with anticipation. Carefully she wiped the dust from the frame.

She looked up into the mirror hung over the dresser. What had happened to that promise? The small pink roses on the wallpaper were faded with time and bleached pale by the sun. When did the vibrant colors of life become so washed out? When had she? A pain shot through the vortex of her body and caused her to nearly double over. With a shock Millie realized that the pang was loneliness. Maybe that's what happened—maybe we only get so many moments—and maybe if we don't use them they leave. Maybe she too had become bereft of moments. Only Millie's were not used up in love, hers had simply expired. *I tried to cut my heart out.* Sharp pangs clutched at her chest. It occurred to Millie, she envied the woman her pain.

The next day dawned sunny and warm. A rebirth. Millie had lost the battle to keep the merry-go-round lady in bed but Millie knew she hadn't really fought that hard. Though her guest was still weak, coughing and hacking, the best Millie could get from her was a promise not to push too hard. Together they drove up to the diner. Millie's home wasn't far, only a few blocks away. She said the directions out loud. Left onto Cedar, right onto Spruce. Millie could smell her fear as they approached, watched as she looked toward the fence. "It'll be alright. Rudy and Joe got them covered." Millie flashed on Tom standing in her kitchen, his face contorted with anger, but she did not mention the cost.

Millie watched the carousel lady's nervous looks toward the yard and wondered if she should have stopped there yesterday to check on the job the guys did. Probably. But it wouldn't matter now. It was going to be what it was going to be. It wasn't like this was something they volunteered for. As it was she had to beg them. All those years of knowing Rudy and Joe— The Norstak Brothers—years of alternately flirting with them, joking with them and occasionally even crying with them, might not have been enough to enlist their assistance if it wasn't for Lyle. Tom had already shared with them exactly what he thought of the situation the other night in the rain. And while not necessarily taking sides, Rudy and Joe were quite clear with their opinion—they just figured this whole thing was weird from the get-go and Millie, Millie taking in the merry-go-round lady like she was some stray cat was even weirder. It just wasn't right and they weren't going to be a part of her craziness.

And then, somewhere in the middle of the parking lot, with words heating up and lines being drawn and friendships being risked, Lyle Johnson just stepped up and told the three of them that he and Millie were going to get on with what needed to be done. Yep. Just get on with the getting and they could either help or not, wasn't for him to say. Yep. Not for him to say. And if he and Millie were so wrong, he had just one question for the Norstak Brothers—were two wrongs gonna make a right? Cause sure as he was Old Man Johnson, he knew she'd be coming back and sitting here and letting her work get ruined seemed mighty selfish just because they thought it was weird. But, wasn't for him to say. Nope. Not for him to say.

Millie looked up in her rear view mirror as she parked, unconsciously bit her lip and consciously wished she had thought to check up on the boys.

She was terrified. She needed to get out of the car, but couldn't. What if Miriam was gone, destroyed? What if she had stripped her bare and the storm had taken her. She began to push back into the seat, began to feel the tremors begin, began to ball up her body.

Millie took her hand. "It'll be all right," Millie assured her, uncurling the fist. She wasn't sure whether she was calming the woman or herself. The condition of the horses had somehow become her own urgent calling too. She looked down at their clasped hands and smiled over at her companion with a courage she knew was false. "Come on." Millie gave their hands a tug, "We'll go look together." The woman gazed at Millie, nodded.

They stood at the fence, two faces squinting and scrunched as they peered in. There was not much they could see. Apparently Rudy and Joe had taken some sort of tent and built out from there, giving the middle of Lyle's yard a circus-like appearance. Millie exhaled loudly. "Well, let's go get some coffee."

§ § §

She sat at the counter, not quite believing it had been only four days since she had collapsed. She watched as Millie filled the salt shakers. A trucker's toot pierced the routine. Millie looked up and grinned. Without saying anything, she set down the ketchups, wiped her hands and came around the counter. She gestured to the woman to follow.

Outside, climbing down from the huge truck—with a great deal of assistance—was Lyle Johnson. Helping him was Rudy, and coming around the other side, Joe. "Hey Millie, look who we found hitching his way over here."

"If we'd known how long it would take to get him up into the cab and back down," Rudy grinned, "we probably would have left him to walk."

Lyle deliberately ignored them all. Putting his walking stick in front of him, with as much dignity as he could muster, he made his way to the fence and began to unlock and unwind the chains.

As the fence opened, the small group stood aside, creating a path for her. She moved forward, glancing at each member as she went. What greeted her inside was extraordinary. They had done much more than tack down the storm-blown tarp. A roof had been erected using a tent. They had stretched canvas onto posts to create what appeared to be a small big-top. All the horses had been moved from the floor and lifted onto remnants from the junkyard. But most amazing of all, in the center, holding court was Miriam. Placed onto a makeshift workbench, kept company by all the tools and materials, she sat high, regally perched, awaiting her next moment of glory.

She didn't know what to do—what to say. It was so overwhelming. Everyone had followed along, a couple of steps behind her and now they huddled anxiously. She could feel her throat closing. She turned back to Miriam, stroking her frame, trying to loosen both her own mind and her throat, trying to find some words.

Nervously, Rudy broke the silence. "Uh, we hope it's all okay. See, me and Joe couldn't use the tarp you put up seeing as the storm shredded it, so Joe had this old tent in the back of his cab and we got it up, but it didn't cover enough, so we added the sides . . . " Rudy's words were cut short as she turned around, with arms shaking from the effort of nearly atrophied connections, and tentatively hugged the larger man.

As Rudy's arms equally tentatively returned the hug, Joe picked up the story, "The tarps have these holes, so if you want you can pull the sides all the way back during the day, but cover it up at night." She moved to hug him as well, but Joe stepped away and gestured back toward the center, "and we all figured you could use a work table or something."

Lyle cleared his throat, "Yep. Didn't seem real smart having you working on the ground. If you're gonna fix them, we figured you needed a way to reach them." She turned toward Lyle. He was leaning on his stick, dangling something from his hand, "Yep. We figured you needed to be able to reach them."

She just stared at Lyle, overwhelmed by what she saw dangling. Shiny. New. A key.

"Yep."

She turned to Millie. There were no words between them. None needed. The waitress had tears in her eyes but she winked and grinned. "Come on everybody, coffee's on me."

Millie linked her arms through those of Rudy and Joe. The brothers might still be a bit out of sorts with the whole thing, and perhaps they were only here because an old man shamed and bullied them into helping, but she felt them return her grasp and Millie knew that at the very least, they were no longer untouched.

As a group they turned to leave—all except the merry-go-round repair lady. But then again, no one really expected she would.

§ § §

The voices rambled on long into the night. They had much to say. The old lady lay awake all night. She had much to hear. She had not thought that telling her story would matter to her, but it did. She often repeated her story to herself but it didn't have the same impact as saying it out loud. In the telling she had thrown open a window to her soul. *Grief will eat you alive*, she told the young woman. She left out the other side— bitterness will keep you alive long after you have forgotten how to live. Through the night, dwarfed by her pillows, the old lady listened to the voices of her ancestors, carried on the wind and landing in her heart. She heard their wisdom. Now she had to own it.

Gran pulled herself up, buoyed by the knowledge that this morning would need to signify a new beginning. She reached for her housedress and pulled it on, listening for sounds that the house was awake. She made her way to the dresser, running her fingertips over the old, polished wood to complete her preparations. Folding. Tucking. Supplies in the voluminous front pocket, she was ready. Satisfied, she stood in front of the mirror she could not see and aligned her face with determination. It was time. It was past time.

Nan was already in motion, pulling on an ill-fitting blazer, getting it together for another day, pouring her coffee and setting out her grandmother's tea.

"I can get that you know."

Time froze. Fear rose in Nan's throat, clogging her passageways, forcing her to gasp for air. She turned, the coffee landing on the floor, and stared at her grandmother, stared at a ghost. The coffee spread, its rivulets drawing a line from one woman to the other, connecting the space that grew larger by the second. "You can talk," Nan Walsh finally managed.

Her grandmother pulled out a chair and sat down.

"Wait a minute," Nan's voice was shaking; her entire body was shaking. She couldn't decide if it was fear, relief, or anger. It was definitely rage. She couldn't for two seconds answer what was going through her mind. She didn't understand.

Her grandmother looked at her. Sorrow was etched in her face, and for a brief moment Nan thought Gran could also see.

"Let me tell you a story" the old woman began, her only way to start—as timeless as she was. "It's a story 'bout growing old and becoming a burden, 'bout losing the joy, the gift, of being needed in this world. I buried my children and never once thought I would still be here. It isn't right, outliving your children. But here I was, still livin' on, year after year with nowhere to go. But then, oh my Lord, a wonderful thing happened. One of my grandchildren took me in, took me in out of love. And we would laugh and we would sit down and have dinner and I would cook for her all her favorite foods. I would sit all day and wait for her to come home so I could be proud—proud I could still get dinner on the table, proud I was independent.

"Only bit by bit things changed. Sometimes she'd come home and she'd just want to eat quiet. She worked hard. And sometimes it seemed like she wanted to go out, but she wouldn't talk about it."

Gran paused, pressed her hand to her lips to cover them, to help swallow the choking she could feel. She could not stop now. "And then," she reclaimed her voice, "then sometime, it seemed to me, her love had become duty."

Nan attempted to jump in, to protest. But her grandmother raised her hand. She would not be deterred. "Just because truth ain't pretty doesn't make it somethin' to be avoided."

"A word meant kindly became a word of criticism. A thought said freely became a conversation to be dutifully heard, then dismissed. Better just to let old Gran have her say and be done. And so I thought, I thought I should learn to be quiet. Because you know, I had my pride. Oh yes, I was proud. So proud, I was so proud I couldn't look to see if there was truth in your feelings. I was too afraid to look to myself for answers. Where would I go if I grew tiresome? It was easier to sit myself on a pedestal of right-eousness, bitter in my silence." Gran looked up, her gaze unerringly pointed at Nan's. "Easier to punish you than look for answers. And my granddaughter, she seemed relieved by the change."

Nan slid down to the floor and sat sobbing, her arms wrapped around her grandmother's legs.

Gran thought to comfort her but realized she had to finish. There would be time for comfort when she was done, but there would be no comfort if she did not finish what she had to say. "Now I realize my time may be limited and when I go, I do not want to go in silence and anger brought on by selfish pride and fear. I want to go with my granddaughter knowing I just might be an ornery old woman, but I love my granddaughter and I need her." Her voice cracked and tears ran from her sightless eyes.

Nan rocked herself, clinging to the legs, "I'm so sorry, Gran, so very sorry."

The old woman stroked Nan's head. "Nothing to be sorry for. You took in this old lady and you put a roof over her head and a bed under her back."

"But I could have done better." Nan's words were gulped as she tried to gasp for air. "I could have listened better. I could have tried harder."

"We all could listen better. But I should have known better."

"I love you, Grandma."

The old woman stopped patting and pulled away for just a moment. Nan felt her warmth leave and looked up at her grandmother through the tear-filled eyes of a little girl. Gran reached into her pocket, deep inside, and pulled out a tissue.

This very simple gesture brought back loving memories of scraped knees and "boo-boo" kisses. Nan's tears began to pour again as her hand grasped and twisted the tissue. Gran leaned back down to her granddaughter. "I love you, my sweet little Nan." Wrapped about each other, rocking and clinging, the poison slipped out the back door.

§ § §

Jess came slowly around to grasp the fence and stared in. The merry-go-round lady was back. Jess had been checking the fence every day, but now that the lady was here she suddenly wasn't sure what to do.

She felt Jess arrive. She looked up from her position. The two of them took stock of each other for just a moment.

In an echo of their first meeting, she broke the silence, "Well, are you going to stand there all day, or are you at least coming to help?" This time though, the question was gentle. And this time, unlike the first time she had asked, she smiled.

It was Sunday and all was quiet. She sat looking at the horses and thinking of the last several weeks. Somehow she had just stayed on at Millie's. They had never talked about it.

The long row of horses stretched wide in front of her. With a sense of satisfaction she now saw that everyone was a "stander," everyone except Miriam. Miriam alone was a galloper. It was ridiculously appropriate.

She had been right—the last three were beyond saving. All the others had been stripped bare. She put the last of her tools away for the day. Next week. Next week was time for a new beginning. Next week.

§ § §

Millie drove the winding roads to the cabin she knew she would find neatly tucked into a small copse off to the left. It was a trip she had made countless times over the years. She drove slowly, partly because the wintry rains left behind ruts and branches and other small nuisances and partly, mostly, because she knew this might very well be her last time to travel this road.

Tom stopped mulching as the familiar car pulled into his driveway. Straightening up he watched Millie climb out, but he didn't move toward her. He didn't understand what had happened and wasn't certain he even wanted to.

She put the car in park and could see the anger and trepidation in his eyes, in the rigid way he held his back and in the legs that never moved to join her. She climbed out but stayed near the driver's door. He was palpable. Millie trembled, as much from her own nerves as Tom's stare. She could feel his unrepentant chill knifing through her with as much ferocity as any icy nor'easter could. Millie wrapped her arms tightly around her body. "Hi Tom."

He hesitated for just a fraction, but when he spoke, his voice was hard. "Millie."

She looked at him, looked around the front yard, the neatly kept house. God she wished she had an easy way to do this. "I came to say ... you know,

I'm not sure I know exactly what I came to say." This was so hard. Millie didn't know if she could explain any of this, even to a willing audience, and Tom's stillness told her he was not going to be that.

"What's going on, Millie?"

"I don't really know." Maybe if she turned away. Maybe if she just didn't look at him she could get this out. Millie tried but it was a coward's glance. She turned back, tried to stand up to his withering stare. "I just know it's not there."

"What's not there?"

"I don't know."

Tom could see the tears in her eyes but his legs refused to move. He had nothing to give her to help her with this. "You're not exactly making a lot of sense."

"I know." Millie ran her hand through her hair, took one step forward. "I don't know Tom. I don't know if I can explain it. Hell, I don't even know if I understand it. I think, I don't know, I think it has something to do with passion. I want, no, I need to believe that if I died tomorrow, someone would love me enough that it would hurt—truly hurt in their soul."

"And you don't think I love you that way?"

Millie shook her head sadly. This was her truth. "No, I don't."

Tom looked at her. His mouth twisted into a sneer, his words defiant. "And what about you, do you love me that way?"

The second it took for her to answer seemed like an hour. "No." This was his truth.

"Well, then I guess there's nothing more to say."

Millie looked at Tom. He was so strong, so safe, so stalwart in his simple presence. "I know you won't believe this," she looked up and shrugged, grinned a bitter grin, "but there is someone who will love you that way, and when she does, and you feel what it means, maybe then we can be friends."

Tom stared ahead for just a moment. Then he leaned over and turned the mower back on, letting the job at hand remove any need to hear any more.

Millie climbed back in her car. Tom was a good man, she thought. She looked in the rearview mirror as she pulled away. She thought she should feel empty. But, as her eyes moved forward she felt the weight of the world lift ever so slightly.

§ § §

She entered the kitchen and found Millie perched on a flimsy looking ladder, blue paint tape being less than carefully applied to the ceiling. Shredded remnants of plastic wrappers and cardboard littered the floor. Millie's voice pinged up and down upon her, "I hate mustard gold."

"Okay." She moved over to steady the ladder. "What color are we painting?"

"I don't know."

"I see." This she understood. "Just time for a change."

For a while they just worked silently, applying blue tape and plastic drop cloths to everything they could. Finally, Millie pushed herself up from draping the small kitchen table. "Well," she asked as she surveyed their handiwork, "What do you think?"

She took a look around, noticing for the first time that the supplies didn't seem to actually include paint. "I think if you don't pick a paint it's going to be interesting eating in here."

"Yeah, well . . ." Millie's voice drifted off.

She watched Millie for a moment. What was she doing here? This connection was exactly what she didn't need. "Want to tell me about it?" she offered gingerly.

"I told Tom it was, we were, over. That I wanted to know what it is to have passion, to know that if I died someone would miss me enough to hurt. But after I drove away I realized that it isn't about dying, it's about living.

"I left this town once. Moved out to go to college, chase big dreams. Mom was sick before I left but Dad took care of her and they were both so proud. Then my father died and Mom needed help and suddenly it's twenty years later and I'm living in their house, in their bedroom, and I get up and I go wait tables and come home and I think I could truly die of fucking boredom, only I would have to get out of my own stupor in order to do it and I can't be bothered."

Millie reached blindly across the table and clasped the hands that rested there. She fought to find voice for her thoughts before they ran back and hid. "And I came back, came into the kitchen and looked at the walls and sat here thinking about how much I fucking hate mustard gold and I didn't even know it and now I just need it to go away."

Giving the hands that clung to hers a shake, she nodded. "Let's go find paint then."

§ § §

Lyle Johnson looked up to see the Reverend approach, not sure what to make of it. Frankly, he wasn't sure what to make of anything these days. His world had been changed the morning he took the chain off his fence and let her in. Yep. He had a routine. Been a good one too, only now it seemed to have been swept away overnight. Lots of people, all stopping to stare, apparently everybody needs to watch the merry-go-round lady at work. He didn't know how she ignored them all. Yep. Didn't seem to matter to her.

"Good Morning, Mr. Johnson."

"Reverend." He might be curious but it wouldn't do to ask. Reverend would speak up when he was ready. One thing about a reverend, they sure know how to talk.

"Just thought I would come down and see for myself what everyone is talking about on Sunday mornings."

"Yep."

The two men watched for a moment. Lyle rocked upon his stick. When nothing further was said, Lyle stole a sideways glance. What he saw nearly made him burst out laughing. The Reverend looked mighty uncomfortable. Fidgety even. Lyle grinned. Yep, he thought, she sure did seem to have that effect on people.

The Reverend made his way toward the young woman. Her head was bent over a diagram. As he stood there he realized it was some type of inventory of the horse laid out in front of her. She didn't look up, just remained lost in her world, a silent intensity in her task.

He realized she would not break the silence. She hadn't asked him to come by and visit. This was on him. He raised his eyes to the sky for a brief second; it was now or never. "Excuse me. My name is Reverend William Dalton. I'm the Pastor up at The Church of Nazareth."

She looked up at him, but didn't reply.

He tried for what he hoped was his winning smile. "Well, I hear a lot about you these days."

She sighed. "Look Reverend, I'm sorry, but if you've come looking for a soul to save, you've come to the wrong place."

"I'm not so sure."

"Trust me. Wrong faith."

"And which faith might that be?"

Her eyes finally met his; her tone was flat and cold. "Any faith."

"Ah, I see." He circled about a bit, using the pretense of looking at the line-up of horses to cover his nerves. Slowly he made his way back up toward her, overstepping his space to force eye contact. "Well, then you might be relieved to know that I'm actually here about the merry-go-round you're building."

"Nope. No merry-go-round. Just a handful of horses."

"Seems to me that if they're not spinning, they're not complete. Seems to me you can't make them whole without giving them back their home."

"Seems to me it's none of your god-damned business." It was snarled and ugly and came from somewhere deep inside. It was a gut-wrenching projectile vomit of a reaction to his accusation. Visceral. Guttural. The scream in her brain overpowered everything else. "You can't make them whole." She thought she would physically throw up from the vertigo that engulfed her to her core. Who the fuck is he to come down here and tell her what she can and can't do! "Can't make them whole." It echoed over and over again. Miriam lay on the ground swimming before her eyes. "Can't make them whole." Finally she blinked and managed to swallow.

Reverend Dalton, reeling from the direct hit, quietly stood his ground, absorbing the verbal blow. "Please think about this," he continued, all the while collecting himself, "I believe we have paths we need to take and somehow ours have crossed."

As he turned to leave he remembered Lyle Johnson watching from his window on the world. "Thank you, Mr. Johnson. See you on Sunday."

§ § §

Lyle watched her leave. Something was not right. Yep. She never left the horses during the day. It was only two o'clock. Nope. Something was wrong. Wasn't really any of his business of course. But soon Jess would be here and she'd be pestering him about where the merry-go-round lady went and then Millie would be getting off work and she'd want to know. Millie! That's what he could do. He could tell Millie and she could figure it out if she wanted to. Lyle pulled himself up to head into the diner. He wondered if he should put the lock on first. See, this was exactly what he was talking about. Yep. Just earlier, he was thinking that ever since she came he couldn't get his days back to his routine. Yep. That's just what he'd been thinking.

§ § §

She floored the gas pedal and drove. "Whole. Whole. Can't make them whole. Have to make them whole." Her voice, his voice, Miriam's voice all echoed in circles. She drove. Didn't know where she was going, just needed to get away.

§ § §

Millie jumped in her car and took off. She wasn't sure where to go, where to look. Millie knew she wouldn't go to the house. Think. Tom had said something about seeing her out at one of the campgrounds. It was worth a shot.

§ § §

She stared at the phone for a long time. She had driven sixty-three miles before an empty tank and a full bladder forced her to stop. If she went any further she might not turn back. She stared at her car through the convenience store door. It was decision time—north, south, east? She couldn't go east, there was no more east to go. Her breath echoed through her ears as she expelled it.

She dialed the number from memory even though it had been a long time. It had been a lifetime ago.

Two rings, maybe she wasn't home.

"Hello?"

She struggled to find her voice.

"Hello?" The question demanded to know if anyone was there.

She cleared her throat. "Hello Mom."

"Oh my God. Where are you? We've been so worried."

The words came rushing over the line to her. This was a mistake. She wasn't ready. Her throat began to close. "Didn't you get the cards?"

Her mother's voice became quiet. "We're all hurting baby."

She leaned her head against the metal box surrounding the phone. "I know Mom. I just don't have any room for your pain right now. I love you."

Click. She replaced the receiver, severing the connection. Tears streamed down. She was wrong. She must have room left for their pain or it wouldn't be hurting this much. She forced her legs to move. Back to her car, back to her steel cocoon.

§ § §

Hours had passed. What if she was gone? What if . . . don't go there. Just think Millie. Let's assume she's here somewhere and figure out where. Daylight was long gone as Millie pulled in and spotted the car. It had taken her a while but she'd found the campground. It would have been so much easier if she could have simply called Tom but Millie knew that was impossible. Instead she had driven frantically from site to site praying that somehow the woman was still there.

Now Millie could see her sitting behind the wheel staring out into the night. Now she wasn't sure if she should have come. Now that everything was apparently calm, Millie was no longer certain what to do. And why should she have to do anything? When did this woman become her problem?

The release of the keys from the ignition also released the adrenaline Millie had managed to contain. Who the hell did this woman think she was? Slamming her car door, Millie approached the woman head on. Any rational or poignant feelings Millie had were swallowed by a tidal wave of fury.

"Was that it? Were you just going to fucking leave? Hit the road. Adios people. Thanks a lot Millie." Rage born of fear, rage born of tension, rage born of embarrassment, rage Millie didn't even know was there spilled wide across the field as Millie stared the woman down over the hood of her car. "No. That's not right. No thanks a lot Millie or Lyle or goodbye Jess. No see you around sometime. Just hit the road. Don't even bother looking in the rear view mirror."

She looked up at Millie. Turned the key and lowered the window.

"So, that about it?" Millie wanted this answer. "Did I get it right?"

She stared directly at Millie. Didn't flinch. "Pretty much."

Millie's hand flapped in exasperation, "Why?"

Maybe it was twenty seconds, maybe it was two minutes, but the answer came out with almost a question. "He told me I had to make them whole."

"Oh." Millie heard her answer, but realized she could actually feel her voice. It felt trampled and whipped, a mix of bewilderment and maybe an edge of forlorn. It was the undisguised, unedited sound of defeat. The rage from just seconds ago, so vehement, dissipated as fast as a summer storm. Millie came around to the side and leaned on the car top, "Want to tell me about it?"

"He wants me to build a carousel." She kept her eyes forward. Staring through the windshield. "Just like that." She snapped her fingers. "Build a carousel."

Millie could do this. No eye contact. Keep looking in the distance. Pretend we're chatting about the beautiful view, the size of the green tree in the distance. "The Reverend?" Millie kept her voice nonchalant. Thank God Lyle told her about the visitor who seemed to set her running.

"Yeah."

"Well?" Ask like you're saying please pass the bread. Just having an everyday conversation about building a carousel. Not a thing out of the ordinary. "Why don't you?"

"I was just passing through. Stopping for a cup of coffee. I didn't expect to find her here. Yeah right. Build a fucking carousel. I can't stay."

"Right."

"I drove away you know." Her hands played about the steering wheel as she spoke, "Went miles down the road but it wasn't working. It doesn't matter, I can't go yet either."

I can't go yet. Millie let that thought echo and finally released the breath she hadn't consciously realized she'd been holding, "Right."

"So . . ." For the first time she looked directly at Millie, "now what do I do?"

§ § §

They headed inside and found the chapel. It was small but elegant. A simple altar, high windows, their stained glass beautiful even against a night sky. The ceiling was arched with a small balcony tucked above. He asked them to take a seat, he'd be right there.

They entered and stepped quietly down the aisle. One row, two; by silent agreement, the third row down on the left seemed to be the space. Millie and the merry-go-round lady sat shoulder to shoulder, butted up against the aisle edge, neither one looking particularly comfortable, neither one able to talk about the last time they had been in a church. They sat poised for escape.

The Reverend paused outside the doors to the chapel. It was late. He couldn't believe they had come. He knew this would be his only chance. Keep it simple, keep it light. Keep her here long enough to hear me out. He looked through the small windows in the door, past the women, over the altar at the large cross and offered up a short prayer that he was capable of delivering this message. No big words, no razzle dazzle. Humor. Humor would be good. He pushed open the doors.

He headed down the aisle and entered the row in front of the one where they were seated. Reverend Dalton wasn't feeling much more comfortable than either woman looked. He had a great deal riding on his next few words and for a man of words he was, on many levels, at quite a loss.

Leaning against the seat back behind him, he cleared his voice and dove headlong into the deep end. "You know, when I first went to become a Reverend and embarked on what I like to call those Reverend-training classes, I saw big city lights in my future. I was going to save the world. So I get my Reverend degree and get posted. So maybe it's not quite the big city. But, hey, it's a start. A small town, neighbors knowing neighbors. And I had a new dream. I was going to have my little church and we would raise up our spirits and the people would become, I don't know," the Reverend paused and smiled ruefully, "maybe the people would become the Waltons or something, and I could grow up to be the new visionary of Boy's Town or some other grand legacy."

Reverend Dalton chuckled to himself. It seemed so silly now, giving voice to this but he knew he had to. He had to make her understand that she had something to give that he, no, that they all, desperately needed. "So I get here and I meet the people and I get to know them and find out they're good people. And I slowly learn something about life. I walk the town and I begin to understand that struggling to stay alive can take its toll. That unemployment and poverty erode dreams. That the daily grind takes some people and slowly forces joy from their hearts and compassion from their souls. That the struggle kills hope. And they don't have time for knowing their neighbors. They don't have time for knowing themselves. And I'm trying. I'm trying to take one hour a week, a psalm, a simple Sunday Sermon, maybe an uplifting "Amazing Grace" and find a way to help them back into loving themselves enough that they can move on and love thy neighbor."

Reverend Dalton paused. This was the moment. Here and now. Time to lay bare his truth. Time to admit that the fantasy of Little Billy Dalton had not become the reality of Reverend William Dalton. "And you know what, I'm losing the battle."

"And then a really funny thing happens. Church lets out and not everyone races off to catch the game. And I realize that I hear my parishioners talking. Talking to each other about the merry-go-round lady. Is she crazy? Have you seen the horses? And, I realize she's contagious. She's the stuff that Don Quixote was made of. She can make people believe in Dulcinea. And I sit in wonder that you can achieve something that I cannot. And at first I think it's not fair."

For the first time her eyes looked up and he laughed. "Yeah, I know, not a very Christian reaction. But, that's why I get to be called 'man' and not 'God'. And I pray for guidance. And I learn in my answer, that in my struggle, I too, had lost hope; had lost faith. Not my faith in God, my faith in humanity. I lost the battle to my own apathy and my own self-pity and my own greed. Yes greed. Instead of being a humble man among men, I wanted to be the spotlight. And if I didn't have the spotlight I didn't know how to walk among the people and listen.

"And in my prayers I heard an answer. I should not commit the sin of envy, I should instead look to you and let your journey carry us all."

She started to laugh. Build a carousel. She wanted to scream at him. Yell he was wrong. Tell him he's an idiot, a religious lunatic. He was wrong. There is no journey. He didn't understand. That's the whole point. Life was gone. Miriam was gone. The journey was over. She sat with tears running down her face, silent sobs shaking her shoulders.

Millie motioned the Reverend away. When it was just the two of them, Millie leaned over and took her in her arms. She sat and rocked her gently. Very quietly she whispered, "When you were sick you told me you needed to be here to save Miriam. Maybe this is where you are supposed to start."

They sat in the pew for a long time. Finally she looked up. "He wants me to build a carousel. How?"

"I don't know. I guess we'll have to ask him."

"Millie?"

"Yeah?"

"I want you to know that once I had words and once I had manners and I need you to know that if I had either of them left I would share them with you."

Not quite an apology, not quite an explanation, but at least an acknowledgement.

She owed Millie so very much but it was all so far beyond her. "I just don't know where they've gone." This would have to do for now.

§ § §

Lying in her bed on the edge of sleep, Millie heard the soft trod on the steps, she heard the front door open and gently close. Millie didn't move. Millie knew she was going out. She even knew where she was going. And Millie was bone tired. She just needed some sleep. She knew she had nothing left to say, no more to give, it was now time to let her find her choice.

§ § §

She went to the fence, took off the key she wore around her neck and let herself in. She sat staring at Miriam.

Jess awoke in the dark. It had been a long time since she had roamed the streets at night, but she knew what she had to do. She slipped from window to tree, down into the darkness and headed out.

Jess found her just where she knew she would be. She came up quietly and slipped her small hand into the woman's. They both stared at Miriam. Finally Jess spoke, her voice quiet but firm. "She says you have to do this."

"She didn't happen to say how, did she?"

"No. Miriam just said it's right and you need to."

"Thank you." She squeezed the small hand that held hers. They stood there in the night, tied together by a voice and a once-proud carousel horse.

Millie came down the next morning to find her kitchen inundated with paper. There were drawings and sketches everywhere. Thankfully there was also fresh coffee, already brewed.

"I figure if *he* figures he's going to have a carousel built, he better have some idea what he's in for." She looked up with a rueful grin.

Millie grunted and poured coffee. It was a bit early for all this activity. Sip. Sip. Blink. Okay. She made her way around the table. "Well ... "

§ § §

Lyle peered over her shoulder as she unrolled the paper on the diner countertop. It was after three, so the diner was reasonably empty. Their little group of Lyle, Reverend Dalton, Jess and Millie staked one end for themselves. She paused, as the plans were laid bare and looked through the diner windows, over toward Miriam. She couldn't see her but needed the connection. Just needed to know she was there.

"Okay Reverend, here's a simplistic big-ticket first draft list. I'm thinking we need a platform about forty feet across. We have thirteen horses here—eight are definitely interior horses—and we'll need thirty-two horses for the carousel plus at least two more, so let's say we need twenty-one more horses. And since our herd is pretty much 'standers,' we'll need 'gallopers.' Of course we also need a couple of chariots, rounding boards, ceiling panels, mirror panels, door panels and about a hundred other panels, and of course, the calliope."

She looked up and took in the stunned faces around her. She looked down at the detailed plans that held them all captive and realized her mistake. She could feel her internal shut-off valve turning on. She struggled valiantly to finish, but now her voice sounded deadly, even to her ears. "Oh, and in case I didn't mention it, we definitely need the whole mechanism and then, just when you think the list might be nearing completion, we'll also need someplace to put the whole thing when it's finished—and a way to house it."

No one said anything. They looked at each other, looked at the Reverend. She had put the idea to paper but now it was big. Now it was crazy.

She could feel the air growing desperate. She didn't know what to say. It was insane for him to have come to her and even more ridiculous for her to have actually given him the time of day. Miriam was wrong. She didn't have to do this. Stupid. She never should have put these plans out there. After all, doesn't everyone know how to draw up a set of blueprints? Open a door to a piece of yourself and next thing you know you are vulnerable. Stupid. Stupid. Stupid. She knew better. Just shut the damn door. She moved to gather the papers back together.

Jess looked desperately over to Millie. She didn't really understand it all, but she knew something was going terribly wrong.

Millie had watched the scene unfold while quietly going about her afternoon cleanup. She didn't need to stand over the drawings; she'd had a bird's eye view of them on her own table just a few hours ago. Sure was something to see—sheets of white paper transformed into all these sketches filled with detail. Now Millie's view from the side let her see the impact those pictures were having.

She couldn't decide if everyone was stunned by the carousel, or simply stupefied by the merry-go-round lady making this whole presentation. Wasn't like you could pick just anyone walking into a diner and find out they could put together a set of drawings for building a carousel. Yet here they were. Oh well, whatever had them all stunned didn't really matter much either way. Millie simply accepted that somehow the save-the-horse crusade had become her crusade. That somehow, on some weird cosmic level, all their fates were tied to saving those crumbling, antique horses. Millie stood by and enjoyed watching the show, but now it was time for action.

With a quick wink at Jess, Millie strolled into the middle of the group and set down the omni-present coffee pot. "Well, I can only speak for myself when I say I'm in. I mean I can't help with carving, but I can lug and I can paint and I'm sure I can do other things once I know what they are, so count me in."

For the briefest second nothing changed and then the Reverend looked up. "I'd like to have a copy of these."

She didn't say anything, just continued to look at him.

"Well, now that you've put it in writing I see that I have a bit of work to do." He reached over gently and took the papers from her hand, "I'll have a copy made," he stated quietly while rolling. "I want to say a thank you to each of you who have just attended the first meeting of the first chapter of the local carousel builder's guild. We'll convene again soon." His eyes circled the group as he spoke, finally stopping where they had started, back to the merry-go-round lady. "We have a carousel to build."

§ § §

Post lunch things were always pretty quiet. Millie motioned to Lacey and stepped outside to grab a quick smoke. As had become her habit, her gaze traveled across the parking lot. The door opened from behind her as Lacey came and stood next to her, letting her gaze travel the same path as Millie's.

"I need to tell you something, Millie."

Millie knew what was coming before it was out. She took a deep drag and blew a perfect smoke ring.

"Tom asked me to go to the movies tonight. I told him yes."

Millie turned the concept over in her mind and shrugged. "Okay."

"Hey Millie?"

She should have known it wasn't going to be this easy. She thought about screaming, "none of your business" but settled on a slightly peevish, "Yeah?"

"You and Tom. I mean, I think, well, you know everyone thought," Lacey struggled to find the words. "Why'd you break up?"

Millie took another deep drag. It crossed her mind that today was a perfectly fine day to quit smoking. She dropped the cigarette to the ground and watched her shoe grind it out. She turned around and her eyes found Lacey's. What she wanted to say was "Because the only thing worse than being lonely yourself is being lonely with someone else," but frankly, it wasn't any of Lacey's business. And knowing Lacey, it probably wasn't even something she would understand. Millie turned to go back in. "Have a nice time," was all she said.

§ § §

She let herself in the front door, drafting pad in hand. It had been a good week. She needed to double check but she was pretty sure she had all of the horses marked out for refurbishment. She checked and noted every seam line—head, neck and legs. She found a wood dealer and brought him a sample. He was confident he could supply enough kiln-dried wood for her needs. Tomorrow she should be able to begin the dismantling for the restoration.

She found Millie sitting alone, in the dark, on the floor in the living room. She could see Millie's back pressed against the couch, the bottle of beer in her right hand lit by the embers of her cigarette glowing in the dark. "Hey," she leaned against the entry and called out softly.

"The Reverend called. He's ready for a second meeting of the carousel maker's guild."

"Oh."

She sat down on the floor, joining Millie in the dark. It had been over a week and she had convinced herself that she had, in the end, scared him off. That all of his wishful chatter was now a flight of fancy long gone.

They both sat in silence when it dawned on her something else had to be bothering Millie. Building some carousel wasn't really Millie's problem. Well maybe sort of in a third person kind of way, but not in a sit on the floor in the dark ... maybe Millie was rethinking Tom. Maybe she was sorry about her choices.

"Well ..." she let the word dangle in the air.

Millie deliberately stubbed out the cigarette then ground each small individual pile of ash down one stub at a time. "He asked if we could meet here—the church has some kind of function and he didn't want to delay."

"Oh."

The ash stubbing was now more like ash swirling. "I told him sure."

"And?"

"And ..." Millie finally dropped the butt into the ashtray, letting out an exasperated grunt, "and so I said sure, hung up the phone and looked around the house and realized that it's like a bad time warp back to nineteen seventy-something in here and it never mattered because I never had people over so it isn't like anyone was looking but now he's coming and he's bringing people and they will be looking and ..." a raspberry was the last punctuating remark.

"Ah."

"Yeah." Millie got up and grabbed another beer from the fridge. "Answer me one thing. How is it possible to go from not even noticing to, I don't know, maybe huge amounts of embarrassment?"

She sat and thought. Her hands picked at the carpeting. She could answer Millie, tell her it's the gift of consciousness, but she couldn't think how to say it without sounding snide. She didn't even need to look around. She knew she couldn't argue with Millie—the place was pretty bad. Not dirty, just kind of ugly in that really badly dated kind of way. She remembered her initial reaction to the puce-colored dishes. It wasn't that the house actually smelled; it was that its sense of being musty was so strong it permeated from your eyes right into your pores. It *felt* like it smelled.

Even in her stupor she had wondered about the house, the incongruity between owner and furnishings. Houses always fascinated her. As Millie talked about her parents, parts of the journey from house to a home back to a house clicked into place. It was such a specific line and always so easy for her to see. House. Home. Structure. Life.

Miriam would have been quick to share with Millie, how much she liked walls. Miriam was probably right. She built walls; Miriam tore them down. Her hands continued to pick at the carpeting. The kitchen paint had helped. It was about the only room that worked. The avocado green refrigerator was so old it had a retro chic about it; with the new white paint the bad seventies hell was pretty well toned down.

"So," she looked down as she continued picking, "this orange shag isn't cutting it for you, huh?"

Millie looked dubiously over. "Not really."

Suddenly she was laughing. It so stunned Millie that for just a second she froze, and then found herself laughing, too. God, she hadn't laughed in so long. Truly laughed. They were going to build a carousel but first they needed to do something about the carpet. Millie realized she had become a visitor in her own life. She could hear Lyle, "Yep. A visitor. Yep." Millie laughed that much harder. She suddenly slipped off the couch and splayed onto the floor, "what," she hiccupped, "what the hell is so funny?"

She could feel the unused muscles burning in her cheeks as she paused and considered the question. "I don't know." That was all it took. They couldn't look at each other and couldn't stop laughing.

"Okay." Millie sat up. "This is not funny. This sucks."

"Alright." She massaged her cheeks trying to calm them down, "Let's think for a minute." She cast her eyes about the room. The furniture was more or less serviceable, the couch was kind of tacky, but a couple of the old dark wood pieces were truly beautiful, especially the china cabinet, but God, Millie was right, this carpet sucked. At least they didn't wall-paper the downstairs. A curious thought came to her. "What's under the carpet?"

"I have no idea."

"Okay." She began to get excited, warming to her thought, "If we're really lucky, your parents were one of *those*."

"Those?"

"Hardwood Floor Coverers! Sorry, but a particularly nasty breed in my opinion. Take a perfectly beautiful hardwood floor and glue and nail orange shag right over it. Happened in a lot of old houses. It was an era, and a bad one." As she spoke she crawled over to a corner, praying for a simple answer. "I get wanting carpet, but take a stand for good taste and get a big area rug."

This was it. Millie was now leaning over her shoulder and watched as she deftly maneuvered her fingers under a corner.

"Yowza! Millie I am proud to tell you that you are the child of *those* people! We have hardwood."

"Great." Millie sat back on her heels, grinning away. It then occurred to her that she wasn't exactly sure why this was good news. "What's it mean?"

"It means we pull it up, pray they just tacked and didn't glue all over the place, polish it up and between the kitchen paint job and the hard-wood, you'll be spiffy enough to entertain." She grinned mischievously. "At least down here." Her laugh rang out as she ducked to avoid Millie's immediate back-handed slap.

In spite of her playful reaction, Millie still looked perplexed at the sudden turn of events. "You really think we can do this?"

"Excuse me?" She could not believe Millie just asked that. "Did I hear that correctly? YOU think we can build a carousel, but we might not be able to rip out a carpet? You're nuts, you know that?"

"Okay." Millie laughed at the exaggerated eyeballs looping around at her. She raised her hands up in surrender, "Point taken. When do we begin?"

"Can you call in sick tomorrow?"

"Call in sick?"

It crossed her mind that Millie was being incredibly dense. "Yeah. Take a day off." Apparently this was not a choice Millie ever made. Apparently it wasn't even a possibility she ever considered. "Take one day, not go in and we'll do this instead?"

§ § §

As Nan tossed a file into the trunk of her car, she saw the merry-go-round lady out front. Nan knew she was staying at Millie's, which was odd enough, but she didn't know what to make of this. That was Millie's carpet. God, she'd know that ugly thing anywhere. This woman was pulling it out the front door.

"Okay, on three, we drag again." She huffed the words out. "Ready?"

They had already been at it for two hours. She had the carpet ripped up and off the floor, now they had to get it through the front door, down the porch steps and into range of the garage so she could somehow get it into stacks for the dump.

Nan continued watching. She spotted Millie struggling and grunting on the other end. "Hey Millie," Nan hollered from her open garage, "need a hand?"

On the offer, Millie dropped her end of the carpet and stood back up. She shaded her eyes as she watched Nan pick her way across the lawn. "We would kill for a hand."

Nan clunked up the stairs. "I can't believe you're finally tearing that out."

"Yeah, well." Millie could feel the embarrassment rush to her cheeks. It hadn't really occurred to her that anyone else might have noticed the carpet.

"Aren't you supposed to be at work?"

"I took the day off." Millie grinned over at the merry-go-round lady and pronounced, "I am modernizing."

Nan was stunned. They'd been neighbors a long time, eleven years, she realized with a start. Nan had been twenty-seven when she bought her house. She realized that Millie and the other woman were waiting for her to respond. "Cool."

"Um, Nan," Millie didn't know where she had ducked out to, but whatever? "Um, what happened to that hand you were offering?"

"Sadly I cannot offer you a hand in the physical sense. I, as you can see, am dressed for work. But, I do happen to have a dolly in my garage, which might provide a bit of assistance. I'll grab it for you."

"Great." Millie's breath expelled as she sat on the rug to wait for Nan's return. She used the front of her sweatshirt to wipe her face as she tried to remember the last time she'd been this sweaty. It felt great. "Here she comes."

Both women looked up in time to see Nan huffing across the lawn, attempting to carry the clunky, dirty, heavy carpet-covered dolly while trying to keep it from touching her or her clothes. Suddenly, she went down.

The two women were up and across the lawn immediately. They looked at Nan and looked at each other and it was over before they could stop it. Hysteria. So much for being dressed for work. Yesterday's new-found giddiness continued, leaving them equally hysterical, on their knees and gasping for air.

Nan sat up with a struggle. Her shoes had sunk into a soft dirt spot and she moved but they didn't. The topple left her splat in dirt, torn knee-highs, a tear in her blazer's shoulder and at the moment, a wedgie from her twisted slacks. "This is so not funny!"

Millie looked over for a moment, struggling to be serious. "Are you hurt?"

"No."

"Oh," Millie grinned at the merry-go-round lady, "Then it is so too funny!" The two of them began another round of laughs.

Nan was still not finding any humor. "Christ, I am going to be late to work."

"I'm so sorry."

"Couldn't you just rip out the damn carpet on the weekend like everyone else?"

"Nope. I am hosting a meeting here tomorrow night and the thought of anyone seeing the shag was too embarrassing to contemplate. A fact which I seem to recall you just confirmed for me."

Nan's anger immediately dissipated in light of this tidbit. Millie was shredding carpet for what? Nan's ears had perked up. "Hosting a meeting, you?"

"It's the second official meeting of the first guild of carousel builders." Millie wrapped an arm proudly around the shoulders of her merry-go-round comrade. She was flying way too high in her new freedom to feel the flinch caused by the casual contact. "You should come." Millie leaned forward and dropped her hands onto Nan's knees, "Even better. You should take the day off to join us and stay for dinner."

"Christ, Millie," Nan just stared at her. None of this was making any sense. Millie was nothing if not responsible. "Have you lost your marbles!"

"Yep." Millie grinned mischievously. She couldn't remember the last time she had felt this, well, goofy. "Feels good. I promise." Millie kept wheedling, "Come along Nan, come lose your marbles with us."

"Oh, I don't think so."

"Come on." Millie jumped up and offered her hand to help Nan get up. "How many years have you been threatening—you're going to take a trip to Paris, you're going to join a health club, you're going to learn gymnastics."

"I'm going to learn what!" Nan shrieked. "Lie!"

"Okay, you never said you were going to learn gymnastics. But you know what I mean. Just play hooky for a day. It'll be fun."

§ § §

They put Gran in charge of dinner. Maybe she couldn't see, but she still could chop and she sure could cook.

Nan still didn't believe she had done this, but it had been fun and it was an unexpected day. She couldn't remember the last time she'd had an unexpected day—correct that—she had been stunned by Gran the other morning, but before that, it had been years. Nan inhaled deeply, the aroma from the kitchen luring her from her paint can in the living room. She couldn't believe she had allowed herself to forget the smell of Grandma's Roast Chicken.

"Okay. Dinner is ready." Millie's voice rang out from the kitchen. "Hey Nan, where'd our contractor go?"

"Thought she was helping you."

Millie paused, turned and headed upstairs. "Be right down, I just need to get cleaned up for a sec." She stopped at the bedroom door and knocked. There was no answer. Millie wasn't expecting one. She turned the knob and let herself in.

She was sitting on the edge of the bed. It had been a wild night and morning. She had come up to use the bathroom when she heard the voice, "Nice. A couple of laughs and we're right out of your mind. Poof. Gone."

"No." She had tried to protest but she knew Miriam was right. She didn't deserve to laugh. It wasn't in her game plan anymore. She knew she couldn't tell Millie that. Millie didn't deserve to be hurt.

"Hey."

"Hey."

"Dinner is ready."

"What about Jess?" She blurted it out. "We can't have a meeting without Jess."

Millie looked at her steadily, "I'll call the Reverend. I'm sure he can talk Jess' Mom into letting her come."

"Thank you."

Millie turned to leave. She knew something had happened, something she would not learn right now. She closed the door behind her.

§ § §

Tap. Tap. Tap. Tap. Millie tossed about in her sleep, trying to change her dream without waking.

Tap. Tap. Tap. Tap. Downstairs, her eyes migrated toward Millie's closed bedroom door above as she got the next piece into position. It wasn't easy keeping the board in position and tapping in these small nails while trying to muffle the sound with a towel. It needed to be done. It wasn't finished. Without the end it might as well not be done. It was better without the carpet and with the new paint, but it still wasn't going to make anyone's feng shui. It needed to reflect all the attention. Tap. Tap. Walls must be finished. Walls keep things safe. Tap. Tap. The last piece of crown molding made its way into place.

Millie rolled over and breathed evenly, nighttime serenity settling in.

She opened the paint can and began the final stage. Quiet. Focused. Disciplined. Alone; every stroke of the brush serving to paint over, reseal, her private pain.

§ § §

The little house was crowded with people. The highly polished floor gleamed a welcome. The crown moldings gave the room a sense of height, a touch of unexpected majesty. She sat quietly in the living room, tucked into a wing chair, still feeling singed from Miriam's message. It had been debilitating work plastering her emotional walls back in place, but it had been necessary. Most everyone else was chatting and scrambling for coffee and donuts in the kitchen. Millie seemed to know she needed to be away from the chattering.

She felt her shoulder being squeezed. It was Gran moving her way to a chair. "Child, you remember," Gran spoke low, it was between them, "It's time."

"It's time, folks," hands rubbing, energy radiating, The Reverend entered the house, Jess in tow, his words an eerie confirmation of Gran's message. As he greeted people, he effortlessly herded them toward the living room. Jess immediately sat and scooted her way to a spot near the feet of the merry-go-round lady.

"Millie," the Reverend continued. "First, I want to thank you for letting us meet at your house tonight. Hopefully we'll be able to use the church most of the time because I have a feeling we're going to need a command central." Millie raised her cup in acknowledgement of the introduction, using the moment to take in the faces, curious to see who the madman had rounded up.

As though he knew what she was thinking, the Reverend continued. "Okay, most of you know Millie, and for those who don't, our hostess here tonight is a founding member of our newly formed guild. Now, over here, this is our boss lady."

The Reverend had thought long and hard how to handle this introduction. He knew no one knew her name and he knew she wasn't about to confide in him. "So," he continued smoothly, "when you hear boss lady, you know who we mean. Next, we have Lyle Johnson who has generously agreed to donate the original horses currently under restoration and has also generously agreed to let us continue using his workspace as our own."

As the crowd politely clapped, the Reverend paused to give Lyle his moment. He was seated directly across from the merry-go-round lady. As he rocked upon his stick, nodding politely, he caught her eye and winked.

"Now, I'd like to introduce several new members and get the business of our evening going. First off, meet Barbara Adler. Barbara is a guidance counselor at the high school and agrees that there are probably several students who can use this opportunity as credits toward graduation.

"And to Barbara's right is Robert Howard. Robert works for the county and is going to help get the permits and land, and with any luck some grant money; all the things we need to put this baby front and center in Miller Park.

" Now, sticking with moving to the right, Nan Walsh has kindly agreed to donate her accounts receivable skills to keep our books. I'm hoping Gran will agree to keep us fed. Rudy and Joe couldn't make it this evening but Rudy let me know they were planning to join us—some quote about their horses going nowhere without them.

"I think that's it." He paused and looked around and smiled. "Oops. I was wrong. Everyone here, meet Jess Kastellon. Now, she may look a little young for the job, but Jess is our deputy inspector. She works directly for and reports directly to the Boss." His eyes met those of the merry-go-round lady. For the first time he could read what was there. It was good.

§ § §

Millie watched as Nan and Gran carefully made their way across the lawn back to their house. Once she was satisfied they were safe she turned back to the room. The merry-go-round lady sat just where she'd been all night, a small body tucked deep in the old wing chair. Millie turned out the kitchen light. "Good night," was all she said; "sleep well" was all she thought.

§ § §

As Barbara Alder pulled into the parking lot, she spotted her three teenage charges shifting about near the diner. Well, at least they had made it.

She still wasn't sure what to make of all this. When the Reverend phoned it all sounded so simple. Of course she'd heard about the merry-go-round lady—small towns being what they are, she'd have to have been dead to miss a tale or two, but meeting the woman yesterday was disquieting. She seemed swallowed up by the room, saying virtually nothing. The whole night resembled a flashback to one of those reach-your-potential EST Meetings. Oh yeah, she'd been there and done that. What was it—something about if you say it, it can come true. Whew. There's a throwback to a presumed dead brain cell. But then again, some people really did seem to make that whole self-empowerment, motivational thing work for them.

"What do I know?" Barbara checked her lipstick in the mirror, "What I know is I've got three kids standing there and this might be the last chance any of us have to save them."

Barbara exited her car, signaled and yelled, all in one practiced motion, "Tommy, Marcus, Cameron—let's go."

§ § §

She watched from her workbench stool as Barbara Adler led the three teens into the yard. She had heard them talking as they arrived. Well, two of them anyway. The two boys had strolled up together, glaring at her, obviously none too happy to be here. She didn't know which was which, but she knew "this sucked" and "that bitch"—presumably either Barbara or herself—"that bitch was full of it if she thought she could make them build horses." The third one, a young woman, arrived last and as far as she could tell, had said nothing.

Barbara stopped at the gate. "Hi Lyle."

From her perch she decided Lyle looked as happy about this as she did.

"Mr. Johnson," Barbara continued smoothly as though everyone here was at some sort of proper affair, "allow me to present Mr. Thomas Ianucci, Mr. Marcus Kim and Ms. Cameron Blair." Barbara flashed Lyle a smile before turning to stare down the trio. Her voice, when she spoke, held a barely concealed undertone of threat, "People, this is Mr. Johnson, the owner of this establishment. You will be respectful of his house. Understood?"

Although the question was obviously rhetorical, Barbara Adler fixed her eyes on each of them and waited. The trio looked remarkably similar in their coats and mannerisms. Barbara's years of reading the nervous tics of adolescence painfully put on public display signaled their secret code for her private translation. Barbara, satisfied with whatever shifts she saw, turned to move inward.

The carousel lady watched them approach as she had watched their earlier movements. She wasn't sure what she was supposed to say. She needn't have worried. Barbara moved this through as quickly as possible, "Okay kids, meet the Boss Lady. She's going to schedule and teach you what you need to know. Each of you owes her a minimum of twenty hours a week. If you think you are going to graduate this year, I suggest you embrace the opportunity."

"Gee, nice bedside manner she has." Oh God, not now, Miriam. I don't have time now. She could hear Miriam coming full bore. This was Miriam's idea of sport. She tried to block her, tried to focus.

When she finally blinked, Barbara was climbing back into her car and three kids were left staring at her. She saw Lyle watching her from the safety of his office. Think. Miriam was laughing, laughing at her, daring her to jump into this pool.

"Um, so, do any of you know anything about carousel building?" The trio continued to stare. "How about woodworking?" she asked, praying she did not sound as desperate as she felt.

§ § §

Lyle couldn't take it anymore. He pushed himself out of his chair and strolled over to the diner, setting himself up at his usual space. Millie, so surprised to see him, passed right by before taking a step backwards and nearly dropping a pile of dirty plates in his lap. Millie felt her stomach flip. "Is everything all right?" she asked anxiously.

"Yep." Lyle smiled.

"Lyle Johnson," Millie saw the laughter in his eyes. "You do not stop in for coffee at nearly three o'clock in the afternoon. What's going on?"

Lyle started to laugh. "Millie, you should have seen it. Yep. That Barbara Adler woman from last night came by with three sorry excuses for teenagers and just handed them off to her. I had to get out of there before I busted a gut watching them all. Yep. Three sorry excuses."

Millie moved toward the door but to her dismay, from what she could see, the makeshift workspace was now empty except for the woman. Her head was bent over one of the horses and she had an Exacto knife in her hand. "Well Lyle, it's safe to go on out. I don't know what she did with them, but they're gone."

"Why thank you Millie." Lyle still was shaking his head, grinning. "But now that I made it up here, I think I'll just have myself a cup of coffee."

Millie turned back, grabbed a cup and saucer and poured. "Lyle, in honor of this untimely visit, today I am buying."

As Millie went to finish her side work for the day, Lyle sat sipping and thinking. This was one fine cup of coffee. Yep. One fine cup.

She lay in bed listening to the sounds a house makes at night. So different from the night sounds of the camp site, she mused. Groans and creaks. The boiler turning on and off. She had been awake for hours, trying to understand what was happening with Miriam. Something was wrong. It seemed only Jess heard her loving voice. She felt lashed at, scathed. Miriam no longer joked with her, but seemed caustic, taunting her. Instead of poking fun, Miriam seemed to delight in her discomfort. Was she angry? Was that it? Was Miriam angry with her?

She bolted out of bed and went to the mirror. She pulled off her t-shirt and looked at the scar. The puffiness had settled. She picked up the Exacto knife she had brought home, ran her fingers gently over the blade.

§ § §

Millie passed by her bedroom on her way downstairs. She didn't hear any sounds coming from inside. It was wrong, Millie thought uneasily. She's always ready on time. Christ! I didn't even think she slept. Maybe she should go back upstairs and check. She turned to go, but something held her back. Okay, she would wait another five minutes. Just make the coffee, sit down and have a few sips. If she wasn't down by then, then Millie would go up and knock.

Half a cup later, she looked at her watch, double-checking that the second hand was in motion. One minute down. Okay, she'd get her stash of uniforms out of the laundry and hang them up. Millie gave her wrist an extra shake and got up. That was something to do. Should kill at least two more minutes.

Millie walked toward the small laundry room and paused. There were her uniforms, all neatly lined up with hangers on the lip above the door-frame. She pushed them carefully to one side and walked in. Millie opened the washer; it was empty. Her hand moved over to grab the dryer handle. Inside she found a set of sheets. Millie hurried upstairs, pushed open the door and their eyes met.

She was sitting up. It had been a night of mind games and night terrors, but she was still here. Her hand reached under her shirt; the scar was still intact.

Millie could still smell the slight odor of vomit.

She looked away, ashamed to meet Millie's eyes. Millie pulled the door shut behind her.

§ § §

It was a day that offered no respite. No rest for the wicked as the saying goes. They were tired before the day began and by the time they returned home, both women were wrecked. "Thank God for peanut butter and jelly sandwiches," Millie proclaimed as she saw from her position on the floor in front of the fire, the boss lady walk in with the plates.

For a while they both sat quietly eating and soaking up the warmth. Millie stared into the flames thinking how tough it had been to keep smiling and working while seeing Lacey snuggle up to Tom in the booth and kiss him hello. It wasn't that she missed Tom, but it hurt, that first witness to a public look at them as a couple. Millie wasn't foolish, she knew they'd been seen around town, but it was still embarrassing. She felt everyone was checking to see her reaction. She knew people thought she was crazy for letting him go, but it hadn't really hit home until today, when he walked in. Millie sucked in a deep breath of air and blew it out. She contorted her body in an effort to reach the kinks. God, she felt like a mile of bad road.

She watched Millie quietly. She had seen Tom go past. She always saw him. He always made sure of it. Always stopping for just a second, just long enough to rattle the cage. "You okay?"

"I think so. I wasn't expecting a, um, what you'd call a public display of affection, you know?" Millie's smile was wry; her words came out in a snort. "Guess it must be true love."

The flames continued their dance.

"How about you?" Millie twisted her shoulder and arm over the front of her left side and the crack could probably be heard down the block. "Ah, now that felt good. Mmmm." Millie continued to twist right and then left. "How goes life with your trio of teen charmers?"

"Sadly they are already only a dynamic duo."

Millie's eyebrow shot up in question.

"Apparently young mister Thomas Ianucci does not feel that carousel building will enhance his career opportunities." She thought back to his face when he stopped by early that morning. He was in full sneer as he explained what a waste of bleeping time this was and how he'd rather flunk out than build merry-go-round ponies.

She looked over at Millie and rolled her eyes. "Then, let's see, I had to explain to Marcus Kim that Jess outranks him and she is not there to be his personal water boy. As you can imagine it was another stellar conversation. Oh, and did I mention that Marcus' basic knowledge of tools is limited to the difference between a hammer and a screwdriver? But not to worry, he apparently does great in math and auto repair. Thank you Barbara."

She paused for a moment, pushing her fingertips against her temples. Her next thought actually brought a grin. "Then there's Cameron Blair. Doesn't seem to talk at all, just stands there wrapped up in her coat against the world and appears to be your basic social misfit trying to get the hell out of high school." She laughed softly, "Now that, that I can respect."

"Ugh. High school. I think the saddest people must be the people who think high school is great," Millie laughed. She reached over and grabbed a pillow from a nearby chair and lay down in front of the fire with her head propped up. "I mean think about it. Everyone is waiting to grow into someone they can live with except the twenty or thirty kids who comprise the football, baseball, prom queen pack. If you put us on one of those legal scales—you know, those justice is blind doohickey things—by sheer volume of the other side, we must outweigh them by at least a million to one. The real truth is they must secretly be the losers for being that intact during those years."

"Okay. I'll buy that."

"Good. Then I have just one question for you." Millie left the statement dangling until the merry-go-round lady looked away from the fire, made eye contact and asked, "Uh huh?"

Millie grinned, "When exactly do I get to sit on the losing side of that scale?"

§ § §

He was alive with an energy he could barely remember and barely contain. His grace was within reach. When he spoke the other night,

William Dalton realized how far he had fallen. At ten he was going to save the world and by thirty he had walked from the battlefield. Today, today was different. He had reclaimed his steel and was ready for battle—and this time he would not lose. His struggles had taken his brashness, his arrogance, and turned them into compassion and understanding. His steel had become tempered.

As the crowd filtered in, Reverend Dalton glanced from his position in the alcove. His eyes were alert, his heart and mind, body and soul, alive and buzzing with his energy. If this was a bad sci-fi movie, he would be one jumbo pulsating blob. He saw them settle, heard the room go quiet. The time was now.

The Reverend forced himself to move steadily to the pulpit. Look up, take a deep breath, smile. "All right people," he paused and made eye contact with his congregation. "A good Sunday morning to you."

He watched as a few people nodded, a few more smiled that little half smile. The Reverend leaned forward and grinned playfully. "I can't hear you," he teased. William Dalton straightened back up and continued, "I know" he paused again, "let's hear a good morning to God."

The room was deathly silent. Reverend Dalton took a step back and waited. Then he stepped again to the pulpit, "Okay, let's pause for just a second. Now the Lord, as I had it taught to me long ago, the Lord is just happy to be remembered with joy in your heart. But that . . . that people was weak. Now, I know first hand that many of you can do better. I've even heard several of you, at one time or another, giving the Lord his due with huge amounts of, let's call it, um, passion behind the words."

This brought forth a few nervous giggles, perhaps a tinge of guilt from those who caught his inference. "So this morning, let's say Good Morning Lord and let's say it with joy—for those of you who remember the sixties—say it loud and say it proud!"

A small if somewhat self-conscious cry of "Good Morning Lord" rose up. It was stilted and off-kilter and muttered, but it was there.

He surveyed the room again and saw a set of laughing eyes, "Jess Kastellon!" Jess froze immediately in place, one knee up on the bench, her hand locked upon the shoelace she had just been toying with. She felt the heat rush to her face. She wasn't laughing at him, she wasn't! "C'mon Jess," Reverend Dalton continued, "I need your help this morning. I need you to yell Good Morning God."

Jess just looked at him, looked around the room. She could feel her mother's hand motioning her to stand up. She could feel her twin sisters laughing at her. This wasn't fair, wasn't fair at all. As she stood, she saw Lyle nodding to her. Jess turned and stared at the Reverend, saw his smile and drew in a deep breath, calling out, "Good Morning God."

Reverend Dalton looked over, "Thank you Jess. Just for that, I grant you one get-out-of-a-lesson free pass." He felt himself crossing a Rubicon as Jess smiled gleefully at his words and others began to laugh. "Mr. Billy Ray Ryan!" he said watching as the red hair now popped out of his chair. "Mr. Billy Ray, can you do better than that?"

Billy Ray turned to look at Jess, his archenemy. When the Reverend called on her, he had nearly laughed out loud, but now, now she could get out of a lesson and he could tell people thought she was cool. Well watch this. Billy Ray Ryan opened his lungs to the Lord and by the time he was finished screaming "good morning!" there was no doubt God was now wide awake!

Reverend Dalton felt the energy growing as he looked around at his congregation. His eyes met Lyle Johnson's and he could hear Lyle as plainly as if he were whispering in his ear, "Yep." This was it; he stepped up and said simply, "Okay folks, let's pray."

§ § §

Sharlyn found herself being tugged along the path by her very anxious daughter. She didn't really know what to make of Jess these days. She no longer got phone calls about Jess being spotted out at night, her grades were up and even her sisters no longer seemed to torment her. Her child was happy and for that, Sharlyn Kastellon was grateful. On the other hand, who was this woman and what did she want from her child?

Sharlyn accepted that Jess was going to help fix the horses; the horses had always been Jess' obsession. Short of keeping her prisoner, it wasn't likely she could stop her. And between work and shopping and homework and bill paying and soccer and just life, Sharlyn had no time for guard duty. Truth is, Sharlyn never had been able to stop her most strong-willed child—even when she was a baby.

Now she was thankful Lyle Johnson was always there. Sharlyn knew he would keep his eye on Jess. "Come on Mom," Jess tugged anxiously, "We're gonna be late."

Sharlyn oddly looked forward to meeting this woman. For the first time in a long time, her solitary, independent daughter was reaching for her, tugging on her hand. Sharlyn laughed and looked at Jess' face, flushed from both the chill in the night air and all her excitement, "Last one to the door is a rotten egg." She heard Jess squeal as her feet took flight. Who knows, maybe this is a very good thing. Sharlyn hurried to catch up.

The room was teeming with people when Millie arrived. It was a reception hall with a dais in the front and several round tables set out. The merry-go-round lady was seated in the midst, yet, as always, somehow set apart. Millie made her way to the dais, pulling back the chair she knew was being saved for her, "Sorry, Gran moves a bit slow." Millie motioned over to Nan escorting her Grandmother patiently to a chair.

The surprised eyes of the carousel lady raised back to Millie who shrugged, "said she needed some excitement a heck of a lot more than we did."

Millie dropped her coat onto the back of the chair and settled in, taking the opportunity to get her first real glimpse of the assembled crowd. She saw Barbara Adler and the two teens she recognized as the "new help." There was Lyle, and the guy from the other night, Robert something or other. Millie turned to her left and smiled with surprise as she saw both Joe and Rudy. Seated with Rudy was his twelve-year old daughter, Kristen. Jeez, she had grown up. It must have been at least a couple of years since she had seen her. Millie realized she was counting. There must be at least thirty people in the room. She knew most of them—if not by name, then at least by face, but it was wild nonetheless.

Millie's musing was interrupted by the arrival of Reverend Dalton. If there had been a ten-foot high stage, he could have easily jumped onto it, such was his energy. Instead, he strode quickly and confidently to the front.

"Thank you, everyone, for being here this evening. We are embarking on an adventure and I welcome you all aboard. I want to say how glad I am that most of you required only a minimal amount of arm-twisting to join us. Our goal tonight is to learn from the Boss Lady here," he motioned with a tip of his head, "what we need to do in order to move forward. I'm hoping that by the time we're done, all of you will join some part of the process. It's an ambitious project and there will most assuredly be enough slots to go around. All help is a good thing." He paused and took a quick look around. "Okay, let's get ourselves educated. Boss Lady, the floor's all yours."

She stood up and felt the eyes upon her. As she unrolled one of her drawings, the one that showed all the parts to be built, her hands shook and the drawing slipped back down. She felt heat rushing over her face. Jess was ready to jump up from her seat right in the front when they both heard the voice, this time gently reassuring. "Breathe. You can do this. This is right."

"Hey Boss Lady," Joe interrupted from his seat. "How about if Rudy and I hold it up so everyone can follow along?" Without waiting for an answer the two men were on the move. As Rudy passed she heard him whisper, "Hey, the breakfast crowd sticks together you know."

Somehow she smiled her thanks and managed to get started, explaining what they wanted to do and what they needed to do in order to accomplish it. She laid out various groups and committees. Finally she stopped talking. It wasn't until she stopped she realized everyone was genuinely listening.

Reverend Dalton stepped up. "Okay, let's get the ball rolling. First, let's welcome Robert Howard. For those of you who have not met Robert before, he is our county liaison. Robert?"

Robert stood up, smiled at the faces around him. "Okay, tonight I can do you all a favor and promise to be short and sweet. Miller Park has an opportunity for us. I need to get further info and do some leg work before I can say it will work if we do x, y and z, but it's worth exploring. The only other item I have is a request. I'm sure most of you are here because you want to help build a horse, but to be frank, I can use a hand with paperwork and scheduling and all the endless calls this is going to take. So, if there's anyone who thinks they might be better sweet talkers than carvers, please see me."

Millie leaned over and whispered, "Okay, better sweet talkers than carvers. Off hand, I think that probably qualifies just about the whole damn room." She met Millie's eyes and just as quickly tried to look away and stifle the laugh, but was only partially successful. Robert turned and smiled uncertainly. Millie sweetly and innocently shrugged and grinned back. Robert turned back around, having now completely lost his place, "Uh thank you," stumbled out as he took his seat.

"Okay," said the Reverend jumping back into the fray. "We now have a starting place for, hmmm, we'll call it an administrative committee. Now, I'm going to introduce a good man and a good friend, Chris Dysart. Chris?"

"Hi." Chris took stock of the crowd. "I know most of you already, but for people who don't know me, I own Dysart Construction. I'm here tonight because apparently I volunteered." Chris glanced over at the Reverend and everyone started laughing. "Apparently I not only volunteered, but I volunteered to donate labor and materials and all sorts of things for the building and foundation work. Is that right Reverend? I'm not leaving anything out, am I?" Chris now had the crowd playing along with him. "So, I gather it's a little early for what I do, except that as Rob gets his committee together, he's going to need specs and things. So, I am going to need a construction coordinator."

Chris turned as he spoke, running his eyes over the crowd. He noted the young teen glancing up at the mention of the job. "I don't need someone who knows how to pour concrete as much as I need someone who can get all the paperwork back and forth, make sure that finance has our estimates and become the point person between me, Dysart Construction and the rest of the project." Chris bobbed his head at the Reverend and took his seat back.

"Now," the Reverend smiled, "Let me introduce Nan Walsh for those of you who don't know her. Nan has graciously volunteered to handle everyone's favorite committee—finance."

By now the gathering was growing more comfortable and with comfort came both humor and noise. Nan rose to a bunch of teasing cat calls ranging from "Volunteered? Huh, Reverend" to "Ooohhh . . . the money lady." Nan laughed, "Hey everyone, I'll be even briefer than Robert. Help!!" People cheered and applauded this succinct plea, the room beginning to swing effortlessly into play mode.

"All right, I get it," the Reverend waved to get everyone focused for just one last round. "Not only is Nan our financial whiz, she was also smart enough to bring her Grandmother, who was kind enough to bring us a couple of pies." Joe's shrill whistle cut through everyone's cheers and stomping. "So, let's move this into an eat-and-chat mode. Anyone who thinks they can help out with some of our nuts and bolts, please talk directly to team leaders, anyone and everyone interested in joining the art department, please talk with the Boss Lady and let's see who can volunteer what kind of time and skills.

Even though food was a powerful draw, the crowd was evenly split between those who stopped to grab pie and those who went to talk to committees. Rudy made a beeline for Millie and the Lady. "Hi Millie." Rudy kept one arm wrapped around his daughter. "You remember Millie don't you Kris?" Kris nodded shyly into her father's side.

"My God Rudy, she's beautiful, practically all grown up. Has it been that long?" Millie wondered aloud. Rudy nodded but his attention had turned to the merry-go-round lady. "Hello Miss, um, this is my daughter, Kristen. She was kind of hoping she could work on this."

"Hey Kristen." She watched as the young girl remained partially hidden behind her bear of a father. "That would be really neat, thank you."

Conversations overlapped as people came through. The Reverend and Millie helped get names, phone numbers, and email addresses. No matter if they were volunteering for another committee, everyone seemed to want to be at least a small part of the artistic group. "Hello Rudy. Hi Kristen, don't you look lovely tonight." A couple made their way through the crowd. He was eighty if he was a day and still walking tall. She was beautiful. She must have been as old as he was, but where he was big and forceful, she was petite and elegant. "Irene thought you might be kind enough to introduce us."

Rudy grinned and leaned over to give Irene a gentle hug. Straightening, he shook the old man's hand and turned toward the table. "Reverend Dalton, Millie, Miss, I'd like you to meet Sam and Irene Goldstein. They're from up near the interstate."

"Welcome Mr. Goldstein, Mrs. Goldstein." The Reverend stood and extended his hand. "Delighted you could join us."

"Thank you Reverend. It's nice to be here. Rudy over there was telling my brother Morris about your project and to be honest, at first we weren't sure what to make of it—you being a Reverend and your meeting being down here at the church and all. But Rudy explained it wasn't a church project so Morris and I," he saw the group look around, "Sorry, Morris couldn't make it tonight. But we both want to be involved."

"That's terrific. Is there anything in particular you and your brother had in mind to do?"

"Yes sir. My brother and I are both master carvers. We apprenticed when we were oh, I think ten and twelve at our uncle's shop, Stein and Goldstein." A gasp interrupted Sam's story. He looked at the boss lady with her mouth agape and grinned, an acknowledgement of her appreciation for the legacy of his uncle's company. "We were hoping to join the carving committee."

She looked at Millie who looked at the Reverend, and although some of the specific impact might have been lost on them, its general meaning was plain and simple This was quite the score. The Reverend again extended his hand, "Mr. Goldstein, I think it is safe to say thank you for coming and welcome aboard."

Jess had made it directly in front of her idol, tugging her Mom along. "Hi, I'm Sharlyn Kastellon, Jess' Mom."

"It's really nice to meet you."

Sharlyn felt herself stiffen, her earlier enthusiasm dowsed by old fears. She was not pleased that this woman would not return the introduction. Yes she was aware that everyone else seemed to accept it, but it rubbed her the wrong way. She felt Jess tug at her again. "Well I just wanted to say hello and say what a wonderful project this seems. Jess is really enthused."

Sharlyn could still feel Jess' eyes on her and she knew she had to get this right. She deeply resented it, but she realized this was Jess' hero and if she did this wrong she'd destroy a piece of her daughter. "I can't imagine myself carving a horse, and of course with work and the girls, and . . . anyway, I do want to be part of this so I thought I could maybe give Nan a bit of time during the week."

"That's really great, Ms. Kastellon." She understood intuitively this woman feared and resented her, but respected how much she seemed to love the daughter she could not understand. "We can certainly use the help." She smiled at Jess who was beaming.

"Hey Boss Lady?" The disembodied voice called out over the general hub.

She looked up toward the yell. Okay think. Speaker. Construction. Chris. Dysart. Got it.

He watched as she classified him. "Okay with you if I swipe one of your kids here for myself?" She peered around and smiled. "I think Marcus is just the guy I'm looking for." She threw him a thumb's up across the room and laughed when Millie leaned over and whispered, "Two down!"

Well, at least he seems happier about this gig than he did when she met him. Thinking of Marcus reminded her of Cameron and she quickly looked around. She spotted Cameron still tucked away in the same corner she began the night in. Still hiding. She motioned to Millie and walked over. The only indication Cameron gave that she had been watching was the quick reflex she used to slam shut the notebook on the table. She shifted her weight so her arms now fell across the cover. "Hey, no pie and no committee? Not the way to score points with Ms. Adler." Cameron shifted uncomfortably but still didn't say anything.

"Look Cameron," she said, squatting by the table. "Is there anything about this that interests you at all?" She pinched the bridge of her nose. "Okay, why don't I talk to Ms. Adler and just tell her it's not for you? Would that help?"

Cameron's left knee bounced a mile a minute and her hands played with a pencil. Finally she sat back, uncovering the notebook she'd been leaning on and looked at the merry-go-round lady. For a moment she obsessively toyed with the cover flap. Up. Down. Up. Down. She didn't say anything, then, decision reached, opened her notebook to the inside flap and turned it around.

The kid could draw. She was stunned. Really draw. It was an amazing sketch of a carousel horse in motion.

Cameron shifted uncomfortably. She looked back down and played with her pencil, twisting it nervously about.

A hand reached in and stopped the pencil. "Want to build her?" she asked.

Cameron looked up and met her eyes and nodded.

"Great." She looked up at Millie and waved, "We've got a keeper for our team." She gave Cameron's shoulder a squeeze as she moved past. "Bring the drawing to the library on Tuesday. She's going to be the first one up."

It seemed as though the heavens not only heard about the new carousel but signaled approval with a Monday morning that dawned bright and sunny and surprisingly warm. As Millie and the-merry-go round lady made the turn into the parking lot, Millie's eyebrow raised in surprise. Joe's cab had already pulled in and Joe and Rudy jumped down as the women parked.

Millie glanced at her watch. It was only 5:52. Millie closed the car door. "Joe, is something wrong?"

"See Rudy," Joe smiled and winked at the merry-go-round lady. "She does care."

"Grrr," Millie rolled her eyes, put the key in the front door. She pulled it back and held it for the group to pass through, "Come in. Must be coffee time." As she turned on lights and set the pot brewing, Millie turned back to the counter. "Okay, so what has you two up at the crack of dawn?"

Joe leaned up on the bar and whispered loudly, "I can't tell you," he teased. "It's a top secret mission."

"Really?" Millie came around the divider and sidled up to Joe, batting her eyelashes. "Not even for," Bat. Bat. "A cup of coffee."

The group burst out laughing as Millie shouted, "Yes!" and continued her victory dance, high-fiving this small crowd.

The door-opening bell rang when Charley entered. If this morning's gathering was a bit out of the ordinary, no one would know it from Charley. He just nodded to the foursome as he made his way back to turn on his grill.

§ § §

It was nearly three when Rudy and Joe pulled back in. This time their rig was attached to the cab and they backed the truck in near Lyle's side of the parking lot. They announced their presence with a toot of the horn.

The Reverend winked at Millie and put down his coffee—she followed him out onto the landing. Before Rudy could even get his door open, the Reverend raced across the parking lot, hopped onto the running board and leaned in the window, "Get everything okay?"

"Yeah. Piece of cake. What time is Chris's crew due over?"

"Any minute. He swears this will assemble pretty quickly so I'm trying to get the worst of it up and out before the dinner crowd." The Reverend glanced back over his shoulder. A small crowd of on-lookers had gathered.

"Okay." The Reverend hopped down and rubbed his hands together. "Boss Lady," he called to her through the fence, "while we were talking it up last night, I realized that Chris was mistaken, we did have an immediate need or two. A little electricity, a little running water would be good. Also, while I understand this little big top here has deep meaning, if we're going to do this, we need something a little less ..." Reverend Dalton paused to search for a polite word, "dubious, shall we say. So, lift the back boys."

Joe came around to the fence side laughing. It never occurred to him that Reverend Dalton had balls, but he was really starting to like this guy. Joe thought the Reverend looked like a kid on Christmas and laughed even harder. He knew when he opened his truck, somehow a bunch of barn board siding wasn't going to be all that thrilling.

Up went the tailgate. Lots of edges of lots of sides peeked out. The Reverend caught Joe laughing and knew he was laughing at him. "Okay," the Reverend merrily confessed, "it might not look like much but these are the new walls for our workshop. Chris has a crew coming by to get this puppy up and we will be rocking and rolling."

Did he really say get this puppy up? She started to laugh, when suddenly the gaiety fled and she felt chilled. Prickly. It wasn't Miriam, but what?

Tom had pulled up during the Reverend's crowd play. He glanced back at Millie, watching from the landing, turned, let his eyes drift over to *her* and then deliberately strolled his way through to Lyle's office.

Lyle sat rocking his stick, watching the shenanigans through his window on the world. This was better stuff than you could find on the TV. Yep. Television didn't have much to offer anymore, but this, this is entertainment.

The sheriff came in and stood watching.

"Hello Sheriff Tom."

"Everything okay here Lyle?"

"Just fine Sheriff."

"Well," Tom paused for only a second, "That's good then." His quick inventory complete, Tom moved back out. His intensity alone seemed to create a direct path through the crowd to his cruiser.

Only Lyle watched him go, wondering at the strangeness of the visit. Yep. It was definitely strange.

Tom pulled the cruiser into the station. "Hey Miller, I want you to go check some permits for me."

§ § §

She had stayed home the next morning. Chris needed his crews to have access so they blanketed the horses and as much of the yard as they could. It was odd to be in the house alone. She'd been there by herself before, but only when she'd been sick or Millie was just late.

It seemed much too quiet in the house alone. She hadn't heard from Miriam since Sunday night. She didn't hear her all the time now. She wasn't sure if that was good. Sometimes it seemed easier, but mostly it hurt. For so long she couldn't get Miriam out of her head and there was comfort in that pain. It meant she was still there. What if she was leaving her? She didn't know if she could stand that.

§ § §

Morris and Sam drove along the back roads. Morris did all the driving; Sam couldn't see so well anymore. "So tell me again Sam," Morris asked for the fifth or sixth time, "she really knew who our uncle was?"

"Morrie, it was great. You could have knocked her over with a feather. Even Irene was impressed."

For a moment that seemed to satisfy Morris, but it was fleeting. Two, maybe three minutes passed before, "And you really think they're going to do this?"

"I don't know. I just didn't think it was my place to tell them they're all crazy."

Again Morris chewed on the information. Sam sat and waited, Morris did not disappoint. "And the Reverend, he seems okay?"

"Yeah. He reminded me of Solly. A little bit meshugah, but a good heart, you know."

"And this girl, this girl who's going to build the carousel, she has no name?" Morris could never quite get past this part of the story.

Sam looked out the window as the road flew by, he turned back to Morris and sighed, "I'm sure she has one. I mean she had to have parents, they had to have given her a name, but she doesn't tell anyone."

"Why?"

They'd been through this half a dozen times already. Sam knew Morris wasn't going to let this go. "I don't know Morrie, I don't know. Maybe she doesn't like her name; maybe she was hurt and forgot it. Just one promise Morrie, don't go in there today and start something. She seems like a very nice girl. If she wants to tell us her name, one of these days, I'm sure she will."

Morris grunted but to Sam's relief, finally quit nattering and drove the car.

§ § §

The librarian, from her perch behind the desk, saw a small group of people waving and smiling as they parked and approached the door. She knew this had to be "the carousel crowd" she had been expecting. She guessed there were about a dozen people. Excellent. She had set aside an area in the back section and it should be perfect.

They filtered in and then they filtered in that much more. The little back room was now standing room only.

Millie pulled up and looked for a parking space. The joint was jumping. She turned toward Lyle in the front and Jess in the back, both of them watching, wide-mouthed, "I think I'll drop you two off in the front and find somewhere to put the car."

Lyle grinned at Millie. "She sure has gotten to be quite the draw. Yep. Quite the draw."

§ § §

She tried standing on one of those rolling footstools, but the crowd was too deep. She couldn't find the Reverend or Millie or even Jess. There was no way she could handle this.

"'Scuse me, 'scuse me," Jess used her head to bull her way underneath people, one hand behind her pulling Lyle along as she pushed.

Millie met up with the Reverend at the front door. They looked at each other in amazement. The Reverend turned to Millie, a twinkle in his eye. "So, should we take bets on whether or not she could find a window to climb out?"

It was a zoo, but they did it. Chairs were pushed and tables pulled and floor space maximized and somehow everyone managed to settle down. Using the projector, she had taken Cameron's drawing and positioned it on the wall. With the Goldstein Brothers' help, they had traced out the very first pony.

The Goldstein Brothers. God, she didn't want to begin to think where she would have been without them. She was completely unprepared to face the over-flowing crowd, but the brothers just stepped in, reveling in the attention. She grinned as they came to mind.

Since she'd already met Sam, she was expecting to see another Sam. But the funny part is they are two similar faces stuck on two completely different bodies. Sam, the older one, tall and assured, Morris, two years younger, ten years more neurotic, and short, barrel-chested and slightly bow-legged. Together they are their own comedy team.

But today, today they were teachers and they came and they taught, much the way someone had taught them so many years ago. "We know most people think that a carousel horse is one big solid block of wood, chiseled down to look like a horse. Well, most people think wrong. A carousel horse is always crafted in eight sections. There's the body, the head, the neck, the tail and of course, the four legs." Morris smiled at the crowd. "Now, if anybody here would like a three-legged horse, we only have to have seven sections instead!"

People sat glued to their every word. But their biggest help was their direct suggestions. They asked people who weren't interested in carving to please switch to the back while those who wanted to learn, or already had experience with carving move to the front. Painters, for example, would come a bit later. The brothers had surveyed the crowd and Sam explained that right now carvers get to be the front line. You didn't need experience, but you did need desire and commitment, "because, I tell you to look carefully at the beauty of the horse Miss Cameron has drawn, such beauty will not happen overnight. A craftsman's job is to slowly and carefully find in this piece of wood, this horse ... Cameron's ...?"

Sam paused to let Cameron fill in the blank, but she just stared. She didn't know she needed to name the horse.

"Um, Cameron's Dancer...." Sam's voice filled the uncomfortable pause and after turning back to see Cameron nod, he continued, "and every horse and every piece of wood will have its own history, just like people, and like people it takes time and love to bring out the beauty hidden underneath..."

And as Sam spoke, she heard the familiar tickle in her ear. "Now see darlin', isn't that just what I always told you." For the first time in so very long, the voice was playful.

§ § §

She slept with a smile on her face. Miriam was playful, prancing right and left. She snuggled down trying to hold on even as events shifted. Even in her dreams she could not escape the tumult of the past week—this person gets to go to carving, that person to painting. The colors splashed over, wood chips flew and an empty carousel turned. The cranks without horses churned end over end. Miriam reared and galloped up calling, "You're needed. You're needed." The cranks continued to churn.

§ § §

Millie heard the doors shut and the car engine turn over. She blinked at the ceiling but didn't move. She tried to roll over, pulled the covers up and the pillows over her head, but it wasn't working. Exasperated, she rolled back over, kicked the blankets to the side. Sometimes, sometimes Millie just hated that she cared. Stuffing her feet into slippers Millie shuffled her way down to the kitchen; maybe some tea or warm milk would help.

Millie switched on the kitchen light and spotted the torn piece of paper atop the counter. "I had to go out, but I'll be back" was scrawled on the strip. Millie smiled and let her fingertips run over the note. She switched the light back off and shuffled upstairs; sleep could now come.

§ § §

She couldn't ignore it. This time Miriam beckoned her to come and give comfort. She pulled into the dark parking lot and glimpsed a small, solitary figure pass through her headlights. She walked up to Jess and put a hand on her shoulder and waited.

Finally Jess' small voice asked, "She told you to come didn't she?"

"Yes."

Jess' eyes were puffy and her lower lip was quivering but she continued to stare straight ahead. Miriam was still wrapped in blankets, turned away from them. The merry-go-round lady kept her hand in place and waited. She understood that sometimes you needed to share in your own time and way.

"What's going to happen to Miriam?"

Okay. Think. Try to understand what she wants to know. "You mean when the carousel is finished?"

Jess shook her head. "No." Anguished eyes finally looked up. "I mean now, now that everyone wants to build and paint. Miriam doesn't belong to everyone. She belongs to you and me." Jess managed to get it out before sobs overtook her.

She gathered Jess in her arms, kissed the top of her head and held on. "Oh Jessie." Her heart pounded wildly, "Jess, I want you to listen to me. Miriam is ours. No one but you and me will restore Miriam. I promise you. No one but you and me." She rocked Jess and looked up into the night, "No one but Jess and me, I promise you."

"Jesus!" thought Millie as the bell signaled the arrival of yet another customer. She was really going to need to talk to Larry about getting another waitress on if this continued. At the very least she needed a damn bus boy. For the last two weeks, the morning gang was now more like Grand Central Station.

A chorus of hellos greeted the newcomer.

"Hey all." Nan struggled with a large carton. "Hi Millie." Joe jumped from his chair to lend a hand. "Thanks Joe."

"My pleasure Nan." Joe quickly shoved Rudy down two stools and put the box on the countertop. A quick bow with a flourish made Nan laugh. "So pretty Nan, what's in the box?"

Millie was more than curious, but Charley was ringing, the place was mobbed and she had no time. Ring. Ring. Ring.

Riveted, she watched Millie run, concerned at the toll the pace was taking on her friend.

"Come on Millie, the eggs are going to get cold."

She glanced over and glared, but it wouldn't have mattered. Charley was as overtaxed as Millie and the frayed nerves could be heard in his command.

"Damn it Charley, I'm serving as fast I can." Millie blew by the group and grabbed the plates.

Rudy felt a tap on his sleeve. He followed the boss lady's eyes, nodded in agreement and grabbed Joe. Joe motioned to Nan that they'd be right back.

Millie turned around to see Rudy, Joe and the merry-go-round lady running through the diner with coffee pots and bus trays and God only knows what else. Suddenly Joe stopped, jumped on a table. "Hey everybody, listen up. You love Millie. I love Millie. But right now, I need Millie over at the counter for two minutes. Then you all can have her back. Two minutes people. Thank you."

Millie looked over at the whooping crowd and shrugged. Joe hopped down, grabbed Millie's hand and raced back to the counter. He grabbed a spoon and mimicking an emcee boomed, "Okay Nan, show us what's in carton number one!"

Nan laughed with the crowd and popped open the ungainly carton. With a flourish she pulled out one of many cylindrical containers, turning back to face the crowd. "What we have here Joe is a beautiful clear plastic container. But wait, there's something written on it. 'A Penny For Your Thoughts—How About A Nickel For Our Horse.' Catchy, don't you think?"

The carousel lady joined the cheers of the restaurant crowd as Nan curtsied first to the left and then to the right. The pick-up bell rang, Millie smiled, turned to run, "They're great Nan."

Joe leaned into the box and took one out, tossing it from his left hand to his right and back again, "Where you planning to put them?"

"Anywhere that will take one. Fundraising 101."

Joe kept tossing the container and jumped back up. "Sorry to disturb you folks again, but, hey, it's your lucky morning. Nan is going to put one of these right along side the register and let's see if we can fill it up this morning. I am personally reaching into my pocket, sorting my change . . . quarter . . . quarter . . . oh heck, it's for Nan and the carousel, take it all! All sixty-eight cents to start Nan's day off right—worth twice the price but I'm broke! So eat up, then dig in."

"Hey Nan?" The shout cut right into Joe's shtick.

Nan spun around and spotted Mike Garrity. "Hey Mike."

"I'll tell you what, I have one dollar and seventy three cents in change." Mike stood up, took his change and showed it around the room. "It's all yours if you can get that bozo to shut up!"

The cheers were raucous.

§ § §

She waited for Lyle to finish his coffee. She could have gone over to let herself in, but it didn't seem proper. Lyle very deliberately took his last sip of coffee and set it back down in its saucer. He leaned over and picked up his stick, rose and turned to her. "Yep. Shall we?"

The men had finished sometime late last night. As they made their way across the parking lot and toward the gate, they were struck by the lack of people gathered near the fence. Seemed like everyday now there were always people, some looking to get involved, some just looking, but this morning the lot was empty.

As they approached, a big sign posted on the gate gave them their answer, "All horses are corralled until 3 p.m. this afternoon."

She peered nervously as Lyle fished for his key. The horses were no longer in sight. Lyle watched her out of the corner of his eye as he undid the chain and opened the gate, remembering the first day he let her come in.

Together they walked to the deeper end of his lot and looked. She turned to Lyle and smiled. Chris and his crew had transformed his junk yard into a working ranch—their own "Ponderosa." The new building stretched the entire width of Lyle's lot, but it was the front that took her breath away. They had put up an extended roof with poles, almost like a veranda, where people could work in the shade or just sit. They'd even stuck a hitching post out front.

Lyle just shook his head; she ran her hands over everything. Together they opened the door. The space inside was simple, one long room with worktable stations. Each table had a light overhead and an outlet on the floor. The front wall was made of roll-away doors so the whole building could be open to outside. The end of the building nearest the parking lot had been changed to be all windows—a showcase for people to see in.

At the other end, farthest away from prying eyes, she saw her. Miriam. Ready. Waiting. She walked down and nuzzled against her nose.

"Yep." Lyle watched her hand gently stroke that horse. "Yep." Reminded himself of that first day she came.

§ § §

Nan raced in the door of her office; she was late. She threw down her pocketbook, booted up the computer and reached for her in-box in one single motion. Before she could get her password typed, her secretary, Sonia, came in the door. "Hey Nan, Mr. Hart's been asking for you this morning."

Nan and her secretary exchanged looks as Nan grabbed a pad and pencil and headed down the hallway. The pounding in her head made her nauseous and the walk seemed forever, although it was only about eight doors down.

Stephen Hart's door was ajar and Nan gave it a light tap. "Nan," Stephen looked up, "come on in." Nan entered and motioned for whether or not he wanted her to close the door behind her. "Closed, please."

He waited for Nan to take a seat before continuing. "I've been speaking with my wife and she tells me you're heading the finance committee for this carousel thing going on in town."

Nan's head pounded. She couldn't afford to lose her job for this.

§ § §

She returned to her office on slightly wobbly legs and slit open the envelope. It was a check for two hundred dollars. Sonia's head came around the side of the door, peered in, and was then followed by her body. "Well?"

"He gave me a check for the carousel!" She motioned toward the envelope now on her desk.

Sonia looked at Nan. "No way!"

"Way."

§ § §

The Brothers Goldstein arrived at the Carousel Corral at noon. They went inside and walked through with the Boss Lady and the Reverend trying to establish a strategy for making this work.

"I think," Sam turned around and eyed the space again, "Miss, tell me if you think I'm wrong here, but I think we should divide into two groups." Sam and Morris had debated this several times while driving over the last few days. Everyone seemed to know about the woman and the original horses, and Sam believed she would want to finish those. He also knew she didn't like to talk all that much and teaching a group of novices was going to take a lot out of her. Besides, if he was honest, this is why he and Morrie came, one last ride before the sun set.

"The first group, your group, will finish restoring the horses we already have." He paused for just a second, trying to see if he could gauge her reaction. "The second group, well, Morrie and I thought we could lead the second group, and we would begin to carve straight from the wood. We thought we could start with three teams. The first team would be led by Morrie working with Cameron, one team would be mine, and then we thought maybe that man who came to the meeting, John Reilly would take one. Morrie and I would each take on a novice or two and we thought

95

John might work with a couple of the guys who have some experience but wouldn't be ready to lead."

"What about the paint crews?" The Reverend was listening, trying to get a fix on all the logistics here. "Should they be situated next to you?"

Morris and Sam began laughing and after a beat, she joined in. "What? What's so funny?"

Morris wheezed for just a minute, "Sorry Reverend. Now we're not laughing at you, exactly. But, I was just wondering, about how long do you think it takes to carve one of these horses?"

§ § §

"I want to thank everyone for their patience today. I especially want to thank Chris Dysart and Dysart Construction for our new, insulated, carving shop—now known as the Carousel Corral." The Reverend positioned himself outside the fence at three o'clock in the afternoon, looking at the group of faces ready to go.

"Now, I spent this morning gathering up some new information regarding our endeavor and I think before we jump in we need to get everyone on the same page."

For the first time since this literal and figurative stampede began, Reverend William Dalton was nervous. He had come so far and yet it truly was only the tip of an iceberg. If he slipped now, there would be no recovery.

He remembered a teacher he had at the seminary. He walked right past everyone, up to the blackboard and in big block letters wrote, "The Truth Cannot Be Soft Pedaled." Now that he understood what was needed, the Reverend knew only the truth would determine if this dream would be hard-earned real, or just a passing fancy. "I learned this morning that to carve one of these horses will take approximately five hundred hours."

In a parking lot with over one hundred people, a pin would be heard if anyone dropped it.

"Maybe even more amazing for any of us who thought to paint our kitchens ourselves, it will take more than one hundred hours to paint one of the horses." As he spoke, the Reverend moved about, keeping his eyes in motion. What he didn't see gave him strength. People listened, absorbing the information, their connection unwavering. No one was turning to go.

"When I learned this, I realized for us to do this right, we need to believe—to believe that in this day and age, when we could probably, easily, buy plastic horses, that we have a commitment to craft, a commitment to art, a commitment to excellence. To believe if we go forward we have made a commitment to ourselves, a promise to stand here today and to still be standing here, together, at the end."

As the Reverend spoke, Millie felt a tug on her apron. She looked down to see Jess looking at her, a question to be asked.

"Hey Millie?"

"Yes?"

"How much is six hundred times 33?"

Millie's nose scrunched and her fingers moved slightly as she calculated the math in her head. "Nineteen thousand eight hundred. Why?"

Jess' smile got bigger as she took in the numbers. "Because that's like forever and she'll have to stay!" She grinned at Millie and Millie grinned back.

"Okay, so to wrap this up, painters will be needed shortly for several of the restored original horses, but we will call. Carvers, get ready. And now that I know all that I know, I'm going to beg one last time for more volunteers for administration and more volunteers for finance." Reverend Dalton grinned broadly at the gathering, "Mr. Johnson, if you will open your fence, let's get building!"

§ § §

Cameron looked up to see Morris signaling to her. He watched her walk and wondered what had happened to the excited girl from the library. He knew walks and today the young lady looked, well, Morris watched her approach for another moment, defeated. Defeated, that was definitely the walk and he knew walks. "Miss Cameron, is everything okay?"

Cameron stiffened and stuck her hands inside her pockets. "Fine Mr. Goldstein."

"Cameron, Mr. Goldstein was my father. Now, it's my much, much older brother's name." Morris winked and motioned at Sam. "I'm just Morris. You wouldn't want to hurt my feelings by making people think I'm as old as he is, would you?"

He saw that her smile didn't reach her eyes. "So, I wanted to show you that I got us the best seat in the house. We're going to be carving partners, you and I, and I swiped us the window seat." Morris stopped talking and waited.

"Mr. Goldstein, Morris," Cameron bit at her lip, "you might want to pick a different carving partner."

"Why? I quite like you, I think."

"I heard the Reverend outside and he said it would take six hundred hours and I'll be graduated by then, so maybe you should find someone who's only a junior or something."

"Just so I understand. You graduate in June and then run off and leave town never to be seen horse carving again?"

"Well, no."

"So, explain."

"It's just that the school sent me over here." Cameron's hands burrowed deeper into her pockets.

Morris couldn't fathom how anyone's pant's pockets could be that deep, but they had to be, considering every time she spoke she jammed her hands further down.

"I figured that when I graduate Mrs. Adler would have someone else she wants to send and it wouldn't be right that they got stuck with my horse when they're going to have to do all the work."

"Ah." Morris thought about her words. He also noticed that her hands must have finally hit bottom as she had begun twisting instead. She may dress tough, but underneath all that bravado is an honest kid. Morris knew he liked her. "Well maybe I won't want another carving partner. They can be very hard to break in."

She didn't smile at his joke.

"Look Cameron, Mrs. Adler can have lots of students and we'll have lots of horses and lots of hours. But I thought yesterday we decided that the first horse to be made was going to be Cameron's Dancer. Now if you don't want to do this, that's okay. Maybe it's like the Reverend said, it's a big commitment. I like to think it's just a pure labor of love. But this is your decision. If you're ready, I'm ready."

"Thank you." Cameron could feel the tears, but she wasn't worried. She never let people see her cry. "I'm ready."

She accepted a shoebox from Sam and went into Lyle's office. "It sure is busy out there."

Lyle peered at her, rocked for just a minute and thought curiously. Yep. She had never come inside his office. "Yep. Not like it used to be that's for sure."

She looked around. It was amazingly neat. She'd always assumed there would be piles—paper, knickknacks—but it was all very spartan. The calendar was the only piece of art, if you could call it that, and it was one of those bank giveaways. The only other wall hanging was a clock, nestled precisely in the center above Lyle's window. "Well," she cleared her throat and taking a step forward thrust the shoebox toward Lyle. "Well, Sam brought this whole box filled with photos of carousel horses, and I thought, well I thought, you should pick one."

Lyle took the box and looked up at her. All he saw was her back as she turned and fled the room.

§ § §

Joe and Rudy carted in the big block of wood Rudy had driven from Sam's house. Sam had held onto it for years, always promising to get to it. Sam remembered bringing it home and Irene hollering at him when he lifted it up and carried it downstairs. That was a long time ago. Now he let Rudy lift and shift the big block onto the table.

Eyes were everywhere, surrounding the work area and even pressing up against the window. Morris was now unleashed in all his glory. "Okay Cameron, it's time to get started." He walked from one side of the wood to the other. "What we're going to do is take the pattern we made at the library, cut out the silhouette and transfer it onto the wood with marker. Now," Morris looked at Cameron with a wink, "now that you know what goes into this, we still could save ourselves a few hours if I can interest you in that three-legged horse," he teased.

Cameron blushed but held his gaze. "No thanks, Mr. Goldstein."

"Mr. Goldstein, Mr. Goldstein," Morris' hands flew up as he whined at the top of his lungs. "I keep telling you the only Mr. Goldstein here is the old codger at the table next to ours. If you keep calling me Mr. Goldstein this is going to be the longest five hundred hours of my life." Morris settled and looked at Cameron. He passed her a pair of scissors. "Okay, where were we? So, how about a three-legged horse?"

The noise didn't seem to permeate their end of the building. They sat all alone. Her body cradled Jess' in their concentration. One arm gently holding, guiding, she patiently helped Jess run the Exacto blade around Miriam's seams. The restoration had begun.

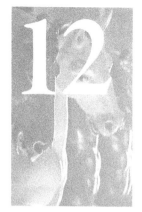

"God, Nan," Millie put down her plate and dropped back into the lounge chair. This was luxury. She felt just the tiniest bit of guilt sitting around while everyone else cleared, but they had all insisted, reminding her she got to wait on all of them all the time. Millie smiled and called over her shoulder, "You were right. A barbecue in your back yard beats the heck out of another meeting in the church ballroom." Millie cringed. Shit! "Sorry Reverend, no offense meant."

"None taken," Reverend Dalton smiled, carrying two large black trash bags out. "I can't be offended when I whole-heartedly agree."

Joe was right on his heels with two other bags, "I'll see your whole-hearted and raise you an 'amen' Reverend."

Barbara ducked her head out from the kitchen, "Taking a count. Coffee or tea. Millie?"

"Coffee would be great."

"Reverend?"

"I'll go with a tea, thank you."

"Hey Millie?" Todd Emerson had joined them and was heading up the painting committee. He moved toward her, precariously carrying the cup and saucer, "Do you need milk or sugar?"

Millie shook her head "no" and took a sip. This was heaven. It was after nine and the sun was now only beginning to fade. A perfectly glorious night.

The kitchen crowd emptied back out to the patio, their job done. Nan was last to go, stopping to hug her Grandmother. "Thanks Gran. Dinner was great."

"Nothing to thank me for." Gran brushed the compliment aside, but her face beamed. "It was my pleasure. Now you just get back out there with your friends and have a good time."

As Nan came through the door, the Reverend nodded, "Let's see where we're at people. Boss Lady?"

"The restoration side is making incredibly good progress. I think we'll be ready to turn the first two over for paint by Wednesday."

To everyone's amusement, Todd whinnied and rubbed his hands

together, "That is going to make a whole lot of very intense, itchy volunteers very happy."

"On the carving side, we're moving. What can I say—five hundred hours is a long time. Morris and Cam are making the best progress. We're currently working three horses. Sam and his part-timers are moving slowly and my big hope is that as soon as John Reilly and Reggie Jefferson finish getting the body carved out, we can split off Reggie to start a body on his own with a new partner while John stays with the horse."

"I think it would be great if we could decide on the next horse and get the tracing done now," said the Reverend.

She looked over at him, perplexed.

"It's inspirational" he explained, "People love to see where we are, where we're going. They adopt the horses we choose."

"Oooh! Oooh! Oooh! Oooh!" Nan's hand shot up, interrupting, "Sorry, but here's a terrific idea. Let's raffle off an opportunity to name a horse. I know we have our first three, but we have like thirty more to go and if I can get a raffle going, we can raise tons of money."

"I like it." The Reverend nodded thoughtfully. "Okay with everyone?"

"It's okay, but the next horse is already spoken for," the boss lady said quietly. She had left Lyle the box and he'd gone through them.

Yep. They were all pretty, but truthfully to him, one horse sure does look like another horse. Lyle continued to thumb through the pictures anyway. And then he saw her. The bluest eyes with roses draped over her saddle. Yep.

If the Reverend was surprised by this news, he accepted it graciously. "Does our newest addition have a name?"

"Elsie's Blue Eyes."

"Okay, Elsie's Blue Eyes is number four. So can we get a tracing?" She nodded. "Great." The Reverend made a check on his list, "Okay Barbara, you're up, what have you got for us?"

"Good news, I think. Mark Stern is the shop teacher over at the high school. He's gotten the board to approve horse carving as a credit for fall semester. So the school will take on building one of our horses." Barbara turned toward Nan. "Mark's even got enough budget to pay for the block."

Nan clapped her hands, "Oooh, a man who has his own money," she fanned herself with her hand. "Why, I feel faint. This is just too much excitement for dear, sweet, little old Nan."

As everyone laughed, Barbara continued. "Mark's plan is to come and join the carve teams for the summer so he can comfortably teach it come fall." Barbara sat back, then leaned forward again. "Oops, one other item." Barbara paused to smile at everyone, "Thanks to this project, both Cameron Blair and Marcus Kim will receive their diplomas this coming Sunday."

As everyone cheered, the Reverend called out, "All right Barbara! Robert? You're up!"

"Aw geez, why do I always have to go after the 'all good news' report?' came the good-natured whine. "All government stuff moving at annoying government stuff pace. Anyone want a job swap?" The group laughed. "Gee, no takers. Thanks. But, I actually have a bit of good news. I tracked down the couple who owns the lot behind Lyle, name of Zaino. I explained a bit of what we're doing and that we'd like to put our paint shop on their property. Just temporary and we'd pay some rent, etc. Anyway, I need to put together a small proposal for them, but they seem open to the idea."

"Let me know if you need anything from me," Nan offered.

"I hate to bring this up, but what I need is some type of small press kit." As soon as Robert said it the group froze. Everyone sitting there had the same thought—the merry-go-round lady.

Before anyone could take out his jugular, Robert raised his hand, "Look, I thought we could just take a few pictures of our work in progress, maybe just a general page and, if no one would be insulted, a photo of the Reverend here and Morris and Sam."

As her jaw and stomach unclenched, she looked up at Robert and smiled her appreciation.

Robert grinned before turning his gaze to Barbara. "So Barbara, have we got any would-be photo-journalists kicking around your office?"

§ § §

It was dark when the group broke up. Millie and the merry-go-round lady picked their way carefully across the lawn.

"Hey, did you notice Joe was there tonight?" At her nod, Millie continued. "I guess he and Nan have gone public. I think they're good together."

"Are you sure you're okay with that?"

"Me?" For a moment Millie was confused. Then she burst out laughing. "Me and Joe? Oh please, he just loves to torture me. Kissing Joe would be like that old expression about kissing your brother or something. Yuck!"

Millie knew she was being teased and reached out and shoved. They were both laughing as they neared the deck. Millie shoved her again, "Me and Joe!"

§ § §

Nan watched the other cars pull away. Joe was still there. "It was a really nice night Nan."

"Yeah, I'm glad we did this." She wrapped her arms around Joe and leaned up for a kiss. "Thanks for helping out."

"Yeah, well, no big deal." Joe kissed her back. "How about dinner Tuesday? I know a place that makes great ribs."

Nan smiled. "I'd love to."

Gran lay in bed and listened. She could hear for miles. Heard the people praise her meal, heard Millie and the young woman walk across the lawn, heard Nan and the young man who was smitten with her talking. She heard all this, but all that mattered was hearing Nan happy, hearing her voice filled with light and laughter and love.

The stairway of faces began to swim in front of her eyes; they were all there, all her children just as she always saw them, smiling their beautiful smiles. The stairway led up and he was at the top, waiting for her just like he always was. "Yes Walter, I'm ready now."

§ § §

Millie unlocked the front door and flipped on the lights. She hadn't followed Millie in. Millie went back to the porch.

She stood in the night, looking up at the second floor room across the way. Miriam whispered in her ear. "It's all right, I've got her. I'll get her home safely. She loves you." Tears streamed down her face.

§ § §

Tears ran down Nan's cheeks as the Reverend began. "Today we say goodbye to a woman we had all come to believe was our Gran."

Nan watched as the pallbearers moved forward. Joe. Rudy. The Goldstein Brothers. Lyle Johnson. Millie. The Merry-Go-Round Lady. It wasn't traditional, but it would have been what Gran wanted. To be carried to rest in a cradle of love.

The day had been long, with easily over two hundred people at the service and even more at the house. Gran's death was overwhelming, but no more so than the outpouring of love. They sat squeezed together on the couch in the darkened living room. Periodically Nan would lean into Millie, a few more tears to give. Millie would hold on until they were absorbed.

Nan turned to the merry-go-round lady, sobbing in a voice so raw it could barely be heard, "It was good, wasn't it?"

She laid her head on Nan's shoulder. "No, it was perfect."

"Millie?" Nan rasped, "Do you know what's sick?"

Millie's arm hugged Nan gently to her body. "No."

"Gran would have been proud today."

"Well, that's good, isn't it?"

Nan turned her head inward, burrowing into Millie's shoulder, "That's not what I mean. Years ago I went to a funeral for a person who died, somebody I worked with. And I remember standing in the chapel and feeling envious. There were so many people there the room couldn't even hold all of them. And I just kept thinking that if I died the next day, there would be no one really to come see me off."

Nan grabbed both their hands, her grip vise-like, "God this is such a sick story."

Millie pressed their clasped hands to her lips, a loving, it will be okay gesture, and Nan struggled to finish. "And today, today we overflowed. That's when I realized that Gran and I have friends and people who love us, and I don't need to go to someone else's funeral and be jealous. I'm not alone any more." Nan sniffled, looked up. "But I'm still going to miss her."

This time they all huddled together in a row, comforting each other.

§ § §

She sat contentedly waiting for Jess, listening to the hum of the shop. Somewhere outside she could hear a voice singing loud, proud and off-key. The memory it stirred made her smile. She glanced over at the horses waiting on her and Jess. She and Jess had stripped and restored, and today they would refit and then it would be time for paint. She leaned against the far-side wall and looked down the rows. When she took a moment to look, to see, this all still truly took her breath away. The doors were thrown open for the summer day and the place was a beehive of activity.

It was funny, the horses in the to-be-restored group remained with her by design, but the people on the team charged with moving them along were fluid and yet composed primarily of the same group that started together. They mostly came on the weekend - Nan and Joe, Rudy and his daughter Kristen, Jess and Millie, even the Reverend when he could. Saturday nights had become pizza-on-the-floor time. They had four horses restored and ready to go, waiting for Rob to find them a place.

It wasn't that they were clique-ish. It seemed that most everyone else simply wanted to be part of the new herd. Reggie Jefferson moved over and was working with Mark Stern on Elsie's Blue Eyes. John Reilly was making great progress on the body of Joan of Arc, his magnificent Medieval design already showing. John found two junior working partners in Barbara's young son, Josh and his best friend, Eric.

Sam's horse was still unnamed. He'd wanted to name it Irene's Gift, but Irene had simply stated it was fine with her if he felt like moving in with his brother.

Morris. Morris and Cameron. Her eyes moved further down to the farthest end. Two heads bent in concentration, the master and the pupil. They were an odd team. Cameron was at least a head taller than Morris and as somber as he was jovial, but it was a terrific pairing. Morris looked up and spotted himself being watched. He grinned and winked.

Her eyes traveled beyond Morris, behind him, through the window over to the diner steps. Millie. She smiled. She needed to talk to Millie later today.

"Hey, Boss Lady," Chris Dysart waved from the other side of Lyle's lot. "Good news. Robert got the deal done and we can probably have a small paint shop over here hot and ready by the end of the week. Anything special I should know?"

She stepped down and walked over to the chain link separating the properties and gave it a small shake, "Any chance of a gate?"

He smiled. "You got it," making a note on his clipboard. "Marcus will be by later to post the permits—terrific kid by the way," he grinned. "He has good running legs. The foreman is a guy named Jack Stavourkis. He's coming by later with Todd to go over the plans, but if you think of anything we've missed or you think we should have, give him a holler and we'll try and get it done."

§ § §

Millie crossed the parking lot after work. "Hi Lyle," she called as she headed through the gate and over to the corral. Everything was pretty quiet. "Hey Boss Lady," she called out as she approached, "slow day at the ranch?"

Boss Lady turned and smiled, shaking her head no. "I don't think so." She took a step onto the porch, put four fingers in her mouth and let out a shockingly shrill whistle.

They poured out from all their hiding places, from behind the building, from Lyle's office and from God-only-knows where else, singing one huge loud off-key rendition of "Happy Birthday to You." Nan and Lyle were the last to leave their hiding place in Lyle's office, with Nan carrying a cake she had crammed with about eighty candles. When Millie saw it, she shrieked, "I am going to kill you both!"

There were hugs and kisses and pieces of cake to be eaten, but soon the ranch was back in full work swing. Millie stood by the far side window towering over Jess and the merry-go-round lady as they worked. Even with the tables, these two continued their tradition of sitting on the floor together. Action across the fence caught Millie's attention. "Oh my Lord, thank you, thank you, thank you."

Millie's voice caught her attention and she stood up, "What?"

Millie made a fanning motion with her hand and looked out the window. "There." She dead panned. "Right there is my birthday wish coming true."

She saw what caught Millie's eye and laughed. "I take it we are talking about the hunk standing next to Todd?" Millie nodded her confirmation without ever taking her eyes off their desired view. "His name's Jack Stavourkis."

Millie's head whipped around, and found eyes that were laughing at her from a safe distance. Millie took one step forward and ordered, "Dish!"

"All I know is he works with Chris and he's going to be the foreman for the crew putting up the Paint Palace next door."

"How old is he? Is he single? Is he straight?" Millie took another step forward, advancing directly at her, backing her up and over the porch. "Answers. Millie needs answers."

"Millie," she dropped down the first step, "let's be honest here." Another step. "I am so not the right person to help you get answers." Her feet hit the ground. "Go find Nan."

"Great idea." Millie leaned over and grabbed her in a quick hug. As Millie took off running haphazardly down the path her voice floated back. The merry-go-round lady stood there watching and laughing. The words she heard were, "Happy Birthday to me!"

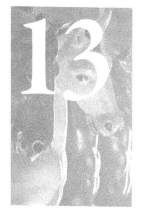

The summer flew by in a whirlwind of wood chips, paint and fundraisers. The committee agreed they would not name the original restored standers as the raffle to "adopt-a-horse" still seemed to be the most effective money maker any of them could devise. It was hard to believe that Labor Day weekend was here and by Wednesday, school would be back in session.

Millie and the Boss Lady arrived at the fairgrounds in the late afternoon. The music from the bandstand stage below, the ringing from the rides to the left and the screaming of children tearing everywhere infused the park with a joyous mood. They strolled about checking out the rides and booths. The raffle drawing for the horse naming wouldn't be until seven that evening.

They found Nan and Joe manning the carousel booth. Large blow-up photos taped to the sides of the tent framed the soon-to-be-adopted horse mounted in the center. "Wow," Millie exclaimed. "This is really great."

Millie slipped behind the table to get a closer look at the pictures on display. Barbara had delivered as promised. She'd sent a young woman, Pam, from the yearbook committee over for the brochure. Pam visited throughout the summer, capturing large portions of the work, now on display. As Millie moved along one side, the merry-go-round lady slipped behind the front table and began her study from the other end; they met at the middle photograph—it was an enlargement from the press kit; Sam and Morris, ages ten and twelve, standing with a carousel horse outside their uncle's factory.

Nan came over to stand with them. "Great stuff, huh?"

"It's amazing." Millie turned toward Nan. "How are you guys doing?"

"It's insane." Nan bubbled over, "The jars keep filling, everyone wants to name this horse."

"Cool, does it make us rich yet?"

"Nope. But I'm hoping it keeps me out of the pokey for ripping off creditors." As she talked, Nan kept glancing back over her shoulder at the table. "One sec," she motioned and walked back over to Joe. "You okay hon?" At his nod, Nan grabbed Millie and tugged her back to the photos. "So this is my new brainstorm—calendars—what do you think?"

Nan beamed at Millie and the merry-go-round lady, clearly enthused. When neither one answered quickly, she demanded, "What!"

"Um, Nan, don't you think it's a bit premature?" Millie stammered a bit, looked to her right to find the merry-go-round lady amazingly fascinated by the young Sam and Morris and knew she was in this one alone. "I mean," she gestured to the photos of disassembled horses, clamped-on body parts and the like, "don't most people want calendars of pretty horses mounted on the carousel?"

"I don't know." Nan felt a little exposed. "Everyone's all wrapped up in this. I think they might want photos of the whole process." As defensively as it was uttered, it gave Nan another idea, "Ooh, there's a thought," she tugged on both Millie and the merry-go-round lady's sleeves. Her energy had her literally bouncing, "A newspaper!"

"Pardon?"

"Well not really a paper per se, but a newsletter, keep photos coming at people, tell the stories of the horses—you know, why someone picks a name, how do you know what color eyes the horse has—is it a dapple or a chestnut?" Nan was on a toot.

"We put it out like monthly and have people subscribe." Nan bounced some more, "This is so good. Okay, I need you two to stay here and help Joe work the booth—I have to go find Barbara."

Nan raced over and reached under the table for her purse. She stopped, kissed Joe as he sat in the chair, and called "Be right back," heading off, leaving three people laughing at her excitement.

"Hi Millie." Millie turned her attention toward the line at the table and looked right into the eyes of Jack Stavourkis. Standing directly in front him were four boys, "I don't think you've ever met my boys, Todd, Jason, Josh and Ty. We've come to buy raffle tickets for a shot at naming the horse."

Millie smiled and pulled the tickets. As she was getting Jack's change, a woman came up. She was tall and breathtakingly beautiful. She looked like she stepped out of the pages of some glossy magazine. Millie watched as she leaned over and kissed Jack before linking her arm through his.

Millie took a deep breath and grabbed the dollar out of the cash box.

The merry-go-round lady saw the striking woman approach. She moved quickly over to stand beside Millie, an instinctive reaction to even the odds and shelter the moment, to provide unspoken moral support.

"Millie, Boss Lady," Jack squeezed the arm that held his. "I'd like you all to meet my wife, Lisa. Lisa, this is Millie, she works over at the diner and this is, well, this is the Boss Lady."

Lisa smiled graciously, took her arm from Jack and wrapped her youngest boy Ty, in an embrace from behind. All Millie saw was her perfect French manicure. "It's great to meet you both. I've heard so much about all this. It's really great just to be here."

Another moment of small talk took place while Jack helped his boys finish filling in the entry slips and they were off, apparently in search of some promised cotton candy.

Millie and the boss lady stood silently watching them go. "Great. It's all just great." Millie let out a snide impersonation. "I hate her."

"It's probably all surgical." She kept her eyes scanning the crowd.

"Ya think?"

"Sure."

"So, you think we can get a phone number?"

She turned to Millie not understanding the question. "For Jack?"

"No you bird-brain," Millie gave her shoulder a nudge, "for the surgeon."

"Ah." Her eyes remained forward but she was grinning.

"Hey Lady!" Billy Ray's voice shrieked through the air, the bright red hair visible long before the body. "The Reverend told me to tell you it's nearly time."

"Couldn't he have sent anyone quieter?"

Millie laughed. "I think that was the point." She turned back to the booth, "Hey Joe, we got everything?"

"Give me a sec. I don't know. Where's Nan?"

"Right here." Nan ducked back into the booth. "Okay, the money has to be locked up, the sold tickets have to be added to the big bin out front, we need Rudy to help get our horse up there and, where's Jess?

§ § §

Jess was busy being delayed by Sharlyn. It was a big day, the carousel committee had decided Jess should pick the winner, and Sharlyn would be damned if her daughter was getting up in front of the whole town and God knows who else looking for all the world like the wreck of the

Hesperus. "Jess," Sharlyn gritted from her clenched jaw, "Jess, hold still and let me finish wiping ice-cream off your face, or you're going nowhere. God, you are filthy. I just don't know how you do it."

Jess squirmed and made a face as her mother went to the spit-and-wipe tissue ritual. "It's a fair, you're supposed to have fun and get dirty," she argued.

§ § §

The Reverend winced as the microphone screamed with feedback. He watched the gathering crowd in front of the stage. It seemed everyone had bought a ticket. Even rides emptied as people flocked to see the draw.

"Good afternoon," the microphone squealed again and one of the technicians ran out for another adjustment. "Sorry about that folks." The Reverend took the microphone back. "Good afternoon and welcome to the Name-Our-Carousel-Horse-Drawing. I promise to be brief, but I want to take a minute and say thank you. A big thank you to Lyle Johnson, to Chris Dysart, to Nan Walsh, to Barbara Adler, to Morris Goldstein, to Sam Goldstein, to Millie Hickson and to the Boss Lady! Let's give them a big round of applause."

As the cheering subsided, the Reverend stopped clapping and picked up the microphone. "Okay, now I want to say thank you to everyone here, each and every one of you is integral to this dream. Without our volunteers, we couldn't do this and without our neighbors and friends buying raffle tickets and donating items for our rummage sales it wouldn't be happening. So before we pull a name, let's celebrate this moment of our journey with a huge round of applause."

Once again, the Reverend led the cheering himself. "Okay, now for the main event. Joe and Rudy, with your help please."

Joe and Rudy came along the side carrying the horse which only minutes ago had been occupying center stage in the booth. They set her down slightly to the right of the Reverend to wild applause.

"As a lot of you know, this is one of the original horses uncovered from Lyle Johnson's shop. His donation of these horses helped make today possible. She is what you call a 'stander' and she is from, and will return to, the inside row of a carousel. Due to the work of our restoration crews, she has been returned nearly to her original condition, which means she is once again an all-wood horse. There are no pieces of metal at all. As soon as we choose her adoptive family today, we will name her, take her to the paint shop, and have the family meet with the head of our paint factory, Todd Emerson."

The Reverend paused to let Todd have his moment with the cheering crowd. "Todd will help choose the color. I know you all heard a minute ago when I said nearly her original condition. We have removed the saddle from this horse. The saddles were actually separate pieces that were attached after the horse was crafted. Once we have a name and a story, then we look to our carvers to craft a saddle embracing her new status."

The crowd cheered.

"Okay," the Reverend grinned. "Since this is one of our restored horses, we thought the honor of pulling the winner should go to a person who has been most instrumental in this phase of our carousel. Jess Kastellon, come on out here."

With a push from Nan, Jess made her way out to stand by the Reverend. She should have just kept her eyes down. She never should have peered out. She could hear her own heart pounding. There were millions of people and they were all watching. She thought it would be fun, but now she was going to be sick. She was shaking so bad she didn't know how she was going to stick her hand in the box. And what if she dropped the winning ticket? And what if she couldn't read the name?

Her heart went out to Jess as she looked on from the crowd. She could read the terror on the girl's face all the way from her very safe space hidden deep in this carefree crowd. They never should have asked Jess to do this.

She felt the nuzzle as though it was real against her neck. She looked up and saw Jess stare directly at her, and she knew Jess felt it too.

To the audience it looked like Jess just pushed back her hair, but as she ran her hand up to feel, she knew she was not out here all alone. As Rudy and Kristen brought the box onto the stage, the Reverend looked over and asked, "Are you ready Jess?" At her nod he picked up the microphone and said, "Okay, draw away."

All eyes stared as the arm and the hand went in pushing and shoving. People from throughout the crowd screamed "Mix them good" and "Pull from the bottom" and about a million other directions. A few inflatable balls bounced through the playful crowed as Jess kept her hand moving.

Someone began a chant of "Jess, Jess" and others quickly joined in, but she didn't hear it. Jess was waiting, waiting until she felt the nuzzle on her neck push forward again and when it did, only then did she grab the entry slip. She opened it and as the Reverend lowered himself and the microphone to Jess, she announced, "Julie Carter."

"Congratulations Julie," the Reverend's voice boomed as his eyes searched. A scream went up from somewhere in the crowd and the polite applause grew stronger. Julie, holding her young daughter, walked up to the stage.

She looked around, a bit dazed. Then, she set the little girl on the horse and everyone cheered.

"Congratulations." The Reverend shook Julie's hand. "And who is this beautiful young lady?"

"My daughter, Courtney."

"Nice to meet you both. So, the question a lot of people out here want to know is—do you have a name for the horse?"

"Oh yes. Courtney has been asking for a horse just about ever since she could talk. So when we saw the contest, my husband and I told Courtney that if we won, she could pick the name, and Courtney decided the horse should be named Christmas. So we'd like to name her Courtney's Christmas."

She smiled from her place deep within the crowd.

The crowd began to thin, but a sizable contingent still remained as the Reverend made his final speech, "Congratulations again Julie and Courtney. We invite everyone to come by the paint shop over the next few weeks, keep an eye on how Courtney's Christmas's new coat comes along. Once again, from all of us, thank you."

The carousel was spinning out of control, Miriam kept whipping by, her head contorted, her eyes wild.

She sat up in bed drenched in sweat, her heart pounding. Something was incredibly wrong. She needed to go. Frantic, she threw on clothes and went tearing into the hallway. Stairs to the left. She hesitated only a second before turning right.

"Millie," she shook her shoulder, her hands shaking.

"Go away."

"Millie," the voice called Millie urgently.

Millie jarred awake, disoriented, sluggish. A bad dream. Millie stared stupidly; the woman was right in front of her. The light from the door let Millie see just enough to know something was wrong, really wrong. Not a dream.

"Millie, please go next door and see if Nan and Joe are there. Something's wrong with the horses, I have to go." She turned to run without waiting for an answer. The last thing Millie heard was a whispered prayer, "please."

§ § §

She pulled up to the junkyard and could hear thrashing and screaming. It was Jess. She was crying and screaming to please stop.

She never hesitated, grabbing a piece of metal from some hunk of junk as she ran. She flew in the door to the ranch. Cameron was holding Jess who was shrieking while Rudy was swinging something at the horses. Several of them were on the ground in pieces. She never thought, she just flew and jumped onto Rudy's back, "Rudy!" She hung on fighting for her life. He was a man possessed. He kicked and she saw Miriam topple, felt her life spin.

"Noooo!" The scream came from deep inside. She no longer saw Rudy, all she saw was an attacker. He would not touch Miriam. She would not let him touch her. All she felt was an attacker. Not again. All she knew was the attacker must be stopped. Never again. This time she was here. This time she would stop him. Must save Miriam. Must save Miriam. Strength that seemed impossible from one so slight burst forward in a flurry of kicks and blows.

Millie's car skidded over the ice as she pulled up with Joe and Nan; Joe flew from the car before she could regain control. She and Nan stared at each other, terrified. "I think maybe we should call Tom."

Jess came running out sobbing. Millie leapt from the car and grabbed her, "Jess, it's Millie, honey, I've got you." Millie pulled Jess inside the overcoat she had thrown on, desperately trying to warm her up in the frigid night air.

Nan came around to Millie's side fumbling with her cell phone. Before she could hit 911, Cameron came running out. "It's okay, Joe's got him."

Jess was still crying. "It's not okay, it's not okay."

"Who?" Millie was still holding onto Jess, trying to understand what Cameron was saying.

"Rudy."

Nan whipped around. "Rudy?" She looked at Millie and took off, vanishing into the building.

Millie disentangled Jess' arms and knelt down. She looked at the tear-streaked face and very quietly asked, "Jess, honey, I'm going to have you stay with Cameron for just a minute while I go back there and see what's happening. Can you do that?" Millie reached out a hand to Cameron. "Can you stay with Cameron?"

Jess nodded and Cameron came over. As Jess was transferred to Cameron's keeping, she gathered her up in a hug. Millie looked at Cameron, wearing only a t-shirt and jeans and silently passed Cameron her coat as she headed through the gate.

Millie approached the ranch cautiously. She shivered, but she didn't know if it was cold or fear. Maybe a bit of both. Her eyes darted around as she moved forward. Everything seemed quiet. The front door was open and she peered in carefully. Nan was behind Joe, who had Rudy wrapped up in his arms. Rudy would look over his shoulder and rock back and forth. He was whimpering, saying something over and over again. As she got closer Millie could make out the choked words, "I'm sorry." Over Rudy's shoulder—it was the merry-go-round lady—she was on the floor, turned away from everyone, but Millie could see she was shaking and rocking the body of a horse. She wasn't making a sound.

"Joe?"

"Rudy came home tonight and," Joe's voice cracked. "Shirley took Kristen and left. Just packed up, left." Joe grabbed his brother. "Kristen's his world and Shirley knows it. She left him a fucking note on the table."

Millie heard his explanation but her eyes had already returned to the rocking body further down in the shop. Millie stepped to get a different angle and felt it hit her in the gut. Millie realized her friend was holding Miriam.

"Okay Joe," Millie tried to keep her voice steady and sound like there was a plan here. "Can you get Rudy out of here and get him over to Nan's?" Millie knew she should probably call the police, but right now her only concern was getting this room cleared.

Millie watched Joe and Nan maneuver the big man. When he first stood, he turned back to say something to her, but whatever it was he could not get out. He struggled to unlock his tongue, to focus his thoughts. No sound. He turned and let them take him from the room.

Millie looked at her, not sure where to begin, not sure what to say. She heard footsteps; it was Jess and Cameron. Good God she'd forgotten all about them. Jess let go of Cameron's hand and walked past Millie, straight up to the lady. She sat down so they touched. "She knows it wasn't your fault."

She looked up at Jess, could barely see her through the tears.

"She said you would understand, but I had to come and tell you first …" This was what had wakened Jess and sent her scurrying into the night. She finished the message, "that pain doesn't let you see."

She reached for Jess, stroking her head. They were both crying. Jess' mission delivered, she reached out to stroke Miriam. "We can fix her, can't we? We can make her whole again?"

§ § §

Millie was living in flashback hell as she raced into the house ahead of Cameron, who was helping the merry-go-round lady out of the car. Somehow they had gotten Jess home and inside through her window. Millie hadn't wanted to let her go, she had wanted to get Sharlyn up, but as Jess pleaded, the carousel lady had finally looked up and just touched Millie's arm. Millie conceded because frankly, she didn't know what the hell else to do.

Millie held the door open, motioning to Cameron and together they managed to walk her upstairs and onto her bed.

She had let Miriam down. She couldn't save her. She was shivering. It was so cold. Jess' words echoed in her head, "We can make her whole again." She couldn't even make herself whole.

"Okay," Millie exhaled deeply, turning to Cameron, "I'm going to run a bath for her. I'll be right back. You've got her, right?"

She could feel the arms holding her, making gentle, circling strokes on her back. For a brief moment she allowed the touch to just feel good, but there was something else intruding. She pushed away and looked into Cameron's eyes. "Why were you there?"

Cameron didn't answer; her hand kept stroking her back.

She shook her head, pulled back and repeated the question. Her tone bordered on accusation. "Why were you there?"

This time the hand stopped. Cameron's eyes fixed on the wall ahead but she couldn't quite hide the clench of her jaw. "I was sleeping there."

"Oh."

§ § §

Her sleep was restless. Wanting. Searching. When Miriam came, she came gently, whinnying and nuzzling and prancing. Her sleep deepened. It would all be okay.

§ § §

Millie rolled over slowly. She had never even bothered to undress. The events of the previous night thrust her to consciousness in a pure adrenaline rush. She jumped out of bed when she smelled it. Coffee. Millie threw on a pair of socks and raced downstairs.

There she stood, looking out the window at the freshly fallen snow. Everything looked so clean, so untouched. She turned as Millie came in. Her hand had been gently rubbing the spot over her heart. Just touching a memory. She smiled wryly, lowered her hand and grabbed Millie a mug. She motioned to the living room. She had spotted Cameron passed out on the couch when she woke up this morning. "She's out cold."

Millie smiled, pointed up. She nodded and they quietly took the coffee back up the stairs and sat on her bed.

"Well," Millie took a sip, "Now what?"

"Oh God, I don't know." She shifted and sat up. "Did you know that Cameron's been sleeping in the shop?" Millie turned and looked at her. "Okay, I'll take that as a no. I found out last night. I couldn't understand why she was there. Well she was there because she's been sleeping there."

Millie lowered her cup. "Jesus."

"Yeah."

After a beat, Millie picked the cup back up and took another sip. "Why?"

"I don't know," she paused, "and I don't think she's going to tell us."

"Okaaay." They both sat in silence for a moment. Millie had no answer for that bit of news so they might as well try another topic. "Well, what do you want to do about Rudy?"

She got up from the bed and walked to the window. The question didn't surprise her; she'd been asking herself the same thing since she woke up. She looked out, thinking. She could see Nan's house from her room. "I don't know."

Millie stayed where she was, propped against a pillow, "Do you want to press charges."

She shook her head no.

"He did do a lot of damage."

She turned around and looked at Millie. "I can fix the damage. The only horse he really hurt was Miriam. But it's okay, remember, I'm a restorer. I'll have to carve a new leg." There were tears in her eyes, but determination as well. "I'll just need to make sure it's better than the old one."

"Hey, it's me, Millie you're talking to." She leaned forward in the bed trying to see if the woman's words matched her eyes. She caught sight of her unshed tears. They glistened in the light. Millie put down the cup and slowly unfolded herself as she rose from the bed.

"He did a lot of damage." Millie repeated herself needing to hear that the merry-go-round lady was aware of any decision she was making. Verifying that it was more than just a broken leg they were talking about.

"Yeah, he did." Her hand moved unconsciously toward her heart, toward her scar. She began to rub and the pent-up tears seeped out and rolled down, "but about the only thing I truly understand in this world is pain."

First Sam hugged her and then Morris. "Thank you for coming."

They were all here now, Lyle, Sam, Morris, Cameron, Nan and Millie. It was later than they'd hoped, but it seemed smart to wait for the Reverend and unfortunately, it was Sunday morning and he had a standing appointment. Now, the Reverend was over at Nan's house with Joe and Rudy.

She had waited for all of them, sitting in Lyle's office, keeping an eye on the window. Millie agreed to meet them at the diner and bring anyone who missed last night's event up to speed on what happened. She and Millie also agreed if they could put the place back together with just their little group, maybe it didn't have to go any further.

There were so many facets to last night's fiasco. She didn't know if she could explain what happened and ask for this kind of help from everyone. She also knew she wasn't ready to face the carving shop alone, so she sat in the office Lyle had opened for her.

Lyle. She smiled. He hadn't asked any questions. He'd just rocked on his stick and come. "Okay missy, you just sit in here and wait for us. Yep. You just wait for us."

From Lyle's window she spotted Jess, peering through the chain link fence. Jess was covered head to toe in winter gear, but the layering did nothing to hide her hesitancy.

She came out from Lyle's door and put her hands up on her side of the fence. "Well, are you just going to stand there and watch or are you going to help?"

§ § §

Finally they were all here, all up to speed and cautiously making their way inside. The place looked like a cliché—the aftermath of a proverbial tornado having ripped through it, which was fairly accurate. She and Jess held hands as they walked through. She noted everything, but still, by the time she and Jess reached Miriam, she was smiling, mostly from relief. She looked down at Jess and squeezed her hand. "It's okay."

It was almost all surface damage. Rudy had overturned worktables and thrown things about, but most of it could be set right with just their group. The toppled restored horses were those still being clamped and set. All the rest were either further back in the shop or had moved over to the paint shed a while ago. That left Miriam. One leg was destroyed and would need a new one carved. The tail was iffy, she would have to check for stress.

Jess asked, "What about her leg?"

"Hey." She gave Jess' hand a shake. "If we can build entire horses from blocks of wood, we can make a new leg, a better leg. You and I can fix this right up."

"We can?"

"We can. I promise you Jess, we can."

Everyone grabbed tables and tools and started to set things right. At some point the group all managed to disappear and leave Morris and Cameron alone. They hadn't known what else to do. All she and Millie knew was that Morris seemed to have a way with Cameron none of the rest of them had.

§ § §

"So," Morris looked up as Cameron placed tools away. "Millie told me you were here last night to help. That's a good thing."

Cameron eyed him warily, but didn't say anything.

"So tell me, is there a reason you like sleeping on a cold floor in a cold building?"

§ § §

They were sitting in the diner having coffee. Well, except for Jess who was busy eating the world's largest ice-cream sundae. The door jingled and Morris came in gesturing. Sam went to rise but Morris' gesturing continued. He didn't want Sam; he was looking for the merry-go-round lady. The adults exchanged looks of silent understanding as she went to meet him at the door.

"Why doesn't Morris come in?" Jess asked, pausing with melting ice-cream half way to her mouth.

Millie watched the gesturing going on. "I don't know Jess, he must just have a question he needs answered."

The boss lady came back to the table and picked up her coat. "Guys,

I've got to run out for just a minute." She smiled at Jess, "Morris is going to use my chair, but just until I get back. Maybe you can get him an ice-cream for all his hard work this morning."

§ § §

She jumped in her car and drove. The only good news about the snow was Cameron could not have gotten too far. She was right. She spotted her making her way, wearing her leather jacket and jeans. God, doesn't she know it's freezing out here? In that moment things began to click. In that moment she realized those clothes were all Cameron owned. She pulled the car over and stopped, threw open the door. Cameron looked at her and climbed in. At least it was warm. She drove. She drove in silence the three miles to the campsite she had found so long ago, letting what Morris had told her in the diner replay in her head. She parked the car.

Cameron looked around but didn't say anything. She had learned her silence was intimidating. She could keep conversation away by refusing to have any.

"You know, you hurt an old man today."

It wasn't what she was expecting. Taken by surprise, Cameron re-heard the conversation with Morris before she could block it. *"Is there a reason you like sleeping on a cold floor in a cold building?" "Yeah sure. I've been thinking about becoming an Eskimo in my spare time so I thought I'd check it out."*

Cameron saw herself sneering at Morris, taking another step toward him, using her height to belittle him. She saw herself explode, *"Because I have no where else to go you stupid old man."* Cameron saw herself as she turned and fled.

"I know." Cameron refused to make eye contact and stared stubbornly out the passenger window. "I didn't mean to hurt him."

"I know." The sympathy in the woman's voice was pure. She knew Cameron would never intentionally hurt Morris, that it was Cameron's own pain that had sprung a leak, precisely *because* she loved Morris. "Why didn't you tell us you didn't have anywhere to sleep?"

"Because it hurts. Okay. It hurts to be a loser. And I didn't want anyone to know. The only thing I have in my life is the horse, and if I didn't have anywhere to stay, maybe I wouldn't be able to carve and I needed that."

Cameron screamed. Before the merry-go-round lady could decide on a reply, Cameron continued very softly, "It's all I have."

"What happened Cameron?" She heard the barely whispered end, knew exactly how she felt. As gently as she could, she asked again, "What happened Cameron?"

"My father threw me out, okay. Are you happy now?"

She didn't want to ask, but she knew she had to. Not because she needed to know, she already knew, but because Cameron needed to get it out. "Why?"

"Because I'm stupid and ugly and a freak. And, and because he hates me. And now you will too."

Gentle. Persistent. "Why?"

"Because now you know. Now you know what a failure I am." The last words were barely audible as Cameron sank down in the seat and turned away.

They sat like that for a few minutes. Two solitary people each in their own bubble. She waited until the moment when all noise fled and the silence became its own echo. Her voice quiet but loud in the now absolute stillness of the car. "This is where I slept when I first came here."

Cameron looked at her in surprise.

"I would work on the horses and sleep here in my car." She paused to let Cameron absorb the information. "Guess that makes me a failure too." She sighed and reached over, brushing Cameron's hair back out of her eyes. "I don't know why anyone, never mind your father, would look at you and not see your talent and your beauty. Shh," She put her finger to Cameron's lips to cut off whatever Cameron was going to say, "but I do know that a group of people back there agree with me and love you. In particular, I can think of one rather short, incredibly chatty, occasionally annoying old man."

In spite of her sullen stoicism, the description made Cameron grin.

"You're not alone and you do not have to hide. The only shameful thing in this world is deliberately hurting someone. Any shame here is your father's shame." She paused, waiting until Cameron blinked her understanding, "Let's go back, huh?"

§ § §

They drove back and entered the diner. The group was all there. Cameron walked over to Morris, waited for a moment and said clearly, "I'm sorry."

"Good." Morris nodded. "I accept." Morris patted the bench next to him, signaled the waitress, "She'll have a hamburger and fries." Cameron started to say something but Morris' eyes twinkled, "Uh. Uh. Uh. I would be insulted and we'd have to do this all over again."

Cameron laughed, "Oh no, I wouldn't think of insulting you twice in one night." She looked over at Jess' empty bowl. "I was just going to say if you were buying I wanted a sundae for dessert."

Millie looked at the rag tag group and offered up a silent prayer in two parts. First, that today would actually come to an end and second, that tomorrow she would wake up and find this had all been a bad dream.

As the end of the prayer passed her lips, the door-opening bell rang and Millie figured God must be in a particularly playful mood. Heading straight for their table was the Reverend. Couldn't a simple fucking unknown anonymous diner who just wants to eat walk in here anymore!

The Reverend stopped as he reached the group. He just said simply, "Rudy and Joe are over in the carve shop."

§ § §

Rudy stood, a lost man in the middle of the floor. All the bulk and muscle that identified him seemed to have melted, leaving a man who took up space but had no definition. "I'm sorry. She took Kristen and I had nowhere to go, so I came here thinking I would feel better, you know, being close to the horses. Kristen loves the horses. And then, and then, it just felt like they were laughing at me and I lost it. I'm sorry."

He looked up at the blur of faces surrounding him. He had said what he could.

She moved to him first and hugged the broken man. "They know."

She could have been talking about the group but he didn't think so. She let her hands gently trace his purpled, black eye—was that from her or just the overall chaos? She hoped that in her caress he could feel her understanding that what had transpired was between them, two lost and damaged souls, fighting demons in the dark.

As she finished tracing her path, he took her hand and gently rubbed her scraped knuckles. "Thank you."

§ § §

Millie climbed the stairs. Cameron was back, settled on the couch in the living room and down for the count. Millie tapped quietly on the closed door and nudged it open without waiting.

She looked up, a question in her eyes. Millie set down the two glasses and the bottle she was carrying.

"You know, this didn't go the way I planned," Millie began. "But," she shrugged and opened the bottle and began to pour. "Today," she glanced at the clock, "well, technically yesterday I suppose, is the one year anniversary of the day the merry-go-round lady showed up."

She looked at Millie, stunned. Time was something she had lost track of such a long time ago. Could Millie actually be right? Could it have been a year? She took the glass Millie offered and clinked when Millie said, "Cheers."

They sat gathered around three long tables, squeezed into the dining room and they barely fit. In the living room there was yet another table, filled with a bunch of laughing and screaming children. The kid's table.

"Tonight," Sam stood and looked down over the seated crowd, "tonight we are blessed to be gathered for Passover Seder in our home. Irene and I are blessed that we have all our children here tonight with us under one roof. We are blessed by the presence of our grandchildren. We are blessed with my brother, Morrie. We are also blessed to have here our many friends. The Jacobsons. The Kradel Family. And finally, we are also blessed to have many new friends among us. We thank you all for coming."

"To start the Seder we have a very special Kiddush," Sam glanced about and explained further, "a blessing for the wine, tonight. Evan, our grandson, had his bar mitzvah two months ago. So tonight, as the young man he has now become, Evan moves from the children's table to join us here at what some might call the adult table." His eyes twinkled as shrieks could be heard from the living room. "Others might call it the boring table. So tonight in honor of this event, Evan will honor us by reciting the Kiddush prayer. It's on page two of the Haggadah." Sam sat down against the pillow placed in his chair as Evan, seated to his Grandfather's right, rose.

They sat politely frozen in their places, interspersed with other friends and family, unsure of what was to come. At Millie's insistence, two days ago, Cameron had finally broken down and asked Morris.

As only Morris could, he turned and looked at the three of them and said, "What's to know? You'll come, we'll sit around a table, read a book and eat."

They were all there; Nan and Joe, Millie and the merry-go-round lady, Cameron, Jess, Lyle, even the Reverend had come. Rudy sat with his arm wrapped tightly around Kristen.

This was a bit more than "you'll read a book." When the old hands turned to page two, the new guests followed along.

As Evan began to chant, she saw all the family and friends smile with pride. Many of them murmured along with him. She felt a chill up her spine. A chill of loneliness, of sadness. She could feel Millie having the same reaction. She moved her hand under the table and grasped Millie's. Millie took her other hand and grabbed for Cameron.

Evan sat down and Sam began to lead the service, using both English and Hebrew, stopping to offer meaning to things that might otherwise not be understood. They all sat very solemn, listening.

"Now it is time for all of you to smile and loosen up a bit," said Sam looking up from his place at the head of the table, "and I think we might just need a bit of help." Sam turned toward Irene as she rose from her place on the other side of Evan.

"We are now going to recite the four questions. These are the questions that the rest of the service will answer for us. They are to be asked by the youngest child. However, we learned several grandchildren ago that the youngest child suddenly seems to forget the words when standing by themselves. So, what can you do?"

Sam looked around the table almost as though he expected an answer. When none was forthcoming, he smiled and said, "You can make a new tradition. So we welcome you to the Goldstein Family Seder Tradition where the youngest *table* asks the questions as one."

Irene and her daughter Amy appeared on cue with the freshly assembled grandchildren. As they came forward in their fancy clothes and began, it was comical to watch those whose chests pumped up and voices shouted, and those who sort of stumbled along, as they delivered their share of the service in an off-key cacophony of sound. Cameron watched quietly as everyone laughed, not at them, but with them, in pride and delight.

The service continued with a more relaxed group. Somewhere between the traditional four cups of wine and Sam's warm leadership, the evening became a source of comfort to all. Finally Sam looked up. "I hope that everyone is by now starving, because according to my book, it's time for the meal."

People got up to help serve, but no one would let the newcomers in the kitchen. As the gefilte fish and matzoh ball soup made its way to the tables, Sam held up one hand. "Reverend," he called out. "We weren't certain," Sam glanced at his brother, "Morrie and I, what should be proper tonight. We never had a Reverend at a Seder before. So we talked and we argued, because as most of you know, we're very good at that. But we came to a conclusion that we would like you to say a little something before we eat."

Reverend Dalton was taken off guard. He'd been genuinely touched by the invitation, and now, now, at their dinner, they were asking him for words. "Thank you Sam, Morrie, Irene. I am truly honored. I came tonight and I wasn't certain what to expect. What I forgot is when love and family are shared freely and generously, you don't need expectation, you need to accept. We are blessed to be here tonight and to share in your family circle. May the Lord bless you all in return."

"Amen."

Dinner was nearing an end when Nan looked up to see Sam looking at her. He winked. She smiled and put her hand to Joe's arm. Joe stood. "Excuse me everyone, but as the Reverend said, tonight is a night for family and we, Nan and I, realize our family is right here. So, um, I just wanted to tell everyone, I asked Nan to marry me and she said 'yes'."

The jubilant shrieking and clapping and hugging put the kid's table to shame.

§ § §

As the kitchen clean-up crew went to work, Morris dragged Cameron away, taking her off on a small tour. He took her to the basement where, amid the kids busy searching for a piece of matzo, Sam still had some tools and photos to show off from the old days. Then, shaking his head and smiling at their antics, he took her back upstairs and into the library.

This was Morris' favorite room in his brother's house. It had high ceilings and a beautiful fireplace. Art decorated one wall, books the other three. There were overstuffed reading chairs and a small couch. Interspersed throughout were photos of a lifetime of family and friends. Morris watched as Cameron stood near a shelf, looking at all the titles, running her hands over the spines.

"So?"

She dropped her hands to her side as if she'd been swatted. "So?"

"So I think you should go to college." He waited and was not disappointed. The hands found the pockets and began to sink inside.

"Oh yeah, sure, no problem."

"Good." Morris smiled, stood his ground. He was fascinated by her ability to shove her hands deeper and deeper.

"Are you crazy or something?"

"Meshugah." Morris shrugged, "Absolutely." He moved and watched as her eyes warily followed him. He knew she had reached bottom; she was starting to twist. Her body was physically closing her off from the world. He needed to move now. "You should study. Get a degree."

"You should go to therapy." Cameron snarled back at him. "Get your head examined."

As their voices grew stronger, the small group at the table grew alarmed. Sam came back from the kitchen and pulled up a chair. He leaned over conspiratorially. "You know," he began quietly, "Morris never had any children of his own." He let them sit and hear his words. "He loves Cameron. She'll be okay."

Morris came out from the library. "Excuse me, Miss Boss Lady, can I borrow you for just one second."

She looked at everyone questioningly as she rose from the chair. When he let her in the library all she could see was Cameron's back, turned away.

"I just need you to answer one question for me," Morris said. "What's your degree in?"

She was shocked. No one ever asked her anything. Everyone knew the rules. She looked at Morris but he wasn't looking at her, he was looking at Cameron. She looked at Cameron through Morris' eyes, her body tightened against the pain, wrapped from back to front to absorb the blow. With a start she realized this was not about her, not even remotely personal. Not about her at all. It caught her off guard to realize how long it had been since that simple concept had been attainable for her.

"Architecture." was all she said.

Morris had what he needed. "Thank you." He meant it.

She turned and left; left them to it. Cameron finally turned back around. The dinner. The offer. Morris Goldstein finally did what even Cameron's father's fist in her face had failed to do. Cameron Blair cried.

§ § §

She came in and went upstairs. The dinner had left her feeling quiet, not sullen, not sad, but unguarded. A moment in which feeling loved hadn't hurt. She picked up the phone and dialed. It rang several times and the answering machine picked up, "Hi. We're not here right now. You know what to do." Beep.

"Hi Mom," she spoke softly. "I'm just calling to let you know I'm doing okay. Better. I love you." She hung the phone up, not sure if she was glad she'd left the message or sorry she couldn't erase it from her end.

§ § §

The door-opening bell signaled the arrival of Nan and Joe. It was funny, Millie mused. Joe used to be here every day, rain or shine. Now they stopped in together about once a week for breakfast, but now Rudy was the one here every day. At least his visitation rights seemed to be holding.

"Just who I'm looking for." Nan grabbed the stool next to the merry-go-round lady and pulled out a folder she'd been carrying. "I need you to tell me if this works."

She looked at the folder as Millie stopped on the other side of the counter. It was an antique mechanism for sale. She flipped quickly through the specs. "I think so. It looks right, but we should probably double check with Sam and Morris."

"Great." Nan jumped up. "Now all I have to do is pray people don't get tired of buying tickets to name horses."

§ § §

She strolled through the paint shop, smiling at the work, eavesdropping on the myriad of conversations. She heard someone yell, "Attention. Boss Lady on the floor." She laughed and watched the teasing camaraderie. She couldn't believe that every day this place filled up with volunteers. It was amazing. Nobody seemed to leave. She stopped to look at the horses being painted. There were three of them, all from the restored group, all "grand prize winners." Courtney's Christmas was furthest along, painted white and contrasting directly with Jake's Midnight Rider, her soon-to-be-black stable mate. The third horse in the group, Andie's Pearl, was just beginning her transformation. Next week, Cameron's Dancer would be the first fully carved horse to be welcomed into the shop.

She didn't envy Todd. Getting Cameron and Morris to step back and let the painters paint was not going to be pretty. She shook her head and laughed.

§ § §

Lyle left his driveway for his eight-block walk precisely on time and just as Chris Dysart pulled up and parked. As he exited the car, another man came out from the other side. Chris asked the man something across the car. "Hey, Mr. Johnson." Chris motioned to the other man and they both made their way across the street. "I'd like you to meet David Rosen. The Rosens are your new neighbors."

David extended his hand, "It's a real pleasure to meet you Mr. Johnson. I've heard a lot about you." Lyle accepted the hand, but looked toward Chris. David Rosen laughed, "Oh no, not from Chris. My wife Sara is working on the horses. She's on the paint committee and I've heard so many stories, it's kind of like I know everybody."

Lyle shook David Rosen's outstretched hand, smiled and turned to resume his walk. He was now going to be late. Yep. He grinned as he strolled. Lyle Johnson was definitely late. Yep. Things do change.

§ § §

She was a June bride. The day was perfect. The church looked beautiful and the reception was to be outside on the lawn. Millie smiled as she remembered Nan confiding that she'd just cry if it rained and the reception wound up downstairs in their committee meeting room. But that was months ago. Now, Millie and the merry-go-round lady were helping a very anxious Nan with her final preparations. They placed the dress on the ground and held the opening for her to step into. Millie stepped back while the merry-go-round lady helped do up Nan's buttons.

Nan looked across at Millie, gently running her hands down the side of the dress. "Do I look okay?"

Millie smiled. "You look beautiful. You look like a fairy princess." And she did. Millie realized that Nan wasn't just glowing because she was a bride and brides are supposed to be beautiful. Millie realized that Nan must have lost forty pounds and her weight-of-the-world cloak. She wasn't suddenly model skinny or anything, but rather, she was simply ebullient. Nan had come into her own and she was glowing because she was happy—happy in life.

Nan smiled and then had another thought. She turned and looked over her shoulder anxiously at the merry-go-round lady. "Do you think Gran's here today?"

Looking up from her job fastening the row of tiny buttons, she smiled. "I know she is."

Nan returned the smile gratefully. There was a knock at the door and three heads poked their way in. It was Cameron with Kristen and Jess. The young girls looked beautiful as well. They were to be her flower girls, but suddenly, looking at them all dressed up, Nan realized they were on the verge of growing up.

And if they were on the verge of growing up, Cameron, well, Nan struggled to keep her jaw from dropping in amazement. Dressed in pegged black slacks and a stylish white shirt, Cameron looked like *she* had lost the forty pounds and grown three inches. But it wasn't weight; it was simply seeing Cameron's actual body for the first time. Nan was shocked. She couldn't think of a time she'd seen Cameron in anything that wasn't three sizes too big and even then she would hunch over. She looked long and lean and wow. Nan leaned forward slightly, peering at Cameron's eyes which yeah, really were wearing mascara. The transformation was stunning.

"Wow. You look beautiful."

Cameron blushed but managed to laugh at Nan's none-too-subtle astonishment. "We just came to let you know Lyle's outside, ready to go."

As she and Joe made the plans, most of the choices had been easy. Rudy was his brother and would be best man. Millie would be Nan's maid of honor. But they sat and stared at the list, wondering who would give her away. She had no parents, and any aunts, uncles or cousins that might be invited certainly weren't close enough for that job. Someone should walk you down the aisle with love. Nan thought about it and realized he was there all the time. She asked Lyle to give her away. Yep. It would be an honor.

The music started and Jess and Kristen squealed. Cameron came around behind Nan to help the merry-go-round lady straighten the train. Nan turned first to Millie and kissed her. "I love you Millie."

Millie hugged her for just a moment, "Me too."

Then Nan turned toward the merry-go-round lady. "I love you too." She hugged Nan. "Thank you."

The music changed to the familiar chords. The girls lined up, then Millie. This was Nan's cue. She smiled fearlessly and walked through the door, onto Lyle's arm and down the aisle. Waiting for her with each step she took stood Joe, Rudy and the Reverend.

§ § §

The merry-go-round lady answered the knock and put her finger to her lips. "Shh," she opened the back door and welcomed Jess, "she's still sleeping."

The two of them made their way quietly upstairs, past the room that now housed Cameron and down to the last door on the hallway. "Ready?" she whispered to Jess. Jess nodded. "Okay, now remember you ask her?" she said.

Jess stopped, "No, you ask her."

"No you."

"No you."

Millie heard the voices in the hallway and rolled over. Jesus! It was not even eight o'clock. Couldn't anyone ever sleep late on Sunday? Her voice croaking, Millie yelled out, "I don't care who asks, but could we keep it down?"

The two of them giggled and shrugged. They pushed open the door and hopped up on the bed, "Good morning sleeping beauty."

Jess laughed. Millie glared. The merry-go-round lady raised her eyebrows at Jess. Jess shook her head emphatically and said, "No, you." The merry-go-round lady stuck out her tongue at Jess. Millie sighed impatiently.

"Okay." The lady tried to gather her thoughts. "Hold your horses!" Jess shrieked and that set both of them off. Millie could not understand what the hell was going on. They were both insane. She glared and waited. Finally the merry-go-round lady caught Millie's eye and tried to settle.

"Sorry, let's try this again. Jess and I have been thinking. Miriam is all finished except for the paint and we decided we would wait to paint her until we knew exactly what the right paint should be. So, while we're waiting to get it right, and with school being out and all, it's time for us to find a new summer project and start carving a horse. And so we decided," she looked at Jess, "we decided together that since we already have Miriam, you should choose this horse."

Millie sat and stared at them. It was a moment of two complete thoughts passing each other by, kind of like side-by-side escalators as one goes up, one comes down. Going up. Did they just ask her to name a horse? Coming down. As it happens, of course she has a horse to name.

Horse, name. As soon as they offered, Millie knew who the horse should be. It was odd, with all the carving, naming going on, she never thought of it before, but as soon as she was asked, the answer was right here in her heart and her head. So many years later it was so very right. "Mikah's Spirit." It came out in a whisper.

"Who's that?" Jess wanted to know.

"He was a young man I knew." Millie sat up in bed and tucked her feet under her. "He had long hair and blue eyes and a beautiful smile. People loved him." Millie's eyes misted and her look was distant as she described him. "And he was very special."

"Oh."

She watched Millie closely. It seemed like a good idea, surprising her, only she realized it wasn't a surprise, but more like an ambush. She had just assumed Millie was going to name her parents and this will be her thank you to Millie and that would be that. Piece of cake as they say. Wow. But she knew Millie's answer was deeper than either she or apparently Millie expected and she needed to give Millie some room here.

"Hey Jess," the merry-go-round lady cut in, "you have to get going. Sharlyn will kill us all if you're late for church."

"Oh yeah." Jess jumped off the bed. "See you later."

They watched her disappear down the hall and heard the door slam on her way out.

"Guess I should have known that when you ask someone to name a horse, somehow, it might mean something, uh, special. Duh!" She smiled wryly at Millie. "Tell me about him."

"I don't know if I can."

She settled herself back against the headboard of Millie's bed. "I won't be able to find him in the wood if I don't know him."

Millie joined her, leaning back, looking straight ahead. She thought back, looking for words that might help. "He was playful. And he could be fierce, fiercely loyal. He had a way of walking through this world that's hard to explain. He just had total acceptance. You were who you were. He didn't need you to change, to be anyone different. His gift was that everyone he knew had value." Millie paused, she needed to get this right. Softly she found what she was looking for. "When you were with him, you knew you counted."

She waited quietly, intuitively understanding that there was more to come and still she nearly missed it.

"And I loved him."

"Thank you." She reached over and took Millie's hand. "I'll find him."

The summer flew by for everyone except maybe one little red-headed, freckle-faced boy. Billy Ray rode his bicycle up to the chain link fence and looked in. He hated summer now. Used to be his favorite time, but that was before the stupid merry-go-round lady came. He and Jess and Zach used to ride around all day and do things. Now all Jess did was work on those stupid horses and Zach's Mom made him go away to camp. Now he had nothing to do. Now summer sucked.

She looked up from their marking, saw the bright red hair. She knew that he came by every day but never came in. Just sat on his bike and stared. She nudged Jess, "I think your friend is here."

Jess looked up and saw Billy Ray. She bent back to her work. "He's not my friend."

Millie and the merry-go-round lady exchanged smiles. "Oh, I don't know?" Millie teased, "I think he likes you."

"No he doesn't either," Jess shouted

The two women looked at each other surprised by the vehemence of Jess' outburst.

"Hey," said Millie. "We're just teasing."

Jess turned her head from one to the other. "Well it isn't funny."

The merry-go-round lady reached out and stroked Jess on the arm. "Guess not. I'm sorry."

Somewhat mollified, Jess sat back down.

§ § §

"Hey Rudy, how we looking?" Joe came out the back door and called to his brother by the grill. Rudy poked the coals and signaled "two minutes" while Joe continued his count. "Hot dog, hamburger, both?"

"Hot dog with the works for me," Millie called from under the big floppy hat she was sporting as she sat planted in her spot on the chaise.

"Sounds good," agreed Barbara.

"Make it two for me," Todd said, walking through the patio door. "Ladies." He pulled a chair up to the table and popped the top on his beer.

"Okay Babe," Joe called into the kitchen. "I've got six burgers and nine dogs, but I still don't have a Reverend yet. I'm just going with an even dozen dogs and an even dozen burgers, okay?"

She looked at the merry-go-round lady. "Let's see, he has a total of fifteen but we're missing the Reverend so let's make it twenty four." Nan shrugged. "Sounds perfectly reasonable." She laughed and whispered, "God, I love that man."

Nan raised her voice. "It sounds perfect hon." She linked arms with the merry-go-round woman and they began to head to the back. "Can you believe tomorrow is another Labor Day Fair?"

"No." answered the Reverend as he walked out and joined the crowd. "Sorry I'm late." He smiled. "It's that darn day job, you know."

"Timing's perfect, Rev." Joe walked by with a plate filled with buns. "Food is up in five minutes.

Stuffed and moaning, it was report time for the committee.

Robert stood. "I would like very much to start this evening or I suppose, this afternoon. I realize my position in this group is to wait until everyone has shared all the good news and then give my update." He ignored the good natured hissing and continued. "So if I might."

Todd stood, lifted his beer, offering a toast. "A toast to long suffering Robert."

"Here, here!" The group clinked glasses around.

"Reverend," Robert implored, "please control your flock."

"Sorry Robert," the Reverend laughed, "I've never seen this flock before."

"Go on Robert." Nan came to his aid. "You just ignore these mean nasty people and you go first." Before she finished Nan found herself being pelted with napkin missiles and the odd ice cube. Aaahhh! "Okay. Never mind Robert, just go last as usual." Nan got up, winked at Robert and flounced inside the door.

"Nan," Millie called after her, "come back. I'm sorry I threw ice cubes." There was no response to Millie's plea. "Okay, I promise Robert can go first."

Robert turned toward Millie and with a bow stated, "Thank you." He turned back, scanned the entire group and said, "My report has only one item." He hesitated briefly before screaming, "We've got the park, people! We've got the park!" Robert dug his briefcase out from somewhere under the patio table and handed the merry-go-round lady an envelope.

She looked at everyone watching and paused, turning and passing the envelope over to Reverend Dalton. He was smiling when he opened it up but that was nothing compared to the grin that split his face when he saw the words in black and white. They had done it; the city had agreed to donate the land. Reverend Dalton handed the paper back to the merry-go-round lady and turned to shake Robert's hand.

Everyone was out of their seats and gathering around. They all wanted to see the piece of paper, read the magical words for themselves. The back door opened and Nan came out, carrying a cake filled with sparklers. "Hey," Millie nudged Chris and yelled to Robert, "How come she knew?"

Nan turned to Millie and said, "I'm special. Any other questions?" She turned back around and saw Robert giving her the not too subtle eye/head bob move. Oops. Nan darted back into the house.

She was back on the patio in seconds, followed by Joe and Rudy carrying a large cardboard-covered something. Everyone immediately gravitated toward them and waited. Joe removed the cardboard from the front, unveiling the sign saying 'Future Home of Our Carousel'. It was lettered over a stunning rendering of the carousel set in the park.

The carousel lady took one look and turned a perplexed eye back toward Millie's house. Her eyes traveled to the second floor window. She nodded in recognition.

"Who did this?" a smiling Reverend Dalton asked.

Before Nan or Robert could answer, she said, "Cameron." Everyone glanced over as she answered. She could see the question in Nan's eyes. "It's beautiful. It's her art."

Everyone was hugging everyone. The Reverend finally interrupted, "Let's go spread the joy, shall we?"

§ § §

They arrived at the shop just a little bit early, and sat, grinning and watching as cars pulled in and people began arriving. The Rosen family climbed out and the boys ran to see who could say "hi" to Mr. Johnson first. Sharlyn pulled up with her girls and Jess came flying out the car door and joined them on the steps. A small caravan of honking teenagers pulled in, jumping and shouting, and found their way loudly through the gate. Three small wagons pulled up and sixty cartons of pizza were unloaded onto tables.

The carousel committee moved about, welcoming the noisy bunch. As she walked through the crowd, she remembered back to their first pizza party. It was funny, she realized, how rituals are created. As horses "grew up" and moved through the different shops, each one needed to be celebrated. What had started as a pizza break with three pies for Courtney's Christmas, was now a full-blown party.

She laughed as Nan came up over her shoulder muttering. "I see one more kid with three pieces of pizza and I'm going to kill him." When she turned, Nan shrugged. "Hey, we're on a budget here."

The Reverend jumped up onto the front steps of the carve shop and waited patiently. As people took notice, the crowd quieted down. "Hello everyone and thank you for coming out tonight in celebration. For our first order of business, let's welcome Mark Stern up here."

As Mark jumped up and waved, a group of teenagers began chanting, "Mark. Mark. Mark." The Reverend embraced Mark and whispered as he stepped down, "maybe you can get them up by my place next Sunday. I like their enthusiasm."

Mark smiled and waved, then motioned his hands to settle them down. "Thank you. In particular, thank you to my fan club back there. Just one question guys, why is it when you have to come to class you aren't cheering quite so loud?" They shuffled and laughed and booed, "Hey, that's whack Mr. Stern." Mark gave them their minute before continuing. "Yeah, yeah, I know." That was his idea of teacher-speak for settle down.

He waited a beat, then winked to them. "Well. We are all very proud to be here tonight. Boys?" Mark gestured to the back and four young men hoisted and carried a blanketed horse up to where Mark stood waiting. The crowd parted to let them through and a hush fell over the entire area. "Now before I introduce you all, I would like to ask my students to come up here and join us."

The applause built as sixty-three more young men and women made their way onto the ranch veranda. Mark stepped back and applauded along with them.

"We began this project as a class assignment last year. I thought I was going to be in a lot of trouble when June came and we weren't finished, but this group, our carving group, kept turning up and kept going. And we made it."

Again Mark paused to let the applause die down. "Unfortunately, it wasn't until our horse was ready that we realized we'd actually only finished the easy part. Now we needed a name and with sixty seven carvers, it wasn't easy. So we finally did the only fair thing, we had everyone choose a number and then drew a winner. Ladies and Gentlemen, I present Hannah Czernich."

"Thank you," Hannah stepped into Mark's hug. Then she turned to the crowd. "I think for all of us, this was the best class we ever had. We learned a lot and we got to make friends and it was great." Hannah signaled and two boys removed the blanket. "When I picked the name, I wanted it to reflect all of us. This is Hannah's Class Ring."

As the cheering began, the Reverend walked up and hugged Hannah. He pulled her next to him and waved for quiet. "We're not done yet."

Nan and Robert made their way from Lyle's office where they had stashed the sign. As they brought it out, they kept it turned from the crowd, whose curiosity had once again caused them to settle down.

"Well," Nan took the lead. "In the words of my fellow sign carrier," Nan paused so she and Robert could turn the sign around, "we got the park!"

As people celebrated, screaming and jumping and hugging, the merry-go-round lady fought her way back through the madness as if on a mission. She found Cameron precisely where she knew she would, tucked away in the back.

She smiled. "You did good."

Cameron looked up and blushed, meeting her eyes. "Thanks." Cameron went back to carving.

All the success unleashed a surge of renewed energy. Following the Labor Day Fair, Maddie's Star became the newest adoptee and within the week, John turned his prize carving, Joan of Arc over to the care of the paint palace. Sam estimated his horse, still unnamed, was maybe another three weeks behind and Reggie vowed to have Elsie's Blue Eyes ready for paint by Thanksgiving.

And it wasn't only energy thrusting toward completion; it was energy in forward motion. Morris and Cameron had begun their second horse and Mark Stern had stepped up to declare two more for the upcoming school year.

And there was still one other truly tangible measure of their success.

Amazingly, all the restored horses had been completed. Although they were being held for adoption, it was a great lift for everyone to see the entire inner row standing triumphantly, ready and waiting.

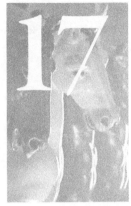

She opened the oven to check on the chicken. It was a rare night at Millie's, all three of them in and having dinner together. There was a knock at the door and Cameron called out "I'll get it," as she came down the stairs.

"Hey all," Nan said as she came in the kitchen. Striding past without another word, she picked a piece of cucumber from the cutting board, shrugged off her coat and flopped into a chair.

"Something wrong?" Millie ventured."

"I don't know." Nan stood back up, paced and this time swiped a carrot from the would-be salad. "I just don't know how to do it."

The three of them exchanged looks as they watched Nan pace about.

This time as Nan approached the salad the merry-go-round lady was ready. "Uh uh," she shook her head and pointed her knife at Nan's hands, "stop picking and start talking."

"I just don't know if we can financially do this." Nan looked at the trio, flopped back into the chair and studied her hands. She had debated this out loud to Joe for the last three days ad nauseum. At first he had been sympathetic and tried to be helpful. By last night they had a rip-roaring fight as he told her she needed to stop talking and do something about it.

Tonight, she had seen the lights on in the house and decided to come over to talk. "I add up the horses we still have available for adoption, the newsletter subscriptions, the donation boxes and every other nickel and dime I can find and I just don't see how we get there." Nan's nails were now apparently fascinating.

"So, I thought finally, okay, I'll have to call the Reverend but guess what, he had a family emergency and is gone for two weeks. Isn't that just fucking convenient?" Nan's mind finally caught up with her mouth. "Jesus! Joe's right, I sound like a raving bitch." Nan fell silent.

Nan's announcement froze the three of them. The impossible had become so possible that no one gave any thought to its impossibility any more. Yet here it was, rearing its very ugly head. Finally Cameron shifted. "Can't we think of another way to get money?"

"If you can think of something, I'm open." Nan looked up. "Lord knows," she smiled and gave a half laugh, "I've wracked my brain, not to mention

Joe's. If I had an idea, any idea, maybe I could get some sleep at night."

They all jumped as the smoke alarm added its blare to the night. The merry-go-round lady turned the oven off and grabbed for a cloth to wave, but she was a fraction of a second behind Millie, who calmly picked up a broom, held the bottom and swung. The smoke alarm was no longer an issue.

§ § §

The old expression "when it rains it pours" became both literal and figurative as winter encroached. First the summer kids took away all their teen energy and headed back to school. Then, when Daylight Savings Time packed it in for another year, its share of people went with it. Now, as Nan struggled with the finances, the creative core also found itself challenged by labor shortages. Everyone seemed to be down with the flu, busy with work, shuttling kids and honestly, when it turns dark by four in the afternoon, people simply couldn't seem to work up the enthusiasm to get out of school or work or the house, and head for the shop. Just as passion is contagious, ennui is equally infectious, virally dangerous and certainly far more devastating. The core gang fought to hang tough, but there was no hiding the rising absenteeism and for so many, almost any excuse began to do.

§ § §

"Hey Boss Lady." Todd came running through the door. "Millie slipped and sliced open her hand. She's bleeding pretty bad. I think she may need stitches."

Primal fear raced through her. Not again. All she could hear was "Millie's bleeding, Millie's bleeding." She went flying out the door of the ranch and into the diner. Millie was seated in a booth with Tom holding a bloody cloth around her hand.

She skidded to a stop. She took a breath. Millie was okay. She could do this. He couldn't stop her. She walked deliberately up the rest of the way. Millie caught sight of her and smiled weakly. "You wouldn't think any of the knives in here could cut a piece of steak, never mind me," she joked badly.

Tom whipped around and snarled. The escalation of tension was immediate. Any relief she felt seeing Millie upright was channeled into resenting Tom's presence. He had no power unless she gave it to him. He couldn't stop her from seeing Millie. She took another step closer. God she hated him, riding in just in the nick of time to save the damsel in distress while she was riding in just too damn late to save anyone.

Millie nodded to her and looked past him. "I think I need to go to a doctor now. Can you drive me please?"

As she drove Millie quietly and efficiently down the prematurely dark road, an eerie thought crossed her mind. "That's two." A sliced hand didn't seem like such a harbinger, but as she sat with Millie in the emergency room, it was a thought that wouldn't quit. First no money, now no Millie. Miriam pranced across her mind, galloping to a tune of "what next, what next, rule of three, rule of three."

§ § §

"Not since 1984." It was a litany repeated everywhere anyone went. The snowstorm dumped over a foot in less than five hours. Cameron got off the bus, grateful the college had cancelled classes so she'd been able to make her way home. She shifted the backpack and looked up curiously. In spite of the flurrying snow she could still make out flashing lights down the road. Dropping her books she ran.

They were working with the "jaws of life" and had just cut him out of the car as she arrived. She stood there, helpless in the snow while the medics moved the stretcher through. Sam, a cut on his forehead, was helped into the ambulance behind his brother.

Cameron stared as the snow soaked up the blood, the stains a silent tribute to a fallen comrade. The door slammed shut in her face and the ambulance raced out.

§ § §

They came around the corner in the hospital. She didn't know if she could do this. Steel bars flashed in front of her, beeps from the machinery grew louder and louder. She thought she might throw up. Millie stopped her, letting the others pass by. "If you can't do this, it's all right."

She looked up at Millie and remembered that first day in the diner, remembered Millie's eyes pulling her through. Looking at her now, somehow, just the recognition, the understanding, gave her the strength she needed. "No, I'm okay," she smiled grimly, "Let's go."

They formed an anxious group. The Reverend went to see what he could learn while the rest of them tried to find comfort in the sterile environment of the waiting room and in each other. Millie motioned to the merry-go-round lady who turned and looked.

She walked over and sat down in the chair next to Cameron. She didn't try to move the hands, white from gripping the chair arms or try to focus the eyes, staring desperately ahead. She quietly reached out her hand and placed it gently on Cameron's knee. She didn't say anything. She knew better than anyone else gathered here "everything will be fine" might be the biggest lie in the world. She just wanted Cameron to know that wherever she had gone to hide, wherever her safe place was, when Cameron came back, she was there; they were all there.

An hour passed. Then another. Every time a door opened, they all jumped, hearts in their throats.

Irene came in and they all stood except Cameron. She couldn't move. "Morris has suffered a stroke," she told them. Somehow, even with all the stress she was under, Irene managed to still seem elegant, to appear somehow composed. She looked to Cameron. Her heart went out to this child; this lost child Morris brought home. "We're all very lucky; the doctors say it's a minor stroke and he should recover quite fully."

Irene crossed the room and gently sat down next to Cameron, taking her hand, "Cam? He'd like to see you if you're up to it."

Cameron jumped, nearly sending Irene to the floor. "Where?"

Irene continued as though Cameron was still seated. "He's not one hundred percent, dear. You just have to be prepared."

Cameron paused. Even in the hallway she could hear the beeps from the room. She timidly pushed the door open. Before she saw Morris, she saw Sam. He looked old, beaten. She nearly backed out.

Sam touched his brother's hand through the bars. "She's here Morrie. I told you she was out there." He motioned Cameron over. "He can't see you over there."

Cameron looked at Morris. He was a tiny frail figure dwarfed by metal and steel. He reminded her of shrunken heads in old horror movies. He was a virtual stranger.

Morris' eyes blinked open and he spoke. His speech was slurred, but miraculously his words were still there. "I just wanted to tell you, don't go finishing my horse without me." It was exhausting for him but he fought to continue. "Don't let this fool you. I'll be back."

Morris stopped talking and closed his eyes. His body needed to rest. The monitors continued their steady beeps.

§ § §

She could see the merry-go-round but it was too far away. No matter how far she walked it just grew smaller. She could hear the music, but there was something wrong with it. It was slow—too slow. The carousel turned slower and slower, grew smaller and smaller. The horses were so very tired.

She woke and looked out the window. Money. Millie. Morris. The three M's. How poetic. God, even more snow. She reached slowly for her boots wondering why she bothered.

§ § §

Millie took her break and made her way to the ranch carrying two to-go coffees. As she let herself in, she stopped and stared. She was stunned. There was nobody there. Just the merry-go-round lady, almost as she had first seen her, sitting on the floor working on a horse. Millie knew a lot of people weren't coming regularly anymore, or some, like Rudy and Kristin were weekenders. Even Cameron lately, between school and visiting Morris in the hospital, couldn't really be counted on. She knew Jess would be there later, but everyone, anyone?

Millie walked over to the end, pulled up a piece of floor and sat. "Weather?"

She smiled sadly. Her eyes flickered about the empty room; from drift to depression to darkness to a death knell, she could see the shop diminish until there was one. Each step of less had been so singular, to not raise an alarm, until the "all of the above" box checked itself off. Her hand rubbed roughly, convulsively over her heart. "I don't think so. I think maybe it's gone as far as it could. Maybe it's over."

§ § §

Barbara Adler looked up in surprise. Standing voluntarily in her doorway was Cameron Blair.

Cameron walked in uncertainly. She didn't know who to talk to. Everything was falling apart. She thought long and hard and the only answer she could think of was that Mrs. Adler was a guidance counselor, which meant she should be an expert in guidance, and at least she did seem to care.

Barbara watched her surreptitiously. The young woman who entered was not the same person who had frustrated her for so long. She remembered the battles, trying to convince Cameron she was bright, that she could have a future. She remembered getting that blank stare each time. She could still see the body slumped in this chair far too often, always wrapped in her too big leather coat no matter the temperature.

But now, now that body was gone. This young woman stood proudly and had eyes that spoke volumes. Barbara realized Cameron Blair was growing up and she wore it well. She wondered what had brought her here.

"May I talk to you?"

"Of course," she motioned to a chair, "please, sit down."

Cameron sat in the hard-backed chair, but she kept herself on the edge, ready to bolt. "I just don't know who else to talk to."

"Okay."

"You see Morris had that stroke and now he can't come anymore because even if he could, Sam can't drive him because Sam can't see, so Sam can't come anymore either, and all these people that Sam worked with don't come because he's not there, and now nobody's coming and the carousel is dying." Cameron rushed all this out and now sat looking at Barbara, needing her to have answers.

Barbara wasn't sure she was exactly following all of this, but she was catching enough. She got up from her side of the desk and took the chair next to Cameron. "Okay, let's see what we can do." Barbara leaned over and reached for her phone, bringing it back and placing it on the desk between them. She gave Cameron a smile and hit the speaker button.

§ § §

Reverend Dalton stood up on his pulpit and looked out. His chapel was packed to overflowing. He had called and phoned and everyone had responded. Many of them were not of his church, many not of his faith. He had prayed and hoped his prayer would be received as well.

He saw his entire carousel committee and took a deep breath. He wasn't certain they would all come. He absolutely wasn't certain *she* would. He allowed himself a brief smile as he thought back to his first conversation with the merry-go-round lady. *And which faith would that be? Any faith.* It was hard to believe how far they had all come since that day. Well now it was time for faith to shine. He had been working the phones for days and he believed he had an answer.

"Good morning. I want to thank all of you for coming." He looked about the room. "I am sure some of you noticed we're a bit packed in here today. I volunteered," he arched an eyebrow and was gratified to get a few laughs, "a few friends to join us this morning for services, so I would like to ask everyone to bear with me and squeeze extra seats into those pews."

He waited as everyone shuffled and shifted and those still standing either found a seat or, in some cases, created one in the aisle.

"I wanted to talk this morning about something very simple. I wanted to talk about faith and a mountain." Reverend Dalton stepped away from the pulpit and the microphone and sat down on the top step.

Barbara Adler pulled her car into the church parking lot and sat waiting. She whispered a silent prayer that this would be all right.

"You see," the Reverend let his hands dangle and kept his voice low, speaking as though he was inviting them all into his parlor. "I went to the carving shop the other day and it was empty. So I opened the gate and went to the paint palace and it was empty. And my first thought was, it must be Sunday." He paused as a few chuckles went through the crowd. "So I looked and went to the diner and just listened. Then I went other places and just listened. I didn't really understand it, but I want to share my interpretation. We all gave time and money and love to build something on faith, but whether it's a bad weather day or a sniffle that came our way or we got bored—I mean, hey, we have been at this for two years now—we decided that the mountain we've been building is not worth climbing."

The Reverend watched as people shifted in their seats as his words hit their mark. But guilt wasn't what he wanted or needed. Guilt can absolve in its own right. He needed more than folks feeling bad; he needed them moved to action.

"Now, I know there's a group of people out here thinking 'who cares'?'" The Reverend laid his arms over his knees and leaned forward. "I mean honestly, we've heard enough about this carousel and let's just move on. Well, you're right. But this isn't about a carousel."

As he spoke, he rose, his voice gathering strength and passion. "This is about life. This is about what we choose when it isn't fun and easy. This is about living. Do we love only in good times? Do we love our children only if they get 'A's? Do we stop giving to charity because the need gets tiresome? Do we root for our ball club only if they win championships? This is the mountain of life and the meaning of faith."

The Reverend stood up on the top step. "I met a man not too long ago. This is a man who understands that the mountain is never built, but always building, it grows with us and if we are blessed, we keep climbing. This is a man who taught me about living on the mountain of faith. He is a man who loves deeply on good days and maybe even just a bit deeper on bad ones. I asked him to come and worship with us today. I ask you all to welcome him."

At his nod, the door to the back opened. Slowly, held up by Sam and Lyle, and followed carefully by Barbara and Irene, Morris Goldstein inched his way forward. It didn't matter that he moved painfully slow, everyone wanted to touch, to touch him, to touch each other with hugs and with their tears.

As he came to the front of the aisle, the Reverend stepped down and embraced the fragile man.

Morris turned to face the crowd. "I have to tell you something Reverend." The speech was slurred, but his voice was strong, "I never knew church could be so welcoming." Everyone laughed louder than the joke warranted. Morris searched the room until he found Cameron. He looked at her as he finished. "I want everyone to know I have chosen the name for my next horse. I'm going to call her Morris' Miracle and I'm going to start carving her on Monday."

Reverend Dalton called Barbara Adler. "Our new carpool committee is on the move."

The Reverend and Barbara pulled up outside the gates and looked around. The parking lot was jammed. They climbed out and went inside to find the joint jumping. Barbara squeezed her son's shoulder as she walked past. The two-some smiled at everyone, keeping one eye on the window.

A car pulled up several rows away from the gate and a woman climbed out. She opened the trunk and leaned over to lift out a wheelchair. Reverend Dalton stepped outside and hurried over to where she had parked. "Mrs. Langstrom, welcome." He leaned in to help lift the chair out and dropped his voice. "Any problems?

"None Reverend."

The Reverend came around the passenger side of the car. It was a two-door, which kept Sam snuggled in the back until Morris could be helped out the front. "Gentlemen, it's truly nice to see you."

Morris smiled and you could see the droop, but he appeared otherwise in good shape. As the Reverend opened the door, he used his arm to help Morris step out, but after that Morris managed to take his cane and steady himself. Sam pushed the seat forward and with the Reverend's help, climbed his way out.

Slowly, the two brothers helped each other to the gate and entered the junkyard. For a moment no one spoke and then the cheers came.

The carousel was back on track.

§ § §

She straightened and then stood leaving Jess bent over the block of wood, her tongue hanging out in concentration, chisel delicately working. She looked down the aisle at the flurry of activity. She smiled but it was bittersweet. She was one of only a few who knew how fleeting this flurry was. She knew none of them had answers for Nan's problems. She glanced down toward Morris, now seated in his wheelchair, pestering or directing Cameron. It was hard to tell the difference.

Her eyes traveled to Sam. He, too, had aged since Morris' stroke. She watched as his team helped him, leaving only the final checks for him to do. Sam finally named his horse, Evan's Wish, in honor of his oldest grandson's desire.

There was so much love in the room—love and blood and sweat and tears and promises and commitment and faith. She turned and walked over to Miriam and nuzzled her nose.

§ § §

Cameron ran the chisel along the patterned, outwardly facing "romance side" of Morris' Miracle. The work was challenging enough, but Morris sat in his chair and kept interrupting. "So Cam, how goes the classes?" She shrugged but kept concentrating. "A shrug. So now it's all clear. The classes go like a shrug." This time she looked up long enough to glare at him.

Morris sat back and watched. Morris knew body language like he knew walks and she was hiding something with that body. "So, tell an old man something, exactly when was the last time you went to class?"

§ § §

She stared at him as though he had grown a second head. He asked her if she could give him a hand with something and she said yes, truthfully thinking a brief escape from all the emotion would be welcome. So she's thinking they will be off to pick up some paper or something else from the church and instead, he drives them to the middle of nowhere and now he is pulling the car up to a, she looked again, yeah, a bowling alley and she is trapped.

The Reverend looked over at her stunned expression and laughed.

"Hey Rev." the badly bleached blonde at the desk greeted Reverend Dalton like an old friend, simultaneously reaching for a pair of two-toned bowling shoes, men's size ten. She and the Reverend both looked to the carousel lady expectantly.

"Uh, Reverend?" The carousel lady began, but faltered before the myriad of colliding thoughts could get from her mind to her mouth. Caught somewhere between 'I don't bowl' and 'have you lost what was left of your rational mind', came the less fearsome, "Size eight."

She hesitantly accepted her shoes and turned reluctantly to follow Reverend Dalton to Lane Twelve, where he was already lacing up.

"Didn't know I was a closet bowler, now did you?" The Reverend motioned for her to start changing but continued talking. "I do my best thinking here. Now, my best thinking and my best praying are somewhat different from each other. There's something about zeroing in, stepping up and setting the ball down exactly right, watching it glide down the lane and when it's perfect, seeing all the pins topple. It not only provides me with stress relief, but a metaphor for life, a lane from which to find my ball and topple my pins. It's interesting, some bowlers use pure strength, throw it hard enough and nothing will be left standing. But great bowlers, great bowlers use finesse. It's all about the placement. About trusting in your release and guiding it to the sweet spot."

He stood up, putting his hand over the air vent, picking up his ball. And then, with unexpected grace, he did just as he said. She watched the pins topple, a strike.

The Reverend came back and stopped in front of her. "It took me eight games to find my lane this time. Rolled a few gutter balls, had a nasty split, but then it all gelled. Started rolling strikes."

The Reverend stopped and turned, sorting through the balls sitting in the return rack. "It's funny how sometimes stopping to see another small piece of someone can change everything." Reverend Dalton stopped his search, picked up a ball and turned back to her. "We've got the money." He held out the ball. "It's your turn."

§ § §

She let herself in and followed the light into the living room.

Millie looked up from the book she tried to convince herself she really was reading. "That was great news, huh? About the donation?"

"She didn't come."

"Who?"

"Miriam. He told me the news and I kept waiting, went by the corral, even went to the old camp site waiting for her to come, but she didn't."

"Is that good or bad?"

"I don't know." She watched Millie put down her book, turn off the lamp. "What are you reading?"

"I don't know."

They made their way up the stairs. As she turned to go into her bedroom, Millie stopped, a question forming.

She turned back and met Millie's eyes.

Millie looked at her, then over her shoulder. "Was it you? Did you do it?" Millie asked and felt a rush of shame from her need to ask even as the question left her mouth.

She smiled tiredly; from Morris to the money to Millie. Three m's again. All in one day. "No."

§ § §

Nan and Joe came into the diner. Nan was seething. Millie was only slightly better.

"Come on Nan," Millie poured four small orange juices and gathered them up in her hands, "If he tells you who donated the money it won't be anonymous."

Nan shook her head. "No. I have begged for dollars and wracked my brains to figure a way out and I can't believe he isn't going to tell me. Me! It isn't fair."

At Nan's look, Joe nodded his agreement. At Millie's glare Joe excused himself and pointed toward the men's room. As he fled past the merry-go-round lady they exchanged amused grins.

Millie darted around the counter, served the orange juice and hurried back for more silverware. "Who the hell are we going to tell anyway?" Nan obviously wasn't finished.

Millie rushed over and placed the serving pieces in the booth, grabbed her pad and wrote up the order. Coming back she stuck the order in the clip and turned to Nan yelling, "order in" to Charley in the kitchen.

Millie returned to the counter and leaned over. "Don't be a spoil sport."

Nan's bark was fast and furious. "Hey, you of all people should understand anonymity isn't right."

The merry-go-round lady could feel her face color. She should have fled with Joe. She slid off the stool and left.

Millie watched her go and turned on Nan, "Great. Just fucking great, Nan."

"Shit." Nan toyed with her spoon. "It was just a joke, Millie. I didn't mean it that way."

Millie sighed. She wasn't angry at Nan. Nan was just being Nan and in fairness, she had every right to be upset. No, this was about last night. Millie was angry at herself because she had asked, because she had needed to know, not Nan.

§ § §

Millie walked into the carve shop. Thank God it was early enough to still be empty. Millie found her sitting on the floor, against the very back wall, her hands wrapped around her knees. Millie slid down against the familiar far side wall and just watched. "Nan didn't mean anything by that."

"I know." Of course she knew Nan didn't mean anything, but she couldn't stop wanting to cry. She looked at Millie who looked like she wanted to cry too and she hated herself. She was being a misery, milking her pain at other's expense and she couldn't seem to stop it.

Millie wasn't sure what else to say. She thought maybe she should apologize but she was afraid to say it, to give it voice, afraid it would somehow make her intrusion more permanent. Maybe it was indelible already. Millie reached into her pocket for her cigarettes. As she went for her light, she glanced around and remembered all the wood and the flammable junk. Sighing, she stuffed the smokes back into her pocket.

"Come on, let's walk. You can smoke outside," she said, smiling at Millie.

She stood and reached down to pull Millie up behind her, grabbed her coat, but left it open, hands in her pockets swinging the coat as they walked. She was trying desperately to get a handle on her mood.

Rationally she knew everything was way bigger than the moment, but she couldn't seem to get rational. Anything said was like a stone dropping into a lake and she couldn't contain the ripples. It made no sense. She knew she was using last night to punish Millie but last night, the question hadn't even bothered her. She'd gone to sleep, tired but amused that Millie even thought the anonymous donor could have been her. But this morning she woke up and was enraged over it. She might have asked the same of Millie only she already knew Millie didn't have that kind of money.

They walked out the gate, toward the street, pausing while Millie lit her cigarette and blew the first drag back out. The next drag became a smoke ring and she now knew just how upset Millie was. This was bad. Millie only blew smoke rings when she was trying to hold onto her control. She was hurting Millie, letting her pick a scab raw on a nonexistent cut.

She rubbed her arms. Why was she being so repulsively petulant? She needed to do something, anything, to set them both right. When Millie went for another drag, she spoke up. "Can I ask you something?"

The smoke ring was perfect. "Sure."

She stopped at the edge of the fence, wrapped her fingers around the chain link and rocked it. "Are you sorry about all this?"

"About what?"

"About me and the horses and the carousel and," she inhaled and used the exhale to force out the rest of the question, "and Miriam?"

A million answers went through Millie's mind. She thought and discarded "are you fucking nuts!" Thought and discarded "yeah, sure, sorry. That's why I've let you stay for over two years." Thought and discarded, thought and discarded. In the end, she simply looked her in the eye and answered, "No."

The merry-go-round lady smiled. "Thanks, Millie."

They had only walked a few steps back toward the diner when Millie realized that the merry-go-round lady was laughing. "Now what?" Millie thought and stopped. A hand pushed at Millie, waving to give her a minute. When she could finally speak, she looked at Millie, laughing, crying, but mostly with disbelief. "Oh my God Millie, I think I'm PMS. It's been so long I forgot." She stared at Millie. "It's my fucking hormones."

Millie just looked at her, her head cocked, processing the information. Then she started to laugh. Hysterically. In a minute they were both laughing so hard, tears were running. They leaned up against the side of the fence trying to catch their breath.

"You okay?" Millie gasped.

"Well some people might say I'm apparently doing better." She had her head bent over her knees trying to get control. "Shit." She looked over at Millie who was on the verge of losing it again. "We can't do this again," she warned. "It hurts too much."

Millie nodded her agreement. She reached down to grab a tissue from her apron. "Fuck!" There was no apron.

"What?" She put her hands on her knees and picked her head up.

Millie started to laugh and hiccupped while struggling to get the words out, "I told Nan," hiccup, "to stay behind the counter," hiccup, "and deal with everything."

"Oh," She looked at Millie. "Fuck."

They both took off running.

It was finally spring and everyone was happy to see winter fade away. One day it will become, "remember when" but for now, everyone was just happy to see it gone.

The flurry of new activity had the shop crammed beyond capacity and the paint parlor wasn't much better. But even allowing for all that, today was unique. With the sun already up and shining at only six o'clock in the morning, about two hundred volunteers milled about outside, chatting at tables filled with coffee and cakes and other donated treats.

"All right people," said Chris, jumping on the back of one of the many pick-up trucks and bull-horning his way over the crowd. "Thank you all for coming. Before we begin, you will see my young associate, Marcus Kim." Chris pointed toward a table along the outside of the fence. Marcus looked up from his carton and waved.

"Everyone here belongs to a team and we have color-coded tee shirts to indicate which team you are on. For example, when we need an electrician, we can look for someone in a red shirt."

Chris held up a red shirt, Dysart Construction stenciled on the front. He smiled and turned it around. The back read "We Build Carousels." The crowd cheered as Chris turned first to the left and then to the right. "Marcus will be helped by Josh Adler and Eric Richfield." Again, Chris paused and let the crowd spot the two waving young men. "So if you will go and get a position-identifying tee shirt, we can have us a good old-fashioned raising of the roof on these buildings and get back to what's important. Thank you."

Robert came to the food table and grabbed a cookie. He spotted the Reverend and the Boss Lady and ambled over. "Promise me one thing," he asked, crumbs falling all around, "promise me we now have enough land and enough buildings, so I will not have to find any more 'gee, was that a ka-ching I heard?' land owners and negotiate rent."

The trio laughed, but truth was everyone was excited. Two more buildings were going up. The first, ready sometime over the next two weeks, would be an additional carve shop. The second was the one they were raising today—a "build it yourself" log cabin kit destined to move with them to their permanent location as an office/museum.

This turnout was unbelievable. Much to Reverend Dalton's amusement, even Martha Washborn, ninety eight, who in a generous moment might be described as sharp as a tack and well, in a less generous moment—tough as nails, had put in an appearance. He watched a group of purple shirts walk by, "Anyone know who the purples are?"

"Dump Movers," the boss lady answered succinctly. "What about the blues?"

"Who or what are dump movers? The blues are mudders, I think."

"Ooh. Joe's not going to be happy. He's in blue and his words this morning were 'put me anywhere but mudding.' Ouch. Dump Movers are tasked with reconfiguring what's left of Lyle's actual business so we can use more ground here and save and salvage the rest."

She turned and looked at Lyle's small office shack. "You know, I forget sometimes that he has a business."

"I asked him about that, way back when. I thought maybe we should move all this up to the church grounds. He told me there were two things I needed to know." The Reverend dropped his voice down in a perfect imitation of Lyle. "One, this was the finest entertainment he'd ever had. Finer than TV." They both chuckled knowing it was exactly what Lyle said.

Reverend Dalton continued in his own voice, "and two, he actually sold more items having all these people in and out than he would have sold if we'd never been here." Speaking again as Lyle, he playfully finished, "All in all he thought it to be a fine investment. Yep."

"Thank you." She turned and met the Reverend's eyes directly, "Not just for telling me, but for having thought to ask."

The Reverend reached over and for the first time, embraced her. The moment was interrupted as a car pulled up and tooted. She turned and peered at the lowering window. She didn't recognize the driver at first, but saw the passenger wagging his finger at them and grinned, "Morris, what are you doing here?"

"Sam and I decided we needed to see this for ourselves. So we got Harry, you remember Harry from the Seder, to drive us over."

She walked over to the open window. "It's nice to see you again," She squatted down to see Morris. "I don't think this is such a good idea."

"Relax. You think we don't know that three old men would be in the way? We called Millie and told her to reserve us a booth with a window view. We're going to sit and have pastrami on rye and watch this glass house get built." Morris managed to lean over Harry to pat her on the arm. "Do an old man a favor?"

She rolled her eyes at Sam in the back and laughed. "What?"

"If you see Lyle, tell him we're here. He's going to have lunch with us."

"You got it." She smiled at Harry. "Nice to see you again."

The car pulled out and aimed for the diner. Harry turned to Morris and Sam. "So tell me again, why she doesn't have a name?"

§ § §

"Ladies and Gentlemen, welcome to our newly built Carousel-In-Progress Center."

As the Reverend motioned to the building behind him, light switches were flicked and through the all-glass front a large, empty log-walled cabin interior could be seen.

The high ceiling of the new building had pole holders installed and as each horse was brought in, it was anchored by a temporary stand with the pole into the ceiling. The exhaustion and filth of the day gave way to the smell of paint and varnish and wood wafting through the air, carrying all the hours of love and dedication into their new home.

The Reverend called the horses out by name as they came into the room, "Courtney's Christmas, Jake's Midnight Rider, Maddie's Star, Hannah's Class Ring, Andie's Pearl, Evan's Wish, Joan of Arc and finally, Cameron's Dancer."

"Hey Boss Lady." Chris came over and wrapped his arm around her shoulder. "Do me a favor and look up." He waited until she was looking and said, "Count the pole holders." Again he waited, but only for a second before he answered his own question. "Thirty two."

She lowered her head and turned to him, a bit unsure of what to say. Chris smiled. "I know, the carousel has thirty three horses—I only put in thirty two holders because if there's room for thirty three of them to sit around in here, we must be doing something really wrong."

She smiled and gave him a hug. As she turned she saw Cameron running her hand down the nose of Cameron's Dancer. She walked over, saying, "She's beautiful."

"Yeah." Cameron's smile was shy but proud as she leaned into the horse.

With Cameron carefully watching her, she took her time walking all the way around the horse. Standing under the lights, polished and gleaming, this was the first opportunity to truly see its finished beauty. Cameron's Dancer was elegantly simple. White with an almost, but not quite black saddle. Espresso maybe. The blanket was a very simple drape in a solid, rich cobalt blue. Where the blanket had its only fold, a silver heart appeared. The bridle and breast collar matched the heart, with minimal and equally simple adornments. Her neck turned down slightly in welcome, her eyes were wide open, her ears alert. She carried all the lines and grace of a dancer, a classically beautiful dancer.

She had completed her circle. "Cam, can I ask you something?"

"Sure." Cameron slipped one hand down into her pocket, but her other hand remained steady on her horse.

"Why did you change your original drawing?" She remembered the horse well. It was basically this horse, but it had stars and the head had been majestically armored. She always wondered about the change, but never felt she could ask. Somehow, with the horse glistening in the lights, it seemed okay.

Cameron blushed furiously but stood her ground, "Morris told me that the stars were okay, but I should use a heart because it was what I needed to do." Cameron managed a wry grin. "That I needed to learn how to wear my heart out in the open."

"And the head?"

Cam leaned in and touched the horse. Head to head her hand stroked the powerful neck. "He told me it would be a sin to hide such a beautiful face from the world."

She took a step closer and looked Cameron in the eye. "Morris," she said, "was right."

§ § §

Honk. Toot. Beep. At exactly seven pm, a festive bedlam began and high-spirited pandemonium reigned. The cars made enormous amounts of noise as they pulled in one after another. Inside the fence parents and volunteers cheered and laughed. The cars circled the parking lot, a giant auto circle dance, all following Mark Stern and several of his team members. The kids shrieked out windows and razzed each other. It was one huge, wild motor-driven pep rally. Tomorrow would be graduation ceremonies, but tonight was a high energy, high volume party of life, achievement and two new carousel horses.

§ § §

Tom's fury showed only in his dead-man's grip on the steering wheel. Lacey looked at the line of whooping kids streaming into the diner parking lot—a line they were trapped directly in the middle of due to bad luck and bad timing. She was so tired of this.

Lacey knew he hated the carousel project and the merry-go-round lady with a nearly violent vehemence, but she couldn't understand why. She tried to ask him once, and although he'd refused to answer, the fury she saw in his eyes was enough for her not to bother asking again.

Tom shifted and his jaw clicked. Lacey leaned over and touched his hand. "Tom?"

He didn't even twitch. "Tom, why don't we turn around and go through Maple Avenue instead?" He never indicated he heard her, just shifted into drive and whipped the car around.

§ § §

Mark's lead car pulled up and his headlights shone directly into the crowd behind the fence. As he stopped, other cars came from behind, splitting off one to his right and one to his left. When they were all in place, kids piled out and waited. Racing in and down the row between the shop and Mark's line-up came a motorcycle. The rider turned off the engine and pulled off his helmet. The kids cheered wildly. David Durban had just arrived. Big, with a cocky grin, David looked more like a boxer than an artist. His reception was most certainly more "Rocky" than "Picasso." He turned to his screaming groupies, looked at Mark and screamed, "Let the show begin!"

Cheers rose as the kids raced off to Mark's truck to carefully pass down the covered horses. As this crowd danced their way into the gates, the crowd inside began a rhythmic clapping, leading them in and up to the center, to the waiting group of carousel committee welcomers.

Millie shouted to make herself heard. "This is wild."

No one bothered to reply, they just kept grinning and clapping to the beat.

Mark arrived behind the snaking trail of bodies, backslapped by his kids every step of the way. He stood for a moment looking up at the gang in front of the big window. "I warned you last year this would be amazing." He took in their faces and laughed.

"Mark. Mark. Mark." The kids had started to chant.

"I think your public awaits." A smiling Reverend Dalton passed him a bullhorn.

"All right guys," Mark yelled, but it didn't seem to settle anything. Mark lowered the bullhorn and laughed. He gave them another moment, then picked the bullhorn back up to begin. "This was an incredible year for us. When I said we would build two horses, even I didn't truly think we would be ready on time. I know Mrs. Adler thought we were crazy." At the mention of Barbara Adler's name another round of cheers exploded. She laughed and gave a wave. "Who would have ever believed that the woodworking club would out pull the football team? But we did it. And tonight, tonight we are going to show the people of this town just how incredibly deep our talent runs." The cheers, already deafening, somehow managed to grow even louder.

"Everyone here tonight knows that because everyone carves, we draw to see who names the horse. Well this year, a group of students came to me, thinking it should be different—that one of their own deserved the honor and they wanted to nominate this person to get it. So, we had a discussion and a vote. The outcome was that every single student who worked on this first horse gave up his or her chance at being the 'namer'. Every single student who worked on the second horse agreed to have their shot at being the namer cut in half by inviting the others into their draw. If that doesn't say something to all of us about respect and generosity, I don't know what does." Mark put his bullhorn between his legs to applaud his students. The rest of the group joined him.

"The honor of presenting and naming our first horse goes to the painfully shy," Mark smiled slyly and the students whooped, "David Durban!"

Amid the screams, David made his way through the crowd, stopping to shake everyone's hands and then clasping Mark in a big hug. "Thank you. I just wanted to say thanks to my friends and thanks to Mr. Stern and I wanted to say thank you to Mrs. Adler." David turned to face Barbara directly. "I got my acceptance to Cooper Union Art School." As she came over to give him a hug, he whispered, "Not bad for, what exactly did you call me, a reprobate tagger, huh?"

"Anyway," David turned back to the crowd, which grew quiet. Mark signaled to the Reverend to undrape the horse. "On behalf of all of us, I want to present David's Road of Life."

Even unpainted, the majesty before them was unmistakable. Her head was carved fully armored and the blanket she wore was oversized and flowing. But it was the detail. The entire blanket was a world. There were trees and curves and water and sun and moon, cliffs and forks, and holding this exquisite tableau together was a path, a road. David's Road of Life.

For a moment, there was absolute silence. Then slowly, the clapping began. It began in rhythm. It was a salute.

She ran her fingers over the wood. It was amazing. It was humbling actually. She was fascinated by its power.

Sam patted Morrie's knee and motioned toward the bathroom, but instead walked quietly from the commotion and slipped behind the building. Cameron slipped into his place next to Morris, who was telling her something, and from the hand gestures, it was most likely about the technique.

Sam walked until he found a place by the paint palace where he could sit for a minute. David's Road of Life. Such a gift he has, this big tough kid. Once Sam had been David, big and tough, but with eyes and hands and a heart that could find the tiny difference between good and brilliant. His eyes and hands were no longer able to give that to him. Tonight, as he saw the art, he felt his heart break too. Sam Goldstein, alone in the night, mourned his own passing.

David finally stepped back down, his fist still pumping the air. "Okay everyone," Mark waved and shouted, "We still have another horse to go."

She spotted Sam slipping away, but was delayed from following as Fay's Champion of Liberty was presented to its own set of cheers. She laughed as she glimpsed Jess still trying to hide from Billy Ray, and by the time she made it around the back, she debated. Should she just return to the party and leave Sam to his own grief?

She came and sat down quietly next to him. "It's hard to see all that uninhibited talent and know it once was yours."

He didn't say anything for a long while, then, "How did you know?"

She shrugged. "Stein and Goldstein. The Central Park Carousel." For a moment they just sat, two people bonded by his history. "But it's more than that, I saw it everywhere in your home. The dining room table, you made it didn't you?" He nodded. "I can't really imagine what it's like to lose that touch," she smiled. "I never had it."

Sam went to say something but she shook her head, stopping him. "I'm honest. I'm good. Solid. He's a different league altogether and so are you." She stood up, leaned over and kissed Sam gently on his cheek. "I know it's hard for you to see this, but it isn't gone, it's only different. It's not the raw talent of a brash young man, it's now the gift of a master."

She left him there, hoping that someone knowing, someone acknowledging his pain, would be enough.

As she emerged from Sam's retreat, she found the party had begun in earnest. A group of students brought their DJ'ing equipment and were busy cranking out tunes. Everyone mingled and stopped to touch the horses, spilling into the parking lot and onto the ranch veranda.

The carousel committee members embraced each other and kept a close eye on the festivities.

She peered through the locked door of the ranch and caught sight of someone inside. Not good. They always made certain the shops were locked against tool theft and paint supplies, which sadly could be huffed. It might be fun but it only took one moron. She fished for her keys while squinting and then relaxed as she made out the figures. Down at their end were Morris, Cameron, and Sam. From the gesturing, a creative difference of opinion was underway.

Shaking her head she stepped down and ran into Nan and Lyle. "I just saw Todd and he needs more horses for the summer run. I'm thinking of a Fourth of July 'Win the Daily Double' promotion. Lyle suggested we do a Triple Stakes. So, I'm taking a poll."

"Sorry Nan," she smiled. "You know the old song, whatever Lyle wants, Lyle gets."

"Gee thanks," Nan stuck out her tongue. "And for the record, that was whatever Lola wants. But nice try."

She stuck her tongue back out at Nan and left her to her polling. She found Millie stashed around the side of the building, sneaking a smoke. "Ooh. Mrs. Adler, come quick." She began to sing song, "Millie's sneaking a cigarette. Millie's sneaking a cigarette."

Millie choked and coughed, her exhale coinciding with a laugh. "Wild night."

"Yeah, but you missed the best part. A group of kids pulled the Reverend out on the dance floor and he may be able to talk, but he cannot dance."

Millie dropped the cigarette and ground it out, "Ooh, let's go see if we can make them do it again."

As they walked off, they heard shouts ahead. Looking at each other, they stopped shamelessly to eavesdrop.

"You're just jealous. That's all. You're mad because I can carve and you can't. But let me tell you something Billy Ray, you can't carve because you're being stupid. My mother says you cut off your nose to bite your face. So there."

"Yeah. Well you're stupid too!"

"Fine. Just stop following me!"

"It's a free country. I can walk anywhere I want."

Millie and the merry-go-round lady leaned back against the wall laughing as two sets of feet stomped off. Millie looked up and said, "How much do you want to bet they're married in another oh, say ten years."

"I won't take the bet, but I will tell you one thing." She looked directly at Millie and said, "We are not mentioning this and we are not teasing Jess about him."

Millie laughed. "Deal." Their grins were both knowing and evil.

§ § §

The night wore on and the party dropped off. Reverend Dalton, Mark and Barbara all agreed to be on the final lock-up at midnight. Millie and the Boss Lady found Cameron trudging her way home and picked her up. She looked completely exhausted.

"Long night?" the amused voice asked as she got out of the car so Cameron could climb into the back.

"Ugh." Cameron slid over to the middle and leaned forward between the two women. "I don't know what happened. All of a sudden Sam comes and gets Morris and me and we go in to the ranch and down to the horse. He and Morris are arguing about the horse and I'm suddenly in the middle and Sam is telling me one thing and Morris is telling me another and I'm just sitting there."

"Why?" Millie tried to keep up. She pulled into the driveway and Cameron kept talking as they walked.

"I don't know. Sam was yelling at Morris that if it was going to be a miracle then it should be a miracle and he wasn't fighting for one. You know Morris, he just kept saying his brother was crazy and I shouldn't worry about listening to him."

They stopped in the kitchen. Leaning against the counter Millie asked, "Well?"

Cameron brushed her hand across her forehead, "I'm not sure. I think Sam wants us to find, as my graphics design professor would say, the USP— unique selling point." She shrugged tiredly. "Should be fun to see what tomorrow brings, huh?"

§ § §

Harry had once again driven Sam and Morris. He liked these people; he always had a good time. And it was nice; he could talk with Lyle about horse racing rather than carving. Neither of them bet, but they both liked to follow the horses, the live horses that is. Harry checked Sam in his rear view mirror. He hated when the brothers fought. "Okay. Enough already. Just make up or I'm not driving you tomorrow."

Sam sighed. Morris refused to budge. Finally Sam said, "Morrie, if it's our last ride, shouldn't it be our best?"

The car drove down the road into the night.

"He shoots! He scores!" Eric blew past Todd on his way to the basket. He turned and low-five'd his teammates as he scrambled back on defense. School was out and everyone was working. A basketball hoop and rim had made their way into the very back corner behind the paint palace and lunch seemed to have turned into game breaks.

Inside the Carousel-in-Progress Center last minute details were being ironed out for the "Triple Stakes of Racing" fundraiser. Nan stole Cameron to help with the flyer design. "Looks good," Nan commented over Cameron's shoulder as she made her way to the back wall. Hanging smack in the middle was Cameron's original rendering for the carousel. Nan's eyes traveled across the room and spotted the small notebook drawing inset against the large tracing, everyone's first vision of Cameron's Dancer. She walked back over to Cameron, observed her concentration. "You're good you know."

Cameron blushed, shaking her head in denial.

Nan laughed. "You need to learn how to take a compliment."

"Thanks." Cameron waited. Nan seemed to have something else to say, but whatever it might have been disappeared with the commotion in the doorway. "Lower," Todd's voice could be heard directing. "Okay, straight back."

Rudy and Joe walked a huge board into the room. "Nan?" Joe called out, "where do you want this?"

"Hi Rudy, Hi Hon." Nan walked toward them. "Just lean it up against those cabinets over there for the time being."

The board might not have been heavy, but it was awkward. Joe looked where Nan pointed and motioned Rudy down. Once it was on the floor, Joe continued. "Nan, in order to move this board against that wall, we are going to need to move three horses. So 'for the time being' isn't really good for us. We need to know where you want this for the definite future."

"Oh." Nan bit her lip and turned herself about in the room. "Cameron, where do you think we should put this?"

Cameron walked over and looked at everyone. "What is it?" she finally asked.

"It's a board."

"I know." Cameron rolled her eyes and laughed. "Even I get that much. What I mean is what's it for?"

"I'm going to use it to build a chart of horses we have, what stage they're in and estimated time of completion." Nan surveyed her room again. "You know, all that jazz." Movement at the window caught her eye. Nan craned her neck. "Hey Boss Lady? I need you."

She came in and took one look at the disheveled group. "You bellowed?" she inquired sweetly.

Nan pointed to the board, "Where would you put this?"

She glanced at the board and then back to Nan. "Where were you thinking?"

"Over there." Nan motioned to the wall.

The merry-go-round lady looked again at the board and then walked over to the space. "It's perfect."

Nan frowned. "You're sure?"

"Absolutely." She nodded firmly, turned to leave them to their task and then pulled up in the doorway. "Hey, are you finished with Cam right now, I could use her help for a minute."

They left the center and made it around the corner, out of Nan's sight before she started laughing. Hesitantly, Cameron joined in. "Thanks."

She smiled. "No problem."

"Can I ask you something?" At her nod, Cameron continued, "Do you even know what the board is for?"

Her smile grew broader, "No," and continued to widen at Cameron's obvious confusion.

"Well then how can you be sure it's in the right spot?"

The merry-go-round lady looked around, then put an arm over Cameron's shoulder bringing her in close. "Let me share a secret with you." She began, keeping her voice down. "When dealing with Nan in circumstances such as these, remember that she actually isn't looking for you to answer, she is looking for you to confirm her thinking. If I had said the other wall, she would have argued I was wrong. If I had said this wall, she would have needed to find another place. This way, she gets to be right and we get to be out of there."

"But what if it has to be moved?"

"Then you know what? When that moment comes, everybody will do whatever it takes to get it moved." She released Cameron and smiled. "Such is life."

"Thanks." Cameron struggled to get out words she desperately wanted to say and seemed never to manage. "And speaking of life," Cameron smiled weakly, "I keep meaning to say, wanting to say, thank you, um, thank you for my life."

"You will never, ever again thank me for something that was rightfully yours." The merry-go-round lady turned and walked furiously away.

§ § §

Boom. Whistle. Boom. The fireworks capped a long day. Nan unwound, lying on the ground, leaning in Joe's arms, watching the display. "I can't believe Millie had to work tonight," she said to the sky.

"Yeah. But I guess when Sharon covered for Millie with her hand this was one of the tradeoffs."

"I know. But it seems like a really lousy deal on a night like tonight." Nan nestled her body even further into Joe's. He figured it was probably pretty hard to see the sky twisted that way. He massaged his fingers through his wife's hair, "Mmm." Nan purred and yawned, "But I am glad we thought to bring the camera, at least this way she can see pictures of the winners."

"Okay." Joe gently pushed his wife up and then stood, reaching his hand back for her.

"What?" Nan looked like a child, tousled and pouty. Joe thought she was beautiful.

"I love you." He leaned over and kissed her. "I love your warmth and your humor and your generosity and your fiscal savvy."

"But?"

"No buts." Boom. A big beautiful blue explosion opened and slowly glittered wide in the night sky. He kissed her slowly, "Let's go get a sundae. You can buy."

They ran into Rudy on their way out and he and Jen, his latest date, opted to come with them. The foursome opened the diner door and laughed. A group of six kids were in the back and other than that, there was Millie and the merry-go-round lady, Jess, Todd and his wife, Lisa, and Robert and his wife, Shelley.

As they were settling, the door opened and Reverend Dalton walked in.

Mixed in between the shakes and the sundaes were the photos Nan had taken at the Triple Stakes Draw. Kathleen's Mocha Cappuccino, Cara's Lucky Number and Arnold's Cavalry Steed.

§ § §

The diner door opened and a man came in. His eyes scanned the room, obviously looking for someone, apparently not finding him. "Take a seat anywhere, I'll be right with you," said Millie, whirling past on her way behind the counter. The man smiled his agreement and headed off to a booth along the window, sitting so he could still see who came in the door.

Millie raced up, tossed a breakfast menu on the table. "Can I get you something to drink?"

He smiled and Millie stopped her hustle for just a minute. He was a rather unremarkable looking guy, but he had a great smile. It caught her off guard. "I'm waiting for someone, but I'd love a coffee in the meantime if that's all right."

"Sure," she shrugged and hoped it was a smile she actually plastered on her face. "Coffee coming right up."

Millie returned to the counter, whipped her order pad out and called into Charley while sticking the ticket in its clip. "Need a French toast and a short stack." She turned to get the coffee.

"Hi Jack," Millie greeted the man's breakfast guest now seated at the table. She set the coffee in front of the strange man who smiled up his thanks. "How are you, how's the family?"

"All good, thanks. Let me introduce you to my brother, Drew. He teaches up at the University and after threatening me for the last couple of summers, actually took this one off to join the carousel crusade."

"Well Drew, welcome," she smiled. "Do you gentlemen know what you're having, or do you need a few minutes?"

§ § §

Drew Stavourkis walked around the Center, but kept turning to peer back out the window, not quite believing what he was seeing. Jack told him stories, even sent him the newsletters, but to be here, to see it, was truly a remarkable sight. He stroked the horse he was standing next to and bent to read the name plated right on her saddle, Elsie's Blue Eyes. He wondered how the names were chosen.

"Hey Drew." Drew's thoughts were interrupted by the reappearance of his brother, this time with a woman in tow. "This is the Boss Lady. Boss Lady, this is my good-for-nothing brother, Drew Stavourkis." Satisfied that his obligation was finished, with a "Duty Calls," and a salute, he was gone. She smiled at Drew and waited.

"This is amazing, truly amazing." He looked around the room again, wondering at the whole process. "When Jack first told me about this, I thought it was crazy." Drew laughed, "and you know what, it is crazy, but amazing."

She laughed. "Jack said you teach at the University?" She left the question in the air as she began to walk and he came with her.

"Social Anthropology." He laughed at her expression. "I think that's why I'm so stunned. Someone should be writing a book about this. I look around and think, if I took an incoming freshmen class and told them all they needed to do to graduate was show up every day and build a carousel, I figure I'd have maybe a half a dozen kids left by graduation day." They had reached the veranda steps and he paused, looking over the rest of the small compound, "Yet, somehow you did this. It's truly amazing."

She watched him carefully, her hackles suddenly raised, wondering if that's why Drew came, to study them and publish some kind of paper.

Almost as if he'd read her mind, or perhaps only that her silence was telling, Drew turned and looked at her directly. "When Jack and I were kids, our grandfather taught us both wood-working." A smile of memory lit Drew's face. "We had the best tree house in the whole darn neighborhood."

"So," Drew's attention came back to the present, "just in case you might have been wondering, I'm only here to spend a summer carving. No hidden agendas. Just a summer of childhood one more time and then back to school for me."

His words proved oddly providential. Drew Stavourkis had an easy smile, a quick laugh and a genuine joy about him. Something about the eager boy in him seemed to help rekindle something in Sam and suddenly the two of them were busy in Sam's space, wood chips flying left and right.

§ § §

Drew pulled in and glanced at his watch in surprise. The noise he heard was definitely coming from the workshops.

For two weeks now he met Sam at ten o'clock to work, and he kept telling himself this was good, it was a vacation, he could just sleep in a bit. Unfortunately, it wasn't working. It was only seven thirty in the morning and he had already wandered around his miniscule motel room for an hour. Drew decided to take a shower and maybe go grab something at the diner. He figured he would eat, maybe if it was slow, chat with Millie; if it was busy, read the paper and burn off enough time to start the day. His eyes glanced over toward the fence, but his feet headed for the diner.

She heard the bell ring and caught the movement from the corner of her eye, "Hi Drew," she spun by, "coffee?"

Drew nodded and sat down on one of the barstools.

Millie surreptitiously tugged at her uniform's skirt as she came by with his coffee. Before she poured, she gestured to his choice of seat and smiled. "I forget, you're not a regular yet. Can't sit there."

"Okay." He agreed, taking a long exaggerated look down the empty counter row, then taking a long look the other way at the empty counter seats. "Okay." Drew nodded his head. "Why not?"

Millie laughed at his antics. "Because, it is about what, eight o'clock, five after? That would be Lyle Johnson's seat and he will arrive before you finish eating and thus you would be in Lyle Johnson's seat. Which is simply not allowed."

"Ah." Drew switched to the other side of the counter divide. "This one okay?"

"Perfect." Millie set the coffee down, pulled the pad out, "Eggs?"

"No, just rye toast, I think." A question raced across his face and Millie paused to see what he needed. "What time does everyone actually start working over there?"

"No real time, it just depends on each person and their schedule. There's just a few who start the day early, we're kind of the group morning crowd. They come in when I open."

Drew sipped his coffee processing the information. "Closed group?"

Millie laughed, "Nah. Just desperate for coffee."

Cameron came into the ranch and dropped her book bag. It was three in the afternoon and there was no Morris, no Sam in sight. She looked up at Drew curiously. "Morris had a doctor's appointment; they needed to leave early today. He asked me to tell you, 'no slacking', he'll be in tomorrow to check." Drew looked at the backpack. "Mind if I ask, what are you studying?"

"Graphic Design."

"Neat." After another moment, "How much longer until you graduate?"

"I have this summer and then two more semesters. It's a junior college."

"Ah."

It seemed to be enough for the moment and both of them went back to work. "Hey Drew?" Mark Stern stuck his head into the shop. "We need you."

Drew looked to Cameron and shrugged. He got up and went to where Mark was leaning in. As he approached, he saw the basketball in Mark's hands. "Oh, I don't think so."

"Come on. It's three on three. We're short a guy. It's you."

"You know Mark, this is going to hurt you a lot more than it's going to hurt me."

Mark laughed and put his arm around Drew. "You're gonna love it."

The cheers and screams brought more people out and soon a good-sized crowd was sitting on the sideline, watching the old guys play the young guys. Jess turned to the merry-go-round lady. "It isn't fair."

"What isn't?"

"They aren't letting girls play. They never let girls play. It isn't fair."

She glanced at Millie and Nan. Jess had a point. She never really thought about it because she had no interest in playing. But Jess was right; it was only always the guys.

Before they could even discuss what to do, Nan was up and marching square into center court. She simply stood in the middle until they caught up and action ground to a halt. Then Nan motioned to Eric for the ball. No one said a word, and when Eric cautiously passed the ball over, Nan finally smiled.

"Okay boys," Nan turned as she spoke, "we have decided that if you aren't going to ask the girls to play, you can't play anymore." Neal, one of

Mark's kids, took a step forward, but Nan forestalled him with her hand. "This, gentlemen, is not a discussion. Make your choice."

Mark was clearly enjoying this, but one hard look from Nan and he quickly called his team around. "Okay," he whispered, "which lady, aside from Nan," he laughed, "do we think has game?"

Drew, doubled over and leaning in on his legs, was just grateful for the break. He looked at Mark and Todd and struggled, "I don't know, but please, pick someone who's got younger legs than mine."

They huddled for another minute until Todd yelled, "Break."

As they stood, they noticed that the 'boys' were all still standing around mid-court. Todd called out. "Nan, as always, you lead us well. We want Cameron."

Cameron was on the edge of the crowd which was now whooping, hollering and chanting her name. Slowly she smiled and conceded, walking out to center court.

Mark turned to Neal. "Well?"

Jess was screaming, "Go Cam! You can whip them!"

The boys looked around. Suddenly Eric elbowed Josh, whispered in his ear. Josh nodded and slapped Neal's arm to get his attention. As he whispered, Neal laughed and nodded, "Okay, you've got Cam, we're taking the Boss Lady."

She stared at Neal like he was insane. Millie laughed and pushed her up, "Oh no, you can't refuse after Nan marched out there."

"Come on, you can do this," Jess said, looking up at her, pleading.

As she looked at them, something inside clicked. She strode onto center court, amid the screams and motioned for the ball. Nan tossed it to her and ran off the court.

The merry-go-round lady stepped out of bounds and tossed the ball into Josh's hands. Josh passed it back. She dribbled up, looked at Todd and grinned, put the ball on the ground and drove past him for a lay-up. Nan, Millie and Jess jumped and screamed as she put the move on. Todd turned to his team, disbelief on his face. "She's a ringer."

The game continued with shrieking and screaming on all sides. It was hard fought and silly and exhilarating.

For the boss lady, the game's tempo ranged from serious one-on-one to fending off Mark's fiendish tickling fingers every time she went to shoot. She walked off the court, pulling at her tee shirt to get air under it.

Cameron followed and sank down on the sideline. Jess came running up to give her a towel; Millie followed, tossing a few more over to Cameron, Todd and Drew.

Todd bumped her elbow. "A ringer? Who knew?"

She just laughed. "Been a long time." She squinted at the group, sweat dripping off everywhere, even her eyelashes. "Feels good."

The Annual Labor Day Committee Meeting and Barbecue came early this year. Reverend Dalton drove up to Nan's house and looked at the cars sprawled between her driveway and Millie's. He remembered when they could all fit in one driveway; now as he drove past and down a bit to park, he mused how even the committees had grown.

Now as he looked back up the block to the party that awaited him, all the Reverend could think is, to quote Morrie, she is going to plotz.

It was a relaxed night, friendly and easy. The Reverend looked around at the group, calm and unhurried.

"I'd like to say a few things before we get down to the business of the Labor Day Fair." He watched as people shifted and laughed. "Relax, I promise to be short." He surveyed the group. "First and foremost, thank you all. You have become my friends and I am both a better Reverend and a better man for knowing all of you and for this I thank you."

A chorus of "hear, hear Reverend" followed his remarks. His heart was filled by the love he saw reflected, reflected at him. When he got to the merry-go-round lady, he nearly laughed aloud. Her right eyebrow arched up and she watched him curiously. He knew that she alone realized there was more to come. It wasn't that she didn't love him, he knew that she did. She just didn't trust a man of faith. Well, in this moment, he couldn't necessarily say she was wrong.

She looked at him, wondering what he was up to. Every instinct told her another shoe was about to drop. She waited. And she didn't have to wait long.

"Now, for my second item." The Reverend looked around again, maintaining eye contact firmly with the group, "I'd like to be able to announce at the fair that we will have our carousel's grand opening," he paused for a brief moment, "one year from now, at next year's Labor Day Fair."

He watched eyes go round and faces pale. The Reverend had spent time thinking and praying about this and he believed he had to make this call. The carousel came into their lives and they were all enriched. They shared births and birthdays, his eyes met Nan's, and weddings and funerals and weathered them all together.

But without a target, all their life enrichment could fall prey to ennui and begin to splinter. Now was the time to pull together and cement relationships forever in celebration, not lose them in dissipation. He continued quietly. "I'm thinking we break ground on the building in the spring and by the end of next summer, spin the wheel." He looked at the accumulated shock. "Well, anybody here with me on this one?"

No one answered. Millie looked across the yard at the merry-go-round lady. "Hey, Boss Lady," she called out. "Is he crazy, or is it a plan?"

All eyes turned. "Yes." was her short answer. She shot the Reverend a bemused look and turned toward the group. She, like the Reverend, took in all the faces, people who had given so much of themselves for so long. She watched Lyle rock, could hear him saying, "Yep. He's crazy."

She looked at the Reverend and as their eyes met, she knew how very right he was. It was time. In project management, one of the skills is knowing how long for how much. The Reverend was spot on. And with a smile, she answered, "Yes he's crazy, but yes, with enough planning and intensity, I mean, it's huge, but we could be ready to ride in a year."

As those words hit home, she thought for sure Miriam would have something to say about this turn of events, but apparently she didn't. Miriam. Could she, would she, be ready to ride free in a year? She could feel her pulse pound her temple, the room closing in, but no one seemed to notice in the unleashed, happy cacophony.

§ § §

The crowd at the fair stopped milling and surged forward. "Thank you all for coming out today, and more importantly, for coming out for us for the last three years." The Reverend smiled as they cheered and whistled. He smiled with anticipation as he thought just how much of an explosion was about to happen. "So, short and sweet, I want you all to mark your calendars, next year, we will open for business at the Labor Day Fair."

The reaction was as Revered Dalton predicted, explosive. Cheering, screaming, hugging, jumping. It was a park jammed with people whose adrenaline was overflowing. She and Millie were tucked back in the crowd. They could feel the reaction pulsating straight under their skin, like a physical being that could actually be touched if you just reached out a hand.

She looked at Millie and realized she was looking directly into herself. The smile on Millie's face and the tears in Millie's eyes spoke directly to the mixed emotions of her own soul. She took Millie's hand. Neither of them had words and it was okay, they didn't need any.

They stood together and watched as the rather elderly Fanny Rose won a horse and named her Fanny's Heart of Gold for her great-granddaughter. They watched as Mark and his students added Candy's Sweeper. Then they watched, and shared, Barbara Adler's tears of pride as her son Josh and his best friend Eric finally had their own horse added to the carousel—Eric and Josh's Ride of the Last Cowboy, complete with a cowboy hat roped to its saddle. They watched, and laughed, as Neal Crowe's horse, Neal's Theory of Relativity was introduced. Even in the horse's unpainted state there was no question whose mane was being celebrated. That famous mop of Albert Einstein had everyone laughing and pointing.

Millie turned, shook the hand she still held and asked, "Want to go home?"

"Yeah."

They walked about halfway up the hill when they ducked to get out of the way of a gang of screaming, tumbling oncoming children being lunged after by a man lumbering with his arms stretched out like Frankenstein. They realized they knew this particular monster and his name was Drew.

"Millie, Boss Lady." Drew pulled up and dropped his arms and shrugged. "Hey kids," he yelled towards the gang at the bottom of the incline, "stay there and wait for me." As four sets of eyes looked up, Drew lowered his voice and playfully threatened, "I have the money and if you want to go on any rides or have any junk food you will all sit down and," Drew paused and waited until he saw four rear ends hit the ground, "and stay still for two whole minutes." He demonstrated his best authority glare then turned back to Millie and the Boss Lady. "Sorry."

The merry-go-round lady looked at him and asked, "Weren't you back on your way to school last week?"

Drew smiled. "Yes ma'am."

"And?"

"Well, I had applied for an emergency sabbatical for the year." Drew's grin was rueful. "I didn't want to say anything because I wasn't sure I would get it all worked out, but I figure we have one year to finish it all and I wasn't ready to miss it. So," this time his smile was full on, "I'm back if you'll have me."

"That's great." She reached up and gave him a hug. "Does Sam know yet?"

"Yeah." Drew laughed and returned the hug, but kept his eyes on Millie. "It was Sam who helpfully pointed out, oh let's call it an even dozen times, that sabbaticals exist exactly for this purpose."

Millie still hadn't said anything. He motioned to the kids who were now standing and yelling "hey, that's more than two minutes!" As he turned to go play uncle, he finally broke her silence. "So, Millie, see you for coffee tomorrow?"

Millie smiled enigmatically. "I'll be there."

He glanced again at his watch. It was three o'clock. Drew stood up, stretched and turned to Sam. "I'm going to go grab a soda," then looked to Morris saying, "can I bring either of you gentlemen anything?" They both declined the offer and Drew set off. As he looked back he could see both of them laughing and was pretty sure they were laughing at him.

He wasn't really comfortable with the idea that they knew perfectly well why he was going for a soda now. As Drew passed and waved to Lyle, he saw Lyle rock on his stick and laugh as well. Christ, he wondered if everyone knew where he was going. No, Drew looked around; no one else was paying any attention. Apparently one had to be over a certain age to figure this out. It occurred to the social anthropologist this was exactly accurate. He knew what each of his brother's kids were doing long before they figured it out. It was generational leapfrogging on full display.

Drew was so busy thinking he nearly collided with Fanny Rose. As he apologized, she explained she had an appointment to meet with a nice young man named Todd to go over the colors for her horse. Drew was pointing out where she should head when he saw Millie go by.

Drew quickly excused himself calling out, "Millie?" He needed to stop her before she disappeared inside the gates and got lost amid the people.

Millie turned and waited for Drew to catch up. "Look," he said, "I haven't done this in a long time and every time I come into the diner there's a crowd, so just really fast, will you have dinner with me on Friday night?"

"Yes." Millie said, turning to walk in the gate before he could see her smile.

§ § §

It was after ten when she finally left for the night. She had carved all day and then turned to the paperwork. Jess hadn't come, but she knew it was her first day back at school and a new school at that. Junior High. God, she had hated junior high. With Mark and all the kids back in school, everyone fell victim to the drop-off in decibel level. It was funny, a carving shop was never really quiet, but today, with all the kids gone, it felt like a museum. There was so little noise yet everyone spent the day speaking in whispers. She realized it was just another one of those periods of adjustment which would be over in another day or two as a new rhythm settled in.

As she pulled into the driveway, she saw a movement by the door and immediately lowered her window, calling "Jess?" It had been a long time since Jess had come roaming at night. She parked and headed up the walkway. "Jess, you okay?"

Jess stepped forward and she could see that Jess had been crying. "What's wrong Jess?" Jess launched herself into the merry-go-round lady's arms, sobbing.

Millie and Cameron heard the commotion and met in the hallway on their way downstairs. As they were about to head out, something, some sixth sense, stopped Millie and she grabbed Cameron's arm and shook her head no. They pulled back into the kitchen.

"My Mom said I had to come and tell you," Jess was sobbing hysterically; big gut wrenching cries.

She held Jess for a while just letting her cry, wondering what Sharlyn would have sent Jess to tell her to provoke all this. Gently, as she heard Jess calming, gasping for air to catch her breath, she inched her back a little ways. "What is it Jess, what did you have to tell me?"

"The teacher at school, Mr. Richards, he asked me to join the Glee Club." Jess flung herself back into the merry-go-round lady's arms.

She was perplexed, but Jess' pain was real, "That's a good thing, isn't it?" Her only reply was a head nod "yes" into her shoulder. "Okay, if that's a good thing, why are you crying?" No answer. "Jess?" She waited. "Look at me Jess."

Slowly the tear streaked face looked up. "I love you Jess, whatever it is, it's okay. You understand, it's okay."

Jess looked into her eyes and nodded. Quietly she turned and said, "Glee Club practices after school, three days a week."

Millie closed her eyes to block out what she was hearing. She opened them and saw Cameron standing next to her. They could do nothing but wait.

The merry-go-round lady turned Jess around and gave her a hug to mask the pain Jess' words brought. As she held her, she realized with a shock how much Jess had grown. Jess came up to her shoulder now, no longer the little girl who wore cowboy boots and prowled around town after dark. This almost-young-woman wore shoes and sweaters and listened to hip music by singers that the merry-go-round lady had never heard of and knew she was already too old to get.

"Oh Jessie," she whispered into the top of her head. "It's okay. It's the right thing to do, join the Glee Club. You'll come see me when you're not singing." But as she said it, she knew this was an end. Jess needed to go and have friends and be in the Glee Club and join adolescence head on. She pulled her close and breathed in the scent of her hair. "I'll miss you."

As Jess turned to leave, she looked back and saw the merry-go-round lady standing on the front steps watching her. Jess stopped and came back a few steps. "Can I ask you something?"

"Sure."

"Do you hear her anymore?"

A tear finally fell down her face. She made no move to brush it away. "No."

Jess nodded. "Me either."

Her hand went to the old scar over her heart and rubbed. "I know."

She watched Jess walk away into the night and lowered herself onto the front step. Millie came out the door and sat next to her. The merry-go-round lady lowered her head onto Millie's shoulder and cried.

Upstairs in her room, Cameron watched them both from her window.

§ § §

The week slogged on. It wasn't only Jess' disappearance that made things tough; everyone was struggling to find new rhythms without the summer help and with all the added pressure of the Labor Day clock.

Friday night finally came, and she and Cameron sat in the kitchen waiting for Millie to make her way down. "Ta da!" Millie turned and showed her outfit to her audience. "Now you're both sure this is okay?" she asked for the third time.

"Yes Millie," they chorused and laughed. The laughter didn't quite reach either of their eyes.

Millie looked from one to the other. What she saw worried her; they both truly looked like crap. Cameron looked like she had enough agitation to launch her body to parts unknown and the merry-go-round lady, Millie sighed, well, she looked like she'd lost a friend, which in truth, she had. "You know," she started, "I think I'm going to call Drew and just cancel. I don't think I want to go."

Cameron looked startled, but the merry-go-round lady jumped. "Don't." She advanced toward Millie, "Don't even think about it. Just because I'm being a depressed person doesn't mean you get to join my bandwagon. You get out there and have a good time. No, you have a great time. You have a great time for all of us. You do not have an invitation to wallow in my misery. Got it?"

Millie nodded, stunned, then she started to laugh, "Remember that Cam, we are not invited to wallow in her misery. Damn, and to think I'd just RSVP'd."

She glared at Millie but it was a second too late in coming. It is incredibly complicated trying to laugh and glare all at once. "Go away."

A car pulled up and Millie peered out the kitchen window. "Gee, it's my ride." Millie looked back into the kitchen, still not sure and gave a half-hearted order, "Don't wait up."

She walked Millie to the door; turned her shoulders forward while leaning over to get the knob. "I really am okay. Sad, but okay." She nodded to Millie. "I promise. Now go have fun and tomorrow, tomorrow, I want details." She smiled and waited.

Millie leaned over and hugged her goodbye. "You got it."

As Millie left, Cameron could feel herself getting nervous. She replayed the conversation with Morris in her mind.

"So what's wrong with the Boss Lady."

"I'm . . . I'm not sure. She just has some things on her mind, I guess."

"Cameron. You are a terrible liar. So, let an old man guess. Her young assistant seems to have gone back to school never to be heard from again. Perhaps that would be in the ballpark?" Morris watched Cameron but she wouldn't meet his eyes.

Cameron was terrified being left alone in the kitchen, not sure of what to say. When Millie walked out the door, and the merry-go-round lady came back in alone, she felt as though she'd been propelled to center stage. The kitchen light was suddenly a huge spotlight shining on her. She believed she should have something to say, but couldn't think of anything. Millie always seemed to know what to say. Cameron felt like a clod, like she was too big for the room, too stupid. She hated this uncertainty; hated feeling this way. She wondered if this inadequacy would ever go away.

She watched Cameron, fascinated by what was going on. Cameron's fists were clenched and yeah, headed straight for her pockets. She wondered if Cameron knew how easily they all read this habit of hers.

Cameron closed her eyes for a moment and tried to remember what Morris had told her. She heard his voice, *Sometimes Cameron, you don't need an answer. You don't need to fix it. Sometimes it's enough just to be a friend, just to let somebody know they're not alone.* She opened her eyes and saw the merry-go-round lady leaning against the counter and looking at her curiously.

Finally Cameron stammered, "I'm really sorry. I mean I know you love Jess and it's probably real painful and there's probably nothing I can do, but I'm really sorry." Cameron cringed at the sound of her voice. To her ears it sounded hollow and echo-y, way too loud for the room.

She crossed the room, took Cameron's hand and gave it a tug. She led her into the living room, pushed her gently down on the couch, crossed to the wing-back chair and sat. She paused and looked at Cameron again. She was at a crossroads and the decision was hers alone.

She held Cameron's gaze and made her choice, slowly unbuttoning the top button of her man-tailored shirt. Then she moved down to the next. When she had finished, she simply opened the shirt. The bra she wore didn't cover much of the old damage.

Cameron looked down and then looked back up, questioning.

Slowly she redid the buttons on her shirt, her eyes never moving. When she was finished, she finally spoke.

"Someone I loved died. And the world just kept on turning. And I hurt so much." The words came slowly, from a place out of time. "And I didn't have any way to get rid of the pain. I didn't have words for it and people meant well, but they moved on. And they moved on before I could tell them the pain wouldn't stop." She took a deep breath before finishing. "So I thought I should just cut it out."

The room fell quiet, Cameron not certain of what she was being told. In a moment, the merry-go-round lady continued.

"When I rub the scar, I'm reminding myself I'm not alone. You know, part of life may be pain, but love is the other part. And now I think the pain actually doesn't go away, it doesn't heal with time, but rather, the love finds a way to embrace the pain, to cosset it and absorb its blows. Almost like a band-aid, the cut is there, but something helps keep it from being ripped open all the time. Love lets the pain live," she paused, looking for a word, "more peacefully, I think."

Cameron looked at her steadily. "Why did you tell me?"

"Because I needed you to know. To show you we are all walking wounded. We just all hide our scars differently." She continued to look across at Cameron. "And because, because I needed to remind myself that Jess growing up isn't the same as being left behind. I needed to say this is good and I needed to say it aloud, to say it to someone who would hear."

Her hand pressed the scar as she struggled to give voice to her thoughts. "I don't know much about life, but I learned you can't keep pain in, because it will find its way out, so I needed to let it out where it could be heard, heard by someone who's my friend." She paused and thought, "and who would understand, truly understand." Finally, quietly, she asked, "I'm not wrong, am I?"

"No." Cameron knew she wasn't wrong. Cameron's hand drifted unconsciously toward her heart. "You're not wrong."

§ § §

Millie and Drew came out of a small Italian restaurant. After following Millie through the door, Drew came along side and took her hand. They strolled along quietly, neither particularly needing to hurry, but moving casually toward the car parked three blocks away. He glanced over at the woman walking next to him and wondered again at the events that brought him here, the call from his brother about the crazy carousel dream and the burn-out of his own once shining star.

From the first morning in that diner, he looked at the red-headed waitress and loved her smile. By the end of the summer he knew he was in love but did nothing. His life wasn't here and she was worth a whole lot more than a summer fling. And then there was Sam. Drew smiled. Sam sat him down and asked why he wasn't staying. Didn't he realize this is what sabbaticals are for?

"What?" he asked.

Sam looked at him and said, "And you call yourself a carousel builder? It's for one more chance." Sam's eyes twinkled. "One more opportunity to grab the brass ring."

As the car came into sight, Drew stopped walking and asked, "Do you know what the best part about taking this sabbatical is?"

Millie looked over, wondering where he was going. "No."

"I get time, unfettered time." Drew began slowly walking the last few steps to the car door. "I realize now that time is genuinely one of life's true luxuries. Maybe even its biggest luxury. Certainly much more valuable than a big screen TV or diamond bracelet. I get time to remember how to laugh and time to remember how to play and be silly and, how to dream."

Drew unlocked the passenger side of the car and opened the door for Millie. As he closed the door, he finished his thought. And maybe, even time enough to remember how to fall in love.

§ § §

Millie let herself into the darkened house. As she climbed the stairs it occurred to her that she wanted her to be up. That she wanted to sit with her best friend and recall all the highlights and be silly and foolish and giddy and feel that tingle and chill and thrill and rush and blush and that wonderful sense of letting the magic of the night crescendo again and again.

At the top of the steps, Millie nearly knocked on her door, just to see if she happened to still be awake, but her knuckles never made contact. It was silly. Just head on down the hall and go to bed and tomorrow you can tell them all about it. But tomorrow would never be the same thing. Don't be ridiculous. Millie forced herself onward.

As soon as Millie opened her door, a smile lit her face.

She sat on the floor, leaning against the side of Millie's bed, her arms wrapped around her knees, waiting. "So . . ." she took in Millie's glowing self, "Dish!" she ordered.

She unlocked the gate and made a sweeping motion for Millie to enter ahead of her. Tomorrow would be a big day—the party to move the last of the horses from the ranch to the paint palace. After that, there would be only one more party left. One final round up as it were. After that the horses would be corralled and the only carving left would be trim and boards. She brought Millie tonight, long after everyone had gone home, because this was private and this was between the two of them. She knew it was good; it was probably the finest work she had ever done. Now she hoped it was right.

Millie followed her into the building. By unspoken agreement she had never dropped in to see the work, never tried to sneak a peek. Millie didn't want to look in bits and pieces and have to decide if it was right; she just wanted to trust.

They made their way together to the far end of the ranch. It was both a familiar and unfamiliar trip. It was a walk they had shared countless times, but never when each of them felt the journey so acutely. Millie's anxiety mounted as they came in. What if somehow it wasn't right? Would she be able to muster exuberance or be betrayed by disappointment? It shouldn't matter, really it shouldn't. The gift should be perfect just for the giving. But, what if it was like sitting in your best dress and waiting for a ring and getting a necklace? God, she remembered feeling this mix as a kid when she played hide-and-seek. You'd go look behind the door and even though you knew they might be there, if you found them and they shrieked, your heart still skipped a beat. Millie half expected, with each step, the horse was going to jump up and yell "boo."

She could feel Millie shake and looked over. "You ready?"

Millie turned to look at this woman who she knew so well and yet not at all. She trusted her with a memory she had never shared. And now? Millie looked into the eyes that connected with hers since the first time they met and reclaimed her center. "Yeah, I am."

They came around to the end and there he stood. Millie stared in shock. His head went straight up, his legs reached out, his muscles rippled through the wood. As she circled around, his blanket showed an eagle flying toward the sun and a lone wolf howling at the moon. The sun and the moon. A yin-yang symbol positioned on a separate layer with a separate saddle blanket hanging straight below the saddle and overlaying the other. He was still untouched, still only wood and yet she had done it, she had captured Mikah's Spirit.

Millie stroked his neck and looked up to see his fierce flaring face.

"He's what we call a stargazer horse," she explained softly. "He'll be the only one on this carousel."

Millie looked up, tears in her eyes. "He's perfect."

This time she held Millie as Millie cried.

§ § §

He drove past on his way home and saw the light. It was two in the morning. Sheriff MacElwain U-turned and pulled into the parking lot. He spotted Millie's car and the chain hanging unlocked on the fence. His inner voice told him he should just leave; his professional voice told him he needed to check this out. He leaned over to place a call to the station to send someone over for backup, but his hand never clicked the radio. Slowly he leaned back in his seat, jaw grinding and tried to pretend he was only doing his duty as he sat waiting and watching in the dark.

§ § §

"You okay?"

They had been sitting for over an hour. Millie had cried for a while and then sat on the floor, wanting only to be close.

She had been content to sit, to watch Millie absorb her surroundings, at peace that she had been able to find this gift for Millie in the wood.

Millie looked up at the merry-go-round lady sitting across the other side of the horse. "I think so."

"You ready?"

"I don't know. I keep telling myself I can come back tomorrow, but it won't be the same. Coming here tonight, in the quiet, it's, it's so beautiful. It's like being in a very old stone chapel, the kind with a really high ceiling and, and instead of feeling an end, it's more like feeling a beginning. It's like being able to actually see his spirit released."

Millie shook her head. "Don't you ever tell Revered Dalton what just came out of my mouth." Tears spilled over Millie's eyes, and her voice turned husky. "Thank you."

As they walked out the gate, she turned to lock up. She was startled by the sound of an engine turning over and wheels peeling out. When she looked to Millie, she saw Millie's arms wrapped around herself, and she heard the lie Millie told. "Just some kids, I think." She let it go.

It was hard to fathom. Not only was Christmas rapidly approaching but its arrival would also signify the end of the horse carving. Morris and Cameron, Sam and Drew, John, Mark, Reggie and countless others worked hard to complete their horses on schedule. Todd was pushing to finish the current paint palace pieces to be ready for the onslaught. The building was filled with even more carvers hustling to get a handle on all the boards that would be needed. Nan was occupied with one last party and one final draw. After this, it was a direct shot at the grand finale.

Morris sat back and watched Cameron work. At this point, his miracle was mostly her work. The stroke had taken too much out of him to do more than small bits and pieces. The horse would be ready, but not without her keeping him going.

"Cam?" Morris stopped her for a moment. "Do an old man a favor." At her nod, he said, "Come and have dinner on Saturday night?"

She met his eyes and nodded before putting her head down and returning to the horse.

§ § §

Cameron parked Millie's car carefully and double-checked the address. She had been leaving to catch the bus when Millie, Drew and the merry-go-round lady descended upon her. Cameron would borrow Millie's car and there was no further discussion to be had.

She looked again at the building. It was a small apartment building, nothing at all like the huge house Sam lived in. Cameron exited and locked the car, making her way up to the entry system.

Morris buzzed her in and watched as she tried, subversively, to check out the room. "So, maybe you thought it would be something like Sam's?"

Cameron turned to deny it and realized she couldn't. Morris always seemed to know what she was thinking. He held his hand out for her coat. She shrugged out of it, passing the coat to him, a bit embarrassed.

"Sam and Irene, they have all their children and their grandchildren. Sylvie and I," Morris gestured to a picture sitting on a corner table. "We

190

were not so lucky, we didn't have any children. So after Sylvie died, I moved here. What would I do with such a big house? This is a good size for one person."

They ate dinner at the small dining room table and when they were finished, Morris took her back to the living room. He stopped at the breakfront and extracted a box of candles and a menorah. "Tonight is the first night of Hanukah and it's tradition I light the candles." He set the menorah near the photo of him and Sylvie. "It's also tradition to give a gift on the first night." Morris signaled her to wait and left the room. When he returned, he carried a box. Morris handed it over to Cameron.

Cameron looked at Morris. "I didn't know, Morris. I didn't bring something with me."

"It's a Jewish tradition Cam. I didn't give you something because I thought you would know and would bring me something. I gave you something because I wanted that you should have it and because I wanted to honor my tradition."

She sat holding the box in her hands. "May I open it?"

"Please."

Cameron grinned and ripped open the paper and then the box. It was packed neatly with Morris' original carving tools. "I can't take these."

Morris touched her hand very gently. "Cameron, I am an old man." Morris' speech still had a slight slurring quality so he took his time, being careful to be distinct. "Tools are meant to be used. Not to sit and gather dust. Not to sit as reminders of ancient days. My days for carving are past me now."

She looked up and he shsh'd her. "It's okay Cam, we both know I am telling the truth. If God had been so good as to have given me and Sylvie a child, I would have wanted that she would be just like you. You are the child of my heart."

Cameron began to sob and Morris held her as he continued to speak. "You will take these with you when you go, and when you use them you will think of Morris."

Cameron's head picked up, "when you go" echoing loudly. "I'm not going anywhere Morris."

Morris gave a big stage sigh and rolled his eyes. "Cam, you'll do an old man a favor." Morris smiled at her. "You'll go and you'll follow your heart. You won't stay here and watch an old man waste away and let life go past." He hugged her. "Promise an old man."

Cameron promised.

§ § §

She pulled the car back in very late. She had left Morris and gone to the ranch. Everything was locked up, but she sat in the parking lot for a long time and just stared.

Millie and Drew were out and as the hours had gone by, the merry-go-round lady became more and more edgy. She heard the car drive up, heard Cameron come in and went to meet her in the upstairs hallway. "Cam?"

It was as if all the crying she had already done never existed. The tears began to run as she sobbed. "He gave me his carving tools."

They sat on the stairs a long time; she rocked and mourned with Cam.

§ § §

The carousel turned brightly, lights flashing, music playing. She felt herself being nuzzled gently and turned from where she stood to see Miriam's nose playing with her. Her nostrils flared and her head pushed into her. Miriam smiled and jumped off, trotting around merrily in time to the carousel's turns. Miriam whinnied and reared.

She awoke with a start. It had been a long time since she had been visited by the dream and it had never been happy before. This time it was.

§ § §

She walked slowly down the long aisle to where Miriam stood, waiting. Tonight she would move from her home here in the ranch. She went over to Miriam and nuzzled the horse's neck. "I'll miss you." She laid her forehead across Miriam's.

She heard footsteps climbing the stairs and pausing. She didn't look up, just took a second to clear her throat and called out, "Are you going to stand out there all day, or are you at least going to come in and help?"

The words were meant reminiscently, innocently but they were like a slap to Jess. She guiltily inched forward, suddenly shamed that she no longer came by. "I'm sorry. I haven't been here very much."

"Hey, it's okay. We resolved that a long time ago." She looked down at Jess and opened her arms. "Come here."

Jess stepped into the warmth. "Did you see her?"

"Yeah."

"She looked happy, huh?" Jess peered up, hoping for confirmation.

She looked at Jess and then looked over at Miriam and smiled, "I think she is."

"So it's a good thing?"

She hugged Jess tighter. "A very good thing, I think."

§ § §

Lyle made his way up the steps to the ranch and opened the door. He looked at her standing alongside the horse and remembered when she first came. "Yep. Guess you were right. You could make them a whole lot better. Yep."

She smiled and turned to hug this man who had given her and Miriam a chance.

§ § §

Cars pulled in and Reverend Dalton met Nan at the gate. "Are you ready for the onslaught?"

Nan smiled at the line-up of people and boxes behind him. "Let's do it."

The crowd entered and disbursed like a well-organized army. Boxes were popped open, ladders set in place and lights unstrung rapidly. Within a few hours, Christmas had arrived at the ranch.

Cameron and her art committee pulled up in Lee's old pickup and somehow Cameron, Lee, Michael and Seth managed to climb out. A second car pulled in behind them carrying another four students. As they lowered the tailgate, they reached in to grab the tubes lying carefully stacked. Struggling to balance they made their way slowly to the Center. Nan looked up as the small crowd came through the door.

"We're here to officially deliver the art for the first fourteen scenery panels." Cameron smiled and handed a tube to Lee. Together they rolled out a streaming balloon, the main piece in a brilliant light purple with partial magenta and blue balloons showing behind it, the stream effect creating a rainbow of color.

Cameron looked over and watched the merry-go-round lady looking at the finished piece.

She could feel Cameron watching, turned around and smiled. It was very much alive with joy. Exploding off its canvas, it really did feel like "joyous movement."

As Cameron's eyes met hers, there was no backing down, no slinking away. Cameron's hands were proudly on her hips. In that moment it was a silent exchange of equals. With a shock she realized this was no longer a confused, hurt teenager before her but a confident young woman, a woman fulfilling her promise. She simply stared as Cameron matched her stare with a growing smile, somehow both defiant and enigmatic.

Before she could define what was going on, Nan interrupted Cameron to talk about the boards as Reverend Dalton came over to the counter. He took in the Boss Lady's perplexed face and then looked to where she was still staring.

"Cameron's growing up to be someone rather special, isn't she?" he said.

§ § §

The night air was frigid but the crowd was friendly and boisterous. The work from the morning had the entire lot glittering in the dark. Nan was busy hanging a new piece of art. Cameron brought with her a print output of the balloon panel they had seen earlier. As she stepped back to check its position, Nan peeked out the Center's window; it was nearly show time. "Well?" she turned and asked.

Reverend Dalton looked up from his notes. "Looks good. I still can't believe this is the last one until opening day."

Nan came back around and leaned on the counter. "I know." She rocked forward. "I can't decide if what I'm feeling is sadness or just plain relief."

Reverend Dalton laughed. "I know."

A tap on the window interrupted. Rudy was signaling; it was time.

"Hello everybody," The Reverend walked out to the cheering crowd, "I want to thank you all for coming out to join us tonight in celebration."

Reverend Dalton paused for the cheers. "It's been our usual practice to have a gathering when the horses are moved from the paint palace over to the Center to wait for their buddies. Tonight, we welcome several new horses, beginning with our striking display of red, Shannon's Spitfire. Shannon Marks walked with Todd and Joe as her horse made its way up the stairs and into position in the Center. She gave the crowd a huge smile and a wave.

"Our next horse, is a bit different." The Reverend continued, "carved by Team North Gardens, her name is Bernice's Step-in-Style and she is the only Clydesdale horse on the carousel." The cheering began as the beautiful legs of a Clydesdale came into view. "I'm not sure a Clydesdale is your average carousel horse, but she sure is beautiful. Thank you Bernice, and all the carvers from Team North Gardens. It took this group nearly three years to bring our latest addition to us, and we thank them all."

As they carried this last horse in, Todd stepped forward at the Reverend's urging and took a bow before the crowd.

"Okay, now before we draw for the last three horses," Reverend Dalton smiled as the screams grew, "tonight we break with tradition and proudly present a line-up for the last horses to leave our ranch and head into the paint palace. Ladies and gentlemen, we hand over to Todd, John's Dark Horse, an homage to dressage, Sam's Day at the Races, Morris' Miracle and, last but not least, Janet's Blessed." The Reverend paused as the horses were moved and the crowds cheered.

He watched as John smiled and waved, as Sam walked proudly across and as Cameron held Morris' arm and they shuffled slowly together. Over their shoulders he could see Janet Thomas waiting. The Reverend remembered the first time he saw "Blessed" and still this horse never failed to move him. She was uncannily simple. Somehow she felt gentler, maybe more nurturing than the others. Suddenly, watching the horse being carried, he realized what was so special. The horse had no bit, no bridle; she was untethered. There was just her face, turned gently to welcome a child to ride.

As the horses moved, Millie turned to Drew, from her perch wrapped in his arms. "Does it bother you?" She pulled away and looked up to see him better when he answered.

"Does what bother me?"

"Having carved all those hours and not having a horse of your own?"

"Nope." Drew watched as his breath carried in the air. He leaned and kissed Millie gently. "No, I got me something a lot more valuable than a horse."

The crowd's stomping and screaming, "Draw! Draw! Draw!" made Reverend Dalton turn and laugh. "Okay, I'm going to ask Nan to come out here and freeze with the rest of us, it's time to draw the last adopters!"

Nan stepped from the inside warmth and was blasted by cold air. She quickly stuck her hand into the raffle bin and called out Pam Kinsey and Madison Nash. A hush fell over the crowd and Nan took the microphone from the Reverend. "This will be the last restored horse to be named. Without all of your support, we wouldn't be here. Thank you." Tears formed. Reverend Dalton reached out and hugged Nan, whispering, "No crying tonight, the tears will freeze."

He took the microphone and said, "Let's hear it for Nan."

She smiled at the cheers through shimmering tears, turning back to the raffle bin. This was it. She didn't yell it, it was barely whispered, "Deb Rakoczi."

The crowd exploded.

Pam's Polka Palomino, Madison's Arabian Flyer and Deb's Daily Double joined the ranks of the paint palace and the party was on.

No one ever went inside the ranch. Only Miriam remained inside.

She had asked Reverend Dalton to bring her over last, to move her privately. As if by unspoken agreement the committee members and myriad of carvers had taken their private moments earlier. Through the night the ranch sat alone, dark to the gathering crowd, its curtains drawn. Miriam alone stood standing the last watch.

The frenzied mood of the Christmas party continued through the winter. There were rounding boards to ready and horses to finish and everyone worked energetically toward their looming date with destiny.

Finally, days began to lengthen again and the promise of spring uplifted the crew.

Nan was busy stripping the bed when she heard the car and looked out from the bedroom window. "Joe," she yelled downstairs. "I think everyone's there."

She laughed to herself looking at Drew's car parked at the end. Nan and Joe often joked about the living arrangement next door. She couldn't imagine Joe having moved in to a full house, and even though Drew still had his apartment, the whole thing was a little weird. But, then again, it seemed to work for all of them.

Next door, Millie, the merry-go-round lady, Cameron and Drew were all in the kitchen catching up and fixing sandwiches. At the knock, Millie called out. "Come in," and Nan and Joe came on through.

"Nice dinner." Nan commented looking at the jar of peanut butter.

"Yeah, well," Millie laughed and shrugged, "you serve food all day and see how much cooking you feel like doing."

"Uh, huh." Nan looked over to Cameron.

"Um. You go to school and make giclee prints all day and see how much cooking you feel like doing."

Nan turned to Joe, "I'm sensing a theme." She turned to the merry-go-round lady, who laughed, shrugged and said, "You go paint horses all day and see how much cooking you feel like doing."

"I think we played this game when we were five." Millie paused mid slice and glanced up. "Didn't it have something to do with going to a market and buying "a" apples, "b" bananas?" Millie took the four paper plates the merry-go-round lady was holding.

"Well?" Nan ignored her and turned to Drew, her right eyebrow arched.

"Um, you live with three women who don't want to cook and see what you wind up eating." Drew ducked as a paper plate rocketed at his head.

Nan laughed and leaned into Joe, resting against him, watching and smiling. These were their friends, their family. Nan straightened back up,

"We have an announcement to make."

Nan turned serious and everyone looked concerned, all of them remembering the last time Nan turned up for an announcement. "Actually, we've been trying to get all of you in one place for over a week and now, looking at you staring at me horrified, well, now I feel kind of ridiculous." She looked at the faces of her friends.

"Never mind." Nan laughed and said, "We're having a baby."

"Oh my God," Millie shrieked and wrapped Nan in a hug.

Amid hugs and kisses and peanut butter sandwiches and glasses of milk, cheers and toasts, Nan basked in the moment. She never thought this would happen. But at eight weeks, she was fine, the baby seemed fine and a new chapter was beginning. It was good to be loved.

§ § §

It was windy and still cool in the early morning, but it wasn't raining and the sun would be out and getting warmer very shortly. She and the Reverend stood side by side. They didn't say anything, just watching as the machinery rolled in and pulled apart the first piece of dirt. Ground had been broken. They waved to a smiling, hard-hat-wearing Chris and Robert.

§ § §

"We need a new committee." Nan announced to Millie in between pick-ups.

Millie grabbed the pancakes with her left hand, reached for the syrup with her right, "Good God, what for?" As she turned she added, "Hold that thought."

Nan played with her spoon while she waited. As Millie came back up, she launched right in. "Look, I am three and a half months pregnant. I lose at least an hour every morning to throwing up. I have a job we need so we can afford insurance and money to raise our child. I just don't have time."

"Okay. I agree. Can't be you." Millie tried to ignore the new customers for a moment but they wouldn't let her. "Be right back." She grabbed the coffee pot, filled their cups, left menus and returned. "So," Millie picked right up where she'd left off. "What's the committee?"

Millie walked into the paint palace, looking around. She didn't see her. She backed out, heading toward the small carving addition in the back. Success. Millie motioned the boss lady out. "We need to talk somewhere."

"Okay."

"Can we go in the ranch?"

"Sure." She unlocked the door and they were both taken aback. The room was barren now. No more wood chips everywhere. Just dust. She swallowed hard, but simply turned to Millie. "Okay?"

"Sure." Only it really wasn't okay. They didn't come here anymore and the emptiness caught Millie off guard. "I'm sorry." This was probably not a bright idea.

"No, it's okay." She smiled. "You know, if you just breathe in, you can still smell the wood. I love that smell."

They stood for just another minute, breathing and remembering. Millie walked down to the far end and sat, an old familiar gesture.

She walked down to join Millie. "So, we need to talk?"

§ § §

She let herself back into the ranch. This had rattled about in her mind over the last two weeks, ever since she and Millie had come in here to talk. It was perfect. Her mind made up, she went to find Todd and enlist his help.

§ § §

Cameron walked out of her advisor's office and headed toward the bus. She was a wreck. She had talked to everyone she could think of, but no one had an answer. They were all very polite but of no help. Cameron wasn't sure what to do. She finally decided to go home and whoever came in first would be who she'd talk to.

The merry-go-round lady came in and found Cameron perched at the kitchen table. "Hi." She looked as Cameron's hand twitched from a pocket and managed not to laugh. "Want to talk about it?" she offered instead.

"You know it's my graduation in two weeks?" At her nod, Cameron went for it. "The problem is we only get two invitations and no matter how I do this, it isn't enough. I need to invite Morris and I need to invite you and Millie and what about Sam and Irene and Nan and Joe and even Drew and the Reverend and I keep trying but I can't get any other invitations." Cameron pulled her hand from her pocket to run it through her hair and then dropped it onto the table.

She sat for a minute before answering. "Cam. All of us want to come, but all of us only want to come because we want to cheer you on. No one cares about the graduation ceremony; everyone cares about Cameron. And you did it!"

She leaned over and grabbed the hand on the table and gave it a shake. "I think you should take the invitations and give them to Morris and Sam. Those two will figure out how to get there and we both know there isn't anyone who's going to be prouder than Morris seeing you standing there in a cap and gown." She smiled. "He knows you're going to wear it well. As for me and Millie and Drew and Nan, you know what? We'll just have to settle for celebrating with you at dinner. Okay?"

"You really think it will be okay with everybody?"

"I'll take care of it."

§ § §

The invocations and speeches droned on. A part of Sam wished he didn't have to be there, but then he would look over at Morris and stop his nonsense. Morris sat bursting with pride. Sam wondered again at their strange bond.

He thought back to the night Morris had come over, the last night of Hanukah. All the kids had eaten latkes and gotten their presents and gone home. When just he and Morris and Irene were left in the library, Morris turned and said, "Sam, I gave Cam my carving tools."

Just like that. Sam was going to ask him why, but Irene gently placed her hand on his arm and he didn't say anything for a while. Just like that. Finally Sam looked at his brother and said, "That's good Morrie." They all sat and watched the fire burn down.

"Cameron Blair, cum laude, with honor." Morris clapped as Cam rose from her chair and moved toward the stage. Sam helped Morris rise.

Cameron accepted her diploma with her left hand and shook all the appropriate hands. As she turned to step down, she saw Morris standing. She hugged her diploma to her and smiled straight at him; a smile of triumph for them both.

§ § §

"Nan," Millie gritted her teeth as she held one end of a congratulations sign over her head. "Let me be clear. If you ever come up with one more committee, and I don't care who it's for, I will personally have to kill you." The chair Millie was on tilted precariously. "Forget that," Millie reached back for the piece of tape Nan held, "If you ever even say the word committee again I will kill you."

"I said I couldn't do another committee. I did not say you had to do it."

"Kill. Are we clear?"

"Okay." Barbara spotted the car out the window. "She's here."

As Harry pulled the car around, Morris teased, "Cam, your friends don't cook?"

Cam laughed. "I told you Morris, we're meeting here because Millie gets off at three and then we're going to some nice restaurant for dinner. I just promised Millie I would come here in the cap and gown so she could see it before I changed."

Harry parked and he and Sam walked behind Morris and Cameron.

Cameron stood dazed and frozen in the doorway. The echo of the shouts rang in her head; she couldn't quite connect it to her. Everybody was here but their faces were swimming, along with her stomach. "So," Morris nudged her arm, "are you going to let an old man go sit down?" Cameron was overwhelmed. She still didn't move. She just stepped aside and let Morris through.

There was cake and of course, coffee, and way down at the end of the counter was one giant card and a big gift-wrapped box. Cameron didn't know what to say to anyone so she just kept walking in circles, being hugged and repeating "thank you" over and over again. Now, as she opened the card, she looked at all the names. There had to be at least a hundred of them.

She smiled across the room at Lee. He had made the card using Cam's artwork on the front. The inside simply said, "We are all so proud." There was a date and below it read, "We love you, The Committee to Celebrate

Cameron's College Graduation."

"So, are you going to open the present now," Drew helped Morris onto a bar stool in a prime position, "or just wait until the anticipation kills us all?"

Everyone gathered closer. Cameron looked at them all, still shaking her head with disbelief, but reached for the box. She carefully undid the ribbon and handed it to Millie to hold for her. As the paper tore, her hands visibly trembled. Everyone cheered as she unveiled the box. It was a state of the art, Mac laptop.

"Speech!" The chant began.

Cameron looked at them, looking at her. She didn't have any words.

As Cameron struggled, someone snuck up behind her at the counter.

She said it so quietly she wasn't sure Cam would even hear. "Just say thank you."

Cameron took a deep breath. "Thank you."

The cheers were loud. It was all they needed.

§ § §

Thursday morning Chris' trucks pulled in at the site, accompanied by a small contingent. He realized it was the original carousel committee and went to meet them. "What brings all of you out here this fine day?"

Robert shrugged. "Orders from the Boss Lady and Todd."

Before Chris could ask further, one of the workmen called out, "Hey Boss?" Both Chris and the merry-go-round lady turned. Chris laughed, "I think this one is mine." He turned. "Yeah Rashid? What've you got?"

"I think you need to come check this out."

Chris walked toward the truck. Todd and the merry-go-round lady exchanged looks and started following, leading the rest of the curious contingent.

Chris pulled up and whistled, waiting for the rest to catch up. They all stood and stared. Rashid was unloading the entire carousel floor, names etched in and refinished.

Reverend Dalton finally broke the silence. "It's beautiful."

Todd smiled. "The Boss Lady's idea. We can all be proud to say that at least one thousand, three hundred and twenty seven people worked on some portion of this baby." Nan and Mark ran their hands over the wood.

The number Todd spit out caused everyone to turn. "That's how many names we have on the floor."

"And if we missed anybody," the merry-go-round lady smiled, "we're going to blame Nan. It was her spotless records we went through to get each and every one. It's really the important piece of the carousel story, the number of people who joined us. And if this is to be here for years to come, this is a piece of the ride people should also experience."

§ § §

Drew and Millie walked through the park. As they came around the turn to the carousel, they stood and watched the work going on. Drew broke the silence, "It's almost done."

Millie nodded but didn't say anything.

"My sabbatical will be over. I'll need to go back." He stepped in front of her. "Will you come with me? Will you marry me and come back with me?"

Millie stood there, hearing the words but denying them in the same instant. Some part of her had known this was coming but she wouldn't let herself go there. Now, here they were and she had no answers. "I don't know."

Drew stood there, not understanding. "You don't know?"

She looked at him, needing him to just go away for a minute. "I need to think."

"About what? I love you Millie, I'm asking you to marry me and come with me and what the hell do you need to think about?" He heard his voice rising and fought to keep control. It was supposed to have been a romantic yes. What the hell was going on here?

"I don't know if I can leave. I don't know if I want to leave."

Something in her voice, the way it was breaking, stopped Drew's anger and he tried to listen. "They're not going to stay forever," he said.

"No." Millie confirmed his words, "I know they won't." She looked at Drew. "She'll be gone soon."

"Has she said so?"

"She doesn't need to." Millie shook her head sadly. "I know it. She knows it. It's just time."

He reached over to Millie, pulled her into a hug. Drew knew the women were an odd trio and some part of him accepted that, and some part of him was jealous of their relationship. But every part of him loved this woman. He held her and spoke softly. "Okay. Then what is it?"

Wrapped in his shoulder, Millie tried to explain. "This is my home. It's funny. It's where I've lived forever, but it wasn't home for a long time. Now it finally is. And then you come along and I fall in love and now if I go with you I'll be what, a professor's wife? Maybe I can find a new waitressing job?" Her body shook with the effort to be honest. "I'm not a kid anymore. I don't know if I can just leave," she hesitated, "I don't even know if I want to."

He gathered her to him, held her and rocked her even as a piece of his heart broke.

§ § §

She opened the front door to the empty house. She carried the brown paper bag upstairs, opened the bathroom door. She set the bag down on the counter, listened carefully to the silence and then closed and locked the door. Slowly she reached in the bag and removed the few items—a jar of bath salts, a can of shaving gel and finally, a package of disposable razors.

She turned toward the tub, leaned over and slowly turned on the taps, adding the bath salts, checking the temperature.

She undressed. Deliberately. She stopped and truly looked at herself in the mirror above the sink. No longer emaciated. She touched the now thin line of her scar. Her hair looked surprisingly good, grown out past her shoulders. She hadn't worn it long since she was a kid. She liked it. She reached over and grabbed a rubber band and tied it up into a pony-tail behind her.

She touched the scar, this time a caress.

She ripped open the package of razors. Took two. For a brief second she felt their weight. She set them on the edge of the tub and climbed in.

With each stroke of the razor, she embraced the young woman she had once been. She remembered the rituals of becoming a woman; the excitement of being deemed "old enough" to shave her legs and the rivulets of blood and the sting from the little nicks, casualties of her inexperience. She ran her hands down her now smooth legs, reveling in their sensual, tactile touch. She could almost hear Miriam rooting her on, congratulating her on her "good self care."

Grabbing her nose, she slid her body forward along the porcelain tub and dunked her head under the water. Emerging, shaking the wet hair back, she laughed and splashed. She finally felt clean again.

They gathered together and walked this last step of the journey as a group. Millie, Nan, Joe, Rudy, Lyle, Drew, Sam, Morris, Mark, Todd, Chris, Barbara, Robert, Cameron and the Reverend. Somehow they had done it.

The ceiling swept from day to night to day in an endless whirl of clouds and different hues of blue. The two chariots had been set in place and thousands of light bulbs were tested and retested. The mirrors were streak-free, the floor polished and spit shined. They waited until all the workmen left and came to see it together, just themselves, just once, before it spun.

No one said very much. Even Sam and Morris were unusually quiet. For just this moment, this was the holiest place on earth and it wouldn't do to scream in a temple.

Reverend Dalton looked up and began to walk the circle as he spoke. "We are blessed here tonight Lord. We are blessed to have traveled this journey, beginning as strangers and ending as friends. I prayed to you for help with my path, my journey and Lord, you sent me a merry-go-round lady!" He paused and grinned ruefully, then catching her eye and winking. "I have to tell you something Lord, something you may very well know. I wasn't actually sure I heard that message right. But tonight I walk this floor humbled by your wisdom. She was a perfect messenger. And all of us who were blessed enough to travel this road say thank you for your blessing. Amen."

It was part blessing, part benediction. He wasn't sure where it came from, but Reverend Dalton knew that tomorrow their road would come to a fork. This was goodbye.

§ § §

"Bonnie's Pegasus. Joan of Arc. Maddie's Star. Emily's Knight in Shining Armor." Reverend Dalton called out each horse as it was moved onto the carousel and took its final position. "Hannah's Class Ring. Cara's Lucky Number. Evan's Wish. Morris' Miracle."

The merry-go-round lady scanned the crowd from her perch far above the cluster. Unlike last night, today was about family and barbecues and the carousel committee, strewn throughout. It was hard to believe they had made it. Labor Day. "Madison's Arabian Flyer. Fay's Champion of Liberty. Mikah's Spirit."

One by one the horses exited their various resting places and joined each other on the floor. "Courtney's Christmas, Cameron's Dancer, David's Road of Life." She spotted Lyle, walking stick in hand, sitting on the park bench closest to the event. He seemed to be highly engaged in a conversation with a very small boy. "John's Dark Horse. Bernice's Step-In-Style. Shannon's Spitfire."

Her eyes continued scanning the crowd. "Ben's Pony Express." She spotted Todd and Nadine, Todd's two-year old daughter held high on his shoulders. To his left she saw Rudy with a tall blonde. She squinted and couldn't believe it. The leggy blonde on his arm was Kristen. "Pam's Polka Palomino. Jake's Midnight Rider. Elsie's Blue Eyes." She glanced back over to Lyle, watching as the little boy cheered and pointed as Lyle's horse was announced.

"Neal's Theory of Relativity." The announcement unleashed its always raucous reception. Her eyes passed over Barbara, standing and chatting with Robert and Shelley. They stopped for a moment as Cameron's cohort, Lee pointed to something. "Fran's Frolicking Filly." She followed Lee's position and saw two children listening intently. She presumed these were his. A woman came up and the little girl held up her arms, pleading. Lee swung her up on his shoulders and wrapped his arm around the woman.

The Reverend paused for a moment, checked the sheet of paper in his hands, "Deb's Daily Double. Andie's Pearl. Eric and Josh's Ride of the Last Cowboy." Finally, the list was down to one. The last to leave its shelter, "Miriam." She was placed in the lead pole.

The merry-go-round lady watched them position her and rose up. Dusting her jeans, she took one last look. It was really quite a sight.

The Reverend turned. "All set, Mike?"

Mike gave the thumbs up as he double-checked each horse.

"When you came into the fair today," Reverend Dalton struggled to be heard over the noise, his voice rapidly becoming hoarse as people sensed it was time. The ground swell of excitement was contagious. "There were tickets given with stars on the back. Please check your tickets. If you have a star, you are invited for the very first ride on our carousel. So, come on up!"

There were squeals and shrieks. The Reverend tried to get out of the way of the squirming advancing mob.

She glanced back down at the carousel below, saw Jess in a group of kids climbing aboard to ride and she began to laugh. There was a young man climbing on next to Jess. She'd know that red hair anywhere.

As she watched the carousel begin to spin, she saw the little boy climb onto Elsie's Blue Eyes. He waved frantically at Lyle. Lyle smiled and rocked his stick.

She watched him rock and a flash of insight came to her. Smiling, she made her way toward her benefactor's bench. "You have a fan club I see."

"Yep. He's a fine boy. Moved in across the way. Yep. A fine boy."

She sat down next to him and for a moment they both watched the horses spin, the little boy waving frantically each time he passed. "Are you going to tell me why you did it?" She gestured at the carousel.

Lyle sat and rocked for a moment. His eyes twinkled as he thought. "Yep. Have you ever read the Letters of Saint Paul?"

"No."

"He says some mysteries are beyond understanding." Lyle met her look. Before he could say anything more, she leaned over and kissed his cheek. "Yep," she understood him well.

As she stood to leave, Lyle called to her. "I'll give you a hint. You ask Millie how old Lyle here likes his eggs. Yep. You ask Millie that."

It was later in the day when she turned to slip away. Before she could get out, Joe called to her as Nan waddled over, one arm supporting her large stomach. "I know you're going to leave so don't bother denying it." Nan reached over and hugged her. "I just want you to know if it's a girl we're naming her Miriam."

At her look of surprise, Nan shrugged. "It beat the heck out of Boss Lady. That was our back-up you know." Nan grabbed her again and whispered fiercely. "She's your niece, you better come back."

"I promise."

"If you don't, when she's old enough," Nan reached back and grabbed Joe's hand, "we'll tell her stories about some weirdo lady who came to town."

"Don't worry." She touched her hand briefly to Nan's stomach. "I'll be back to tell her myself." She smiled and headed off.

As she climbed up the hill, she could see Millie picnicking with Drew and Cameron and Jack and his family. She smiled as Drew and Cameron charged toward each other, the littlest boys on their backs kicking and screaming. "Come on, Uncle Drew, get her."

She slipped quietly away.

§ § §

Millie climbed the steps of the ranch. She didn't really want to turn the knob; it would make it all real. She wiped a tear, took a deep breath and pushed the door open.

Millie stood uncertainly in the doorway. "You're leaving." It wasn't a question. It was a simple statement of fact.

She nodded, her eyes gently drinking Millie in, memorizing this moment and this woman who had given her so very much, no questions asked. "Tomorrow. It'll be time. Before that I still have something left to do."

"What?"

She took several steps toward Millie. "I need to introduce myself. My name is ..."

"Anna." Millie finished the sentence.

She dropped the hand she stretched in front of her and stared at Millie, not understanding. "How did you know?"

Millie could see the night as if it were unfolding in front of her now. Tom standing in her kitchen seeming calm as could be to anyone who walked in, but not to her. She knew him too well. The too-calm warning, "She can't stay here."

His voice tightened when she disagreed, the venom spit out saying what he came to say. "The woman in your bedroom is named Anna Martin. The Miriam she keeps talking about isn't some goddamn horse; it's a dead woman. Do you hear me? Anna Martin is a fucking dyke and Miriam was her girlfriend and she's not sleeping in your house."

His fear. His hate. Millie hadn't really listened; she didn't care. Millie had seen the scar. The woman had nowhere else to go. Millie had calmly picked at some lint on her shirt and when she was done, she had shown Tom out. Best damn choice she ever made.

Millie's tone was flat, matter-of-fact. "Tom."

She wrapped her arms around herself, gave a half laugh. "I guess that explains it."

"Yeah." Millie walked forward, closing the gap between them. "He blamed everything on you. You, my friend, are a corrupting element you know."

"Apparently," came the wry reply. "You never said anything, why?"

"Anna wasn't who you were when I met you. Anna was lost. I just kind of figured you would tell me when you were ready." Millie snorted. "I didn't think it would be over four years later."

She laughed with Millie, then fell silent. She thought about asking Millie if she knew the story, but couldn't. She wanted, no she needed, Millie to hear the story from her. "My friends call me Annie." Slowly she turned and walked down to "their wall."

She patted the floor space next to her but focused across the room as she began. "We had been together for nine years. I came home from work; I was tired. I had been drafting all day. I still remember the project. It was what we always joked was a San Francisco Special—squeezing four thousand square feet into a two inch by four inch lot with lots of amenities." She chuckled for a moment.

"Miriam wasn't home yet. I fell asleep on the couch. The phone woke me up." In her head she could still hear the ring; she could always hear the ring. She shook her head to clear the noise and continued, slowly fighting for and forming each word. She needed them to count. "It was the police; they found our number in her purse. She'd gone to dinner with friends of ours and was walking back to her car. It was only a block away from the restaurant. They held her up for her wallet. She gave it to them, but I guess it just wasn't enough money. They pulled a gun. Shot her. Tossed the wallet in the street."

"They, the police, they explained it was a random act of violence." She tried to form a wry smile, but failed. "I rushed to the hospital, forgot to bring our medical power of attorney forms. They didn't even want to let me in the room." She could see herself standing there, pleading. "I begged. Finally a nurse, I can't even remember her name, let me go in. She was lying there, hooked up to a hundred machines. Her organs were dying. The disease they had inflicted was terminal and it was ravaging her. I sat on the other side of those bars." She looked over to Millie, using her hands to help paint the scene, "you know the ones they put on the bed. It was

210

like a prison. Metal bars. She was in lockdown."

Her mind continued to drift back to the images, her voice grew harder. "I spent the night sitting there, too afraid that if I moved, Miriam would leave, so I just sat there all alone because I couldn't leave to call anyone. But in the end it didn't matter. I couldn't hold on hard enough. She left. Here one minute and gone—poof—just like that."

Anna stopped, lost in the memory, alone again. Millie sat transfixed, her eyes locked on the vein thrusting in Anna's neck as though it was trying to escape, to break free. She moved her hand reassuringly down Anna's arm; Anna allowed the contact, allowed it to bring her back.

She marshaled her fears and pain and expelled them in a deep breath. "That nurse, I guess her shift was changing, that nurse came and helped me get up."

Anna looked directly at Millie for the first time since she began. "Somehow I kept going. Arranged the funeral. Took a few days just to weep. And then, then, I tried to go back to work."

"But I couldn't seem to make people understand that whoever the goddamned stapler belonged to, well it just didn't matter. What mattered was Miriam was dead. Who cared if the proposed fucking balcony wasn't looking like a piano but more like a cello? Please." Her hand gestures waved her disgust. "So, per everyone's kindly phrased suggestions, I took some time off. I couldn't eat, couldn't sleep."

"And for a while people really tried, but you see, they had a life to go back to and mine was gone. That first year I survived in a sort of state of grace. I was numb and people were kind, patient, tolerant and sympathetic. But then I learned some things I hadn't known. Grief has a time limit; six weeks for some, six months for others, move on, pull it together. I learned that how you grieve is something to be measured and judged."

"And I tried. God I tried. I tried to boot strap myself right back up." Anna looked up and out the window, but it was a memory she was seeing. For a moment she gritted her teeth and swallowed the clog in her throat. "And then, then the anniversary came and it was worse, like a big cosmic joke; the numbness was gone and now, now one year later, the pain was so real. I imagine it's like a horrible burn. You don't feel it at first; the nerve endings are gone. But when they come back, oh God, the pain. And I couldn't take the pain."

Millie moved toward her and this time she held up her hand; she couldn't be touched, she needed to finish. She stared at a spot across from her and wondered aimlessly if when wood gets knots it hurts.

She shook her head, wondered where she left off. The pain. "And there was no one left to tell because they had all returned to the land of the living. And it was a year later and I was simply supposed to be okay. You see that's how it works. I had used up my healing time. Only I wasn't okay. So, one night I just picked up that knife. And when I got out of the hospital, I got in my car and drove. And I drove. As long as I could see those little white lines, I followed them.

And then one night I stopped to sleep, get gas." She rested her head against the wall, her eyes closed. "You know the rest."

They just sat together for a while.

"I dreamed of Miriam not too long ago." She opened her eyes and glanced sideways at Millie. "She climbed off the carousel and she ran free. I think she's okay now."

For another minute they just sat. "You know," Millie mused, "Tom isn't actually such a bad guy." Millie grinned as she watched Anna's eyebrow shoot up, even while her eyes remained closed. "He's just, well, I guess kind of limited. Okay. Really limited. He was just so afraid of you. And you know, in one way Tom was right."

Anna's eyes popped open as she tried to let the thought register and then her head lifted up. Millie laughed at her expression. "Well, obviously not in that way." The thought made Millie laugh again.

"It wasn't until I met you and saw the scar and understood how much love you had lost that I realized how lost ..." she struggled to find words, "how lost I was without love. If you hadn't stopped for gas, I'd still be out there. You made me find me."

She smiled at Millie and shook the hand that had taken and held hers at some point through her story. "Okay. In that case I'm going to make you find you again."

This time Millie looked over.

"Marry Drew, he's head over heels in love with you." She watched Millie watch her.

"He told you?"

Anna smiled. "Of course he did. Which part of head over heels are you not hearing?" She leaned over and used her shoulder to nudge Millie. "Come on now. How many times does the universe just drop a Greek God right into your lap?"

Millie was not laughing and Anna thought she'd been pretty funny. "Okay, back up, let's just forget about Drew for the moment. What's important here is I know you're crazy about him." Anna let the statement stand as a challenge.

"Fine. I love Drew. I'm crazy about Drew. Okay." Millie shot right back. "Now answer me this. What if we get back to his nice little college town and I don't have anywhere to go, or anyone to be?" Millie returned the challenge, "What then?"

As she was about to return the volley, Millie's words really registered and she paused for a moment, then leaned her head back. It was a valid question.

Suddenly she popped up and scooted herself cross-legged in front of Millie, "Then you know what. Take a sabbatical." She pointed at Millie, "He took one for you. Rent the house or close it up for a year and go with him. If it doesn't work it won't be because you were afraid to try."

"I could do that." Millie swatted her hand and sat back. "What about Cameron?"

"What about Cameron?" Her eyebrow rose way up.

"You can't just leave her here. You blew into town, transformed her life and she just idolizes you, you know?" At her wary look, Millie laughed. "Oh puhleeze, everyone knows Cam thinks you can walk on water. Everyone. Except maybe Tom, I don't think anyone told him." Millie chuckled, finding herself very amusing. "Come on." Millie shoved the knee in front of her, "Give. You do know?"

"Yeah." An image of Cameron smiling at her as she presented the rounding board art flashed briefly before her. She looked at Millie and smiled gently, almost wistfully. "I know."

"Okay. So you need to take her with you because what's she going to do now, stay here and what, carve another carousel?" They both laughed. "We can't just leave her here and she's not coming on my honeymoon. You need to get out of this town and you need to take her with you, okay?"

Millie waited for a moment and then arched her eyebrow. "Okay?' she repeated warningly.

"Okay. I give." Anna brushed back her hair and then let it fall, "You can put the eyebrow down. Cameron comes with me."

Anna's head was spinning with the turn the conversation had taken. She blew a raspberry into the air as the thought of everyone knowing reminded her of something else she had meant to ask. "So who else knew?"

"I don't know." At her look Millie reiterated, "I don't. Now, I don't think for two seconds Tom didn't tell other people, but no one said anything. Ever. It's odd when you sit here now and think about it. Kind of curious. I didn't think about it then, it just kind of happened."

Millie's face scrunched up as she thought about it, "I guess Joe and Rudy probably know. Can't imagine Tom not sharing his feelings that night. But then again, I can't imagine Joe not telling Nan, not that Nan would care, but I just can't imagine her actually keeping anything secret."

Anna laughed at that, Millie had a point.

"But, they were out there tacking down that tarp with Tom that night. I don't know. Maybe Lyle, I'm not sure. Tom probably would have felt the need to warn the Reverend. But you know, no one, no one, ever said anything." Millie looked directly at her, "I honestly don't know."

They both thought about that for a while.

"I think," Millie broke the silence, "to people here, you just kind of became the merry-go-round lady and you're always going to be the merry-go-round lady. And people here like her. And they needed her. I don't actually think anyone else cares about the rest."

They dropped into silence again.

"Hey Millie?"

Millie lifted her head up. "Yeah?"

Anna's eyes stayed closed. "How does Lyle like his eggs?"

"Pardon?

She opened one eye and smiled, "How..."

"Never mind. I heard you the first time." Millie wondered what the hell had gotten into her now. "Why?"

"I just need to know." She looked at Millie, "Please."

"Well, he has, well," Millie thought about it for a minute. Once the answer would have been so simple. "Every day for the last million years Lyle comes into the diner and orders his eggs poached with one piece of whole-wheat toast. Yep. Don't need two pieces, Millie. Would just go to waste. Yep." Millie laughed.

"Then one day, oh I don't know, a couple of years ago now, it was so strange, he suddenly ordered scrambled. I almost fell over on the counter. Then he ordered pancakes. He was so pleased with himself. It was weird."

She smiled. She understood. Like her, Lyle had been reborn. He had saved the carousel because it had saved him.

Millie looked up and touched her knee. "I'll miss you."

"Me too." She looked up. "You know, you're my best friend."

"Yeah, mine too."

Once again silence descended. She needed to stretch, "Hey Millie?"

"Yeah?"

"At this time of year, exactly how late does it have to be before there's no more sun?"

Millie spun around and looked out the window. It was dark. They had been there for hours. They looked at each other. "Shit."

§ § §

Anna asked her to make one more stop. Millie watched as she opened the back door of the car, leaned in and fished about between the back of the front seat cushions. Finally, she grasped a cord and gently pulled it out. Standing up, Anna walked back over to Millie, all the while unknotting the leather cord.

"This was Miriam's ring. It was her Grandmother's wedding ring. It was to be ours but she didn't live long enough to see that day." She smiled and held out her hand, "I couldn't wear it. I couldn't even let anyone see it. I wasn't ready to share it with anyone. And now, now, I would like you to have it." Anna's eyes met Millie's head on, "I think so would Miriam."

Millie's immediate thought was to protest, but it died in her throat. Some other voice told her to take this ring. Her hands gently wrapped around the thin sliver of rose gold.

§ § §

They came over the rise and let their eyes search the park. She saw them first and nudged Millie. The group was more or less where they'd left them. Jack looked to be asleep. Lisa was rocking Ty, her youngest in her lap. The little boy who had been "riding" Cameron was now sleeping in her lap. Drew was helping another nephew make s'mores.

They walked down together. Millie walked directly up to Drew; saw the questions in his eyes. "Yes."

"Yes?"

Drew stood up and picked Millie up, swinging her around.

Anna walked past the happy couple and sat down next to Cameron. For a moment she said nothing. They both just watched Drew and Millie. "Hey Cam, I have a question for you." Cameron turned. "No promises, just a question."

Cameron nodded, understanding.

"Want to go on a road trip?"

Cameron smiled. She didn't need any promises. "Yes."

Cameron put her laptop and backpack in the car. Anna lifted Cameron's duffel bag and made room for it in the trunk. "Ready?" They stopped and took one last look back at the front porch, the kitchen windows, the bedroom windows, a place they both had called home.

She made a left onto Cedar for the last time. They drove past the diner, looking but they didn't stop. Their goodbyes were said last night. Millie was probably running about with her coffee pot in hand. She had informed them both she had no intention of sitting in the house this morning and watching them drive away.

They drove for a few minutes when she spotted what she was looking for and turned on her left turn signal. She parked the car and asked Cameron to give her just a minute.

Across the street, he stopped his patrol car and just stared.

Anna opened the trunk and slowly untied a bag. She leaned in and took a deep breath, but she couldn't smell anything. It was gone. She put the tie back on and lifted the bag out, walking it into the Goodwill Store. She set the bag on the donations counter and turned to leave. She made it to the door before turning back and quickly untied the bag, reached in and took out an old frayed nearly bleached out blue man-tailored shirt. She touched the collar to her nose. Whether the scent was there or just a memory, it didn't matter. She threw it on over her t-shirt, retied the bag, smiled at the man and left.

As she went to get back in the car she spotted a pay phone against a wall. She signaled to Cameron and walked over.

Cam smiled her understanding, took a sip from her bottled water and sat back to wait.

"Mom. Yeah, it's me. I miss you too. Look, I was just wondering if you felt like making chicken on Friday night. Yeah. It'll be great," she smiled and turned, looking over toward Cameron as she spoke. "Oh and Mom, yeah, I'm bringing a friend with me, okay? No, Mom." She rolled her eyes in exasperation but had to chuckle, it felt good. She realized in that moment how much she'd missed her Mom. "Just a friend. Great. See you Friday night."

She climbed back in and started the car. She noticed Tom when she was in the store. She said nothing; just sat unnaturally stiff, her fingers clenching the wheel and drove very carefully. Limited? Anna thought no, that's not it, keeping an eye on him through her mirrors. Jackass? Better.

As they cleared the county sign, Anna looked in her rear view mirror and watched the patrol car stop and then U-turn, fishtailing as he raced away.

She rolled her shoulders and relaxed, letting the tension in her body and mind deflate. As her nerves settled, she looked over, smiled at Cameron and turned on the radio, "How about some tunes?" They rolled down the windows and cranked up the sound and drove.

§ § §

I felt a rumble in my heart

Over the mountains

As the engine ate the spark

Spitting out the miles . . .

Still after all is said and done

This train still runs

Doesn't matter where its gone

This train still runs

Though the baggage weighs a ton

We carry on

No one is forever young

I'm not done

This train still runs

Janis Ian & Jess Leary

ACKNOWLEDGMENTS

It's a funny thing being asked to write the acknowledgements for your book. It's the one time you must sit and truly reflect on the journey from the blank page to the printing press. And it's a really long list from there to here. So, in my most basic truth—No Fay Jacobs, No Bonnie Quesenberry, No Book. There are not enough thanks for their love and support. Fay—hard to believe you can edit me that much and still keep us laughing. Thanks to Kathy Galloway, Pam Kozey, Anita Pettitt and Fran Sneider. Any errors—grammatical or typographical are probably only due to my negligence, as I know you found them all—at least once! David Perl—thank you for letting the gift of your art grace my cover. To Steve Elkins and Murray Archibald, thanks for giving me a place to write way back when, and to Sue Stember, thank you for almost making that photo painless. To all my friends, from RB to LA to TO and even to the UK, who read the book and said, "this is great, keep going," I am truly grateful. Your support allowed me to move forward and get here. And again, and always, I thank my family. Their belief in me is always there, even when mine falters.

AUTHOR

Television producer and writer Stefani Deoul has long been an East Coast gal with a West Coast and Canadian TV career. Now she's enjoying spending time near her native New York, coffee cup in hand, hunched over her laptop, engaged in her passion for writing. In addition to *The Carousel*, Stefani has written for numerous publications, penned short stories and film and television treatments and has produced *The Dead Zone*, *Brave New Girl* along with being the executive in charge of production for the series *Dresden Files* and *Missing*.

Bywater
BOOKS

At Bywater Books we love good books about lesbians just like you do, and we're committed to bringing the best of contemporary lesbian writing to our avid readers. Our editorial team is dedicated to finding and developing outstanding writers who create books you won't want to put down.

We sponsor the Bywater Prize for Fiction to help with this quest. Each prize winner receives $1,000 and publication of their novel. We have already discovered amazing writers like Jill Malone, Sally Bellerose, and Hilary Sloin through the Bywater Prize. Which exciting new writer will we find next?

For more information about Bywater Books and the annual Bywater Prize for Fiction, please visit our website.

www.bywaterbooks.com